About the Author

T.J. Oswald, was born in 1992 in Sunderland, where he grew up on the estates of Thorney Close and Farringdon. He was educated at Durham and Oxford University. He has always been driven by a unique passion for his hometown and the North East of England. He speaks Mandarin Chinese, Japanese and Korean.

The North Star

T. J. Oswald

The North Star

Olympia Publishers
London

www.olympiapublishers.com
OLYMPIA PAPERBACK EDITION

Copyright © T. J. Oswald 2024

The right of T. J. Oswald to be identified as author of this work has been asserted in accordance with sections 77 and 78 of the Copyright, Designs and Patents Act 1988.

All Rights Reserved

No reproduction, copy or transmission of this publication may be made without written permission. No paragraph of this publication may be reproduced, copied or transmitted save with the written permission of the publisher, or in accordance with the provisions of the Copyright Act 1956 (as amended).

Any person who commits any unauthorised act in relation to this publication may be liable to criminal prosecution and civil claims for damage.

A CIP catalogue record for this title is available from the British Library.

ISBN: 978-1-80439-895-1

This is a work of fiction.
Names, characters, and incidents originate from the writer's imagination. Any resemblance to actual persons, living or dead, is purely coincidental.

First Published in 2024

Olympia Publishers
Tallis House
2 Tallis Street
London
EC4Y 0AB

Printed in Great Britain

Dedication

To Nana, the person who I owe the most to in my life, who provided for me when my parents could not, who exerted every burden and sacrifice to ensure my childhood was never wrought with poverty, misery or despair.

Contents

Chapter I: A Girl Called Sophie 11
Chapter II: A Dun Cow 24
Chapter III: The Creature in the Night 30
Chapter IV: The Rally 35
Chapter V: A Holy Trinity 42
Chapter VI: No Turning Back 51
Chapter VII: Magical Narcotics 57
Chapter VIII: Making Sunderland Great Again 62
Chapter IX: The Terror of Foxy Island 71
Chapter X: The Legend of King Oswald 83
Chapter XI: The Reckoning 94
Chapter XII: Politics & Propaganda 101
Chapter XIII: A Working Class Traitor Is Something to Be .. 110
Chapter XIV: The Schoolgirl Fugitive 118
Chapter XV: Playing Hard Ball 132
Chapter XVI: A Chinese Mackem 146
Chapter XVII: The Promise 156
Chapter: XVIII: The Southwick Job 169
Chapter XIX: The Pilgrim's Path 181
Chapter XX: Evil Reborn 194
Chapter XXI: Honest Questions 203
Chapter XXII: The Forest of Tribulation 212
Chapter XXIII: By the Glory of the People 227
Chapter XXIV: From the Ashes, and from the Heart 235
Chapter XXVI: The Light at the End of the tunnel 251

Chapter I: A Girl Called Sophie

A young woman ran down a dark forest passage as the cold wind howled into the night. As she ran, an unseen growling and snarling sounded from behind her, drawing closer and closer, as if it were giving chase. Her chest squeezed in pain as she desperately gasped for breath, eying an opening in the trees, of which a tarmac led behind. With her last burst of energy, she darted forwards in a bid to reach the exit, but suddenly the figure of a man appeared in front of her, causing her to fall backwards. He was dressed in dark green robes, his face unseen amidst a veil of blackness. As she looked upon him in horror, he then began to speak, hissing "Sophie…", "Sophie…" as a mysterious banging sound then began to echo around her, growing louder and louder, as the figure began to approach her.

"Sophie… Sophie! Gerrup ya going to be late!" A voice was then heard yelling, and Sophie shot up in bed in a state of panic. But she was no longer in a strange dark forest, but a bedroom, and the persistent banging she had heard was coming from her bedroom door as a ray of sunlight poked its way through the curtains. "You're going to be late!" the man's voice continued to shout. "Ha'way man, its breakfast time!" he barked.

"All right, Dad… I'm coming," Sophie then replied in a tired voice, before dragging herself up out of the bed quickly.

Opening the door, her father stood with his arms folded impatiently. He was a bit overweight, his belly poking out, his face aged and worn, bearing the look of cynicism and displeasure, while his hair was short and brown in colour, with streaks of grey.

"Are you just gonna stand there and do nowt?" Sophie commented antagonistically as she approached the bathroom. He declined to answer and walked downstairs.

Entering the bathroom, Sophie glanced at herself in the mirror for a moment. Her hair was blonde and wavy, her eyes a deep blue, while her face embodied an innocent look. As she prepared to shower, she looked around at the bathroom in discomfort, which much like the rest of the home she lived in, was displaying signs of age and neglect. Some of the tiles were cracked and yellowing, while outside the wallpaper was of a similar colour, and even peeling at the ends. The red carpets which lined the house were of a musty smell.

Having showered, Sophie got ready quickly into her school uniform, before glancing quickly at a pocket planner book, which read. "St Genesius Catholic School & Sixth form for girls". As she opened it carefully, her eyes fell on the square marking the current date, which read *Mock exam results returned.*" Her face scorned.

"Crap…" She whispered to herself, before stuffing it in her backpack and trundling downstairs.

As she entered the dining room, her father, known as Eddie, sat disgruntled at the table, the look of displeasure on his face not having shifted at all. Passing him as if he didn't exist, Sophie then started to frantically prepare breakfast at a small and burnt looking stove, while combing her still wet hair simultaneously. "Hurry up man, I haven't got all day!" Eddie then grunted selfishly at her, breaking the silence.

"Neither have I!" Sophie snapped back, "you know I've got my A-levels I can't be on with this!" as she combed her hair anxiously in frustration.

"Selfish as always I see, I wouldn't expect anything less," he then retorted. On hearing this, Sophie's restraint snapped.

"Excuse me! I'm the one who's selfish?" She then retorted in a very defensive manner. "At least I'm trying to do something with my life unlike you, you lazy sod! I'm having to work to pay off your bloody mess! When was the last time you even worked? Or did anything?"

"Sophie, I've tauld yer! My career ended with the shipyards. Now less of yer lip luv and get on with it man!" He growled.

"Aye, well mine hasn't even started yet!" She then snapped back. "Do you think I want to be trapped in this squalor of a Thorney Close council house with you for the rest of my life? Just because you stopped caring, doesn't mean I haven't!"

"Just get on with it man or it will be my fault ya late anarl." He then moaned sarcastically, as Sophie sighed and turned away. Once his breakfast was done, she carried it over begrudgingly in a rush, before rushing for her school jacket and bag.

"There you go, I've got no time to eat now so see you later!" she said in a disgruntled voice, before quickly dashing across the room and out of the house. Eddie said nothing and simply started eating.

Slamming the door shut, Sophie emerged out of a small semi-detached home, which was sandwiched in a long symmetrical row on a hilly bank. Shutting the gate, she then paced down the concrete steps and onto the jagged pavement road, before dashing down the street to the bus stop, passing a sign that read "*Tilbury Road.*"

"Morning, Soph!" an ageing voice suddenly grunted as she ran.

Looking back in surprise, she then shouted back in a friendly voice, "Morning, Goya!" as she hurried into the distance. Goya, or "Joe Goya", he was Sophie's elderly yet energetic next-door neighbour. He looked very cheerful and energetic, dressed smartly in a jacket and hat.

"Look after yersel!" he yelled as Sophie scurried on, sticking up his thumb cheerfully.

Finally arriving at the bus stop, Sophie stopped and panted for breath, checking her phone anxiously for the time. She then breathed a sigh of relief on realising she had not missed her morning bus, and then awkwardly began combing her hair, still wet and unarranged, from having rushed out of the house. Then, finally, a big blue and white bus rolled out from round the corner, came down the street, and stopped abruptly in front of her. The bus, thankfully, wasn't too busy. She sat down on a fabric blue and orange seat, picking up a free-distributed newspaper next to her, whose title read *"The Sunderland Shine"*.

Sophie glanced at the main headline, reading *"Politician vows to heal Sunderland's wounds!"* which had been written by a journalist called Katie Clough. *"Mayor hopeful William Parker-Fulton vowed today to 'heal Sunderland's wounds' by cracking down on delinquency and crime amongst young people. The candidate, known nationally for his populist policies, told the Sunderland Shine on Sunday that the city was facing an epidemic of crime and that young people had lost all respect for society..."*

Disinterested, Sophie put the paper down and started looking at her phone as the bus trundled around the town, winding its way from suburb to suburb. It soon arrived in a neighbourhood which was leafy and affluent in appearance, its landscape scattered with big churches, old churches and classical buildings, reflecting a Victorian romanticism of sorts. Sophie, distracted on her phone, then jumped as the announcer pinged "Next stop, Ashbrooke!" and raced to get off.

Sophie got off the bus and then nervously headed towards her school, where numerous other girls were also making their way casually towards the gate. As she entered, she looked up at the sign which read "St Genesius Catholic School and sixth form for girls". Established by a covenant of nuns over a hundred years ago, the school was known for its very strict and pious ways, before gradually relaxing in the latter part of the last century.

Still, it was undoubtedly one of the best schools a young woman in Sunderland could go to, and was a cut above the rest, especially the often-chaotic state schools, where few had a serious appetite for learning. Its students were made to follow a strict uniform code consisting of navy-blue jackets, skirts and tights, along with a sweater and tie.

As Sophie walked into the schoolyard, she looked around anxiously, standing alone in a sea of other girls chatting, socialising, and waiting for school to start, before another girl ran up to her by surprise and embraced her in a hug. She had fine long black hair, olive skin and glistening brown eyes. This was Millie Chen, who was Sophie's best friend at the Sixth Form.

"Sophie! Are you okay?" Millie said in a warm and caring voice.

"Millie! So good to see you! Feels like ages since the half term holidays," she replied in a slightly emotional tone as she hugged her.

"Fine I guess... he's just been a prick as usual." Sophie continued, as the two then walked further into the yard. "What about you?" she then asked.

"I've just been studying, dad's takeaway is doing well these days," Millie replied.

"Now if only I had the time to study..." Sophie replied cynically.

Sophie befriended Millie after joining St Genesius, with her having been there since the lower grades. The two had bonded on the common experience of "being different" in a world where they never quite fit in. Millie, like Sophie, was also extremely intelligent, perhaps even more so, with a deeper enthusiasm for her studies, a product of parental expectations Sophie did not have. She was also much more proactive, positive and confident than Sophie was. Because of this Millie often found herself looking out for Sophie, and was always prepared to stick up for her friend no matter what.

"Demanding his breakfast this morning as if I'm a bloody slave, I just can't wait to move out and move on with my life." Sophie moaned as they walked.

"I'm sorry to hear that, I don't know how I'd cope if my dad was like that. But as I keep telling you, you also need to stand up for yourself more! Things will never change if you don't try." Millie said in a kind, but urging voice.

"Anyway, did you remember our mock exam results are coming in today?" She continued.

"Oh no, I didn't have time to even study for that because I was too busy with my shifts at the Dun Cow, so I'm dreading it..." Sophie replied showing discontent.

"Oh Sophie... I'm sure you will be fine, and if there is anything to improve on, now is the time!" Millie responded reassuringly.

As the two girls continued to walk, suddenly, another girl stepped out of nowhere and stood in front of them, imposing herself on them and deliberately blocking their way. Sophie froze in shock, while Millie's face displayed clear displeasure.

"Bertha... what do we owe the pleasure?" Millie then asked her sternly. This girl, Bertha Bagshaw, was much taller than both Sophie and Millie, and had long brown hair and a mean pointed face. Bertha was a mean and vindictive girl who was jealous of Sophie, and used her intimidating posture and size to bully, demean and push her around out of both sheer spite and sadistic pleasure.

"Well... look who it is, Sophie slag and her little mate. What's happening then Soph? Still being a daddy's girl?" She scoffed, cackling insidiously.

"Bertha, not now please..." Sophie responded in a lowly voice, seeking to avoid raising tensions.

"Not now?" She laughed dismissively, "why, what are you going to do about it princess? I can throw your face in that mud owa there if I wanted to." She scorned.

"Bertha! Enough! Why don't you just shut up and knock it off? Sophie, let's go..." Millie snapped, attempting to be firm but calm.

"Ow... I didn't say you could leave. This little dog fights all of your battles for ya doesn't she? Tell ya what, let's see your mate stick up for ya!" Bertha said menacingly.

As Millie attempted to pull Sophie away from the scene, Bertha followed and shoved her intimidatingly, leading her patience to snap.

"Come on then! Stick to me you vile pig!" She yelled, and stood forwards towards Bertha. The two readied themselves and prepared to fight, but before either could throw a single punch, they were abruptly interrupted by a funny looking man with curly bushy brown hair and glasses.

"Good morning girls!" he said cheerfully and obliviously, not having noticed the emerging situation and by sheer luck, forcing it into a state of awkwardness.

"Oh... good morning, Mr Marchant." Millie responded awkwardly. Bertha immediately retreated to an innocuous posture.

Gary Marchant was the girls' history teacher. He was a bit of a legend amongst the students at St Genesius, known for his highly eccentric and jovial behaviour, but with an inherently good nature.

"Jolly day today, isn't it? I hope to see you all in the best of spirits in class!" he bumbled. Before another word could be spoken and Millie could alert him to the situation and begin to explain, a school bell rang out across the yard.

"Thar she blows! Hurry along to form now!" He clasped his hands firmly and walked off, leaving the girls standing with each uncomfortably.

"You got out of it this time babes, but watch your backs!" Bertha hissed quietly with a scowl on her face, before proceeding to walk off.

Later that day, Sophie and Millie sat in class as Mr Marchant waffled on regarding the Mock examination. While Millie showed attentive enthusiasm and eager anticipation, Sophie's mind was beset with anxiety over her performance.

"As you know, your university applications are underway! Although this examination doesn't count, you need to make sure you can prepare with the best grades you can possibly get in the view to secure your offers... so anyway, now I have said enough about that, I have your results here and will be handing them out!" Marchant said cheerfully, before pulling out some sheets of paper from a file and proceeding to strut around the class to give them out.

He put a sheet of paper down on Millie's desk. She picked it up urgently and looked, a bright smile beamed on her face.

"Yes, I got an A star!" she whispered in excitement. Sophie looked on uncomfortably. On approaching her, Mr Marchant then stopped suddenly.

"Sophie…" he then said in a serious voice. "Before I hand you this, I'd like to talk with you one on one after all, is that okay?" he asked in a concerned voice. Sophie's face drained of colour, and she replied in a defeatist tone.

"Yes, sir…"

A row behind, Bertha sat smugly watching on and sniggered to her friends.

"Looks like Sophie no brains strikes again. The blonde bimbo get."

Mr Marchant proceeded to finish handing out the exam results and returned to the front of the class, where he proceeded to commence a lecture. He leaned over to his computer and turned on a PowerPoint presentation, and on a luminous screen the word "NORTHUMBRIA" appeared and beamed across the room.

"Okay… quick recap , the Anglo-Saxon Kingdom of Northumbria! The heritage of the North East of England…" he began. "Long ago, the Anglo-Saxons came to this country and established seven kingdoms, which would one day all be united to form England… in the early period, before the onslaught of the Vikings, the strongest and most prominent of these Kingdoms was Northumbria, which itself was a union of two smaller kingdoms which preceded it. Bernicia here in the North East, and Deira, in Yorkshire."

"Northumbria gained its name because it referred to the people North of the River Humber, where Kingston Upon Hull is today. It was also, as we discussed, a centre of religious learning and scholarship. Figures such as the Venerable Bede, who lived here on the banks of the River Wear in Monkwearmouth Priory, brought the country out of the dark ages and penned the earliest versions of English history." As Marchant waffled on, Sophie struggled to concentrate, a thousand things racing through her head at once… panicking almost, in the painful revelation her exam had not gone as well as she hoped.

After school finished, Sophie nervously re-entered Marchant's classroom, where he sat marking papers on a desk.

"Hello! Hello! Hello! Thanks for coming, Sophie," he said carefully as she walked in.

"So… about your mock exam… do take a seat!" he said in a more serious tone, as he retrieved Sophie's feedback sheet from his drawer.

"So, you know I think highly of you, and with high abilities comes high expectations! You and Millie are the best in my class, but I have to say with all my concern, that your exam was poor. You did outstanding last year on your AS levels, all A's… but then suddenly the quality of your work has slumped. I read this, and it's just as if you don't know the content, as if there was no effort or thought put into it. Is something bothering you? What's wrong?" he asked, striking a more concerned tone.

Sophie paused for a moment, as if she was struggling to be honest as to why.

"I'm sorry sir… It's everything going on at home. With my Dad, he has just become a distraction. He's overwhelmed himself with debt and I have to work part-time to keep us going…" she said anxiously, her heart beating. Mr Marchant reacted with alarm on his face, his eyebrows twitching with shock.

"I'm sorry to hear that. If I wouldn't get sacked on the spot I'd go round there and give him a jolly good what for! But don't quote me on that! What I can do is ask for the pastoral tutor to try and call him about it. This is just a big year for you, and I don't want to see you not get the grades you deserve."

"Thank you, sir. It just feels like things are coming at me from every angle and I just don't know what to do. He's never been the same since my mam passed away, and sometimes I feel like I'm carrying the whole world on my shoulders." Sophie then opened up striking a much sadder tone, as if she was going to cry.

"Sophie, my advice is to be cheerful and never forget who you are. You aren't stupid, you aren't lazy and you aren't incapable, but I do feel you are lost right now in the unfortunate circumstances people face in life. But I'm sure that if you find yourself, you can overcome it," Mr Marchant replied in an inspired voice.

"Don't give up... Now is there anything else we can discuss while we are here?" he asked kindly.

"No. Thank you sir," she said in an empty voice, before getting up and proceeding to walk to the door.

"Have a good afternoon Sophie," he said as she swung the door shut.

After School, Sophie got the bus home and walked up the street. As she approached her house, she noticed an expensive car was perched on the pavement in front of their gate. Her face filled with dread and even anger. She walked up the steps and opened the door, entering cautiously.

"Dad... I'm home," she spoke in a nervous tone, before entering the living room to see Eddie sat at the table with another man. The man was large in size, bulbous and gluttonous, dressed in a black leather jacket which looked as if it could scarcely fit him. He had a mean smirk on his face, coupled with a dimpled chin so deep the Grand Canyon would blush. His eyes were sharp and hungry.

"Look Tony, I've tauld yer, I just need a bit more time for the rest." Eddie was heard talking to him in a very pleading voice. "I've got some bets am certain I'm garna win over the next two weeks or so, and I'll get it to yer then." Tony looked at him unconvinced.

"That's what you say every time man. Not a very good gambler for someone who can't stop, are ya?" He snarled.

Having seen Sophie enter the room, his eyes shot at her.

"Oh hello Sophie!" What a nice surprise!" He sniggered in an inconsiderate and insincere voice, before getting up and walking towards her.

"Your father and I were just discussing our... business... we still have a few outstanding bills to settle..." he hissed.

He then proceeded to flutter a few bank notes in full view of Sophie, before stuffing them in his pocket.

"You're looking pretty today... aren't you?" he said rashly.

"Tony, get out of our home." Sophie reacted angrily. "You know we can barely pay it, why can't you just cut your losses and get out rather than sucking the blood out of him?" she snarled.

"Now, now, your dad needs to be a man of his word. I'm not a charity pet. This is a business, and if he can't pay, there's plenty of things in here that can foot the bill..." He replied before then looking around deliberately at the ornaments and furniture around the room.

"What are you looking at? We've got nowt man!" she snapped at him.

"Nowt? I don't see nowt in here," he smiled, before picking up a golden plated photo frame depicting a wedding between two people, presumably Sophie's mam and dad.

"No! You can't have that, get away from it!" Sophie then

screamed in horror as he contemplated it.

"Tony..." Eddie then attempted to plead with him in a very soft voice. "Don't take it please... we'll pay... promise" He gasped.

"Well then Eddie, you better cough up... because if you don't you'll be coughing up blood son. Anyway, I've got to be off now, so you be a good girl Sophie and get to work this evening, and you'll be hearing from me soon enough!" he said menacingly, before proceeding to exit the house.

Sophie glared at her father, crying, who looked at her helplessly.

"This is all your fault!" she yelled, before storming upstairs and secluding herself within the sanctuary of her modest bedroom. She laid herself on her bed aimlessly for several moments, looking up at the ceiling as thoughts raced through her head.

"Will I ever escape this life?" she then asked herself out loud, before seeing the time on the phone. It was time to get changed and go to work.

Chapter II: A Dun Cow

That evening, Sophie reluctantly set out to work. Heading back into the City Centre, she got off the bus and walked towards a pub standing on its own to the west side of the city. It was a beautiful, imposing building, with a black and gold sign reading 'The Dun Cow'. It was of a baroque design, standing three storeys high with a domed tower peeking out of the top, complete with a signature clock on it. The interior of the pub was equally as beautiful and antique, with a shiny and well-polished ornate bar. The building had stood proud for over a century.

But what ,of course, exactly was a 'Dun Cow'? and why did it have such a name? 'Dun' in old English, refers to a light shade of brown, meaning, of course, the pub is named after a 'Brown Cow'. But this wasn't a randomly assigned name, but derived from local legend. Long ago, a series of monks who settled in County Durham sought to find a new place of burial for the leader of their community, St Cuthbert. They allegedly had a vision that they should go to a place called 'Dunelm' but did not know where to find it. That is, until they encountered a young maid who had lost her cow in this exact location.

Following the maid, the community were able to find 'Dunelm', which, of course, became the site of the great city of Durham, Cuthbert's final resting place, and of course, the place Sophie so desires to go. While everything about the *Dun Cow* pub was grand, her job was not grand and unsurprisingly, she loathed it. Working as a barmaid, she often found herself working strenuously long into the night, distracting from her much cherished studies.

On entering the bar, she was immediately greeted by a young man. He looked slightly older than Sophie, with short brown hair, gelled slightly, along with a bit of stubble around his chin. He had a confident, but not overbearing look on his face.

"Areet Sophie!" he said out of loud as Sophie came in and placed her bag behind the bar.

"Aye, all right, Micky…" she then replied in an unenthusiastic tone, showing little appetite for conversation as she put down her coat.

As the evening went on, the pair of them laboured strenuously behind the bar, but Micky, always someone to speak his mind, noticed something was a bit more off with Sophie than usual.

"So Sophie, yer look a bit down there. Rough day at school like?" he asked with a glimmer of concern in his voice.

"You're not kidding, Micky… Not only school, but home too…" she replied in a hoarse voice as she washed pint glasses without enthusiasm.

"Well it hasn't killed you yet anyway, you're almost at the end, not much longer to go!" said Micky as he attempted to reassure her.

"Yeah… and then it starts over and over again. Look today has been awful, exam results a mess because of this, then all that at home," she groaned.

"Chin up Soph, I know one day you'll get out of it all eventually," Micky said in a more hardy voice.

"Not the only thing I want to get out of though is it?" she snarked.

Just as they were chatting, a little bald pot-bellied man

scurried towards them out of the blue, with an angry look on his mole-like face.

"And you'll both be out of here right now if you don't stop messing about and get back to work. Sophie, I want all those glasses cleaned before you finish!" He snapped.

"Yes Derek… sorry." Sophie sighed as she continued working.

"As I've told you before, remember, when you work for me, no slacking!" He grunted, before storming out back to where he came from.

"Ha'way, I'll give you a hand" said Micky in a reassuring voice, sensing Sophie's anguish and volunteering to help her. "Do you want a lift home as well?" he then asked kindly.

"Cheers Micky, but no I don't need a lift home, and no I don't have time to hang out this weekend. I've enough on my plate right now," she said defensively.

"Talk about being overly defensive like. I'm just trying to help a canny lass out, that's all."

Sophie then sighed deeply.

"Thanks, but no thanks. There's nobody that can help me but me, if I ever could…"

Micky's face showed frustration, he then tried again.

"Well anyway, I'm going to the rally tomorrow, sure you don't want to come?" he asked politely, but Sophie wasn't impressed, and lightly slapped the towel down on the bar.

"See, there you go again Micky! I just told you I don't want to meet up, and no I couldn't care less about politics, those liars couldn't care about us man." She snapped.

"Sophie… chill… I agree with ya, that's why this man. Fulton, he's different. That's why I'm going," he said in an unsettled voice.

"Micky I still don't care, I have many other things to worry about, my life is turning to mud mate..." she replied, still displeased. "Now look, let's just get on with this because I want to get this shift done, I come here to work because of my lazy lump of a dad, not to talk with you," she snapped. An awkward silence then fell on them both as they continued to work.

Later, after finishing her shift, Sophie grabbed her coat and quickly stormed out of the pub. Micky looked on and shook his head, muttering to himself:

"I'll never know what's up with that lass..." Angry and in despair, Sophie did not head for home, but proceeded to walk, aimlessly, through the town. Seemingly unphased by any physical tiredness that might have beset her, the racing thoughts in her mind led her to walk, walk, and walk more. Leaving Sunderland city centre, she passed houses and fields alike. By this point, the darkness of the night had beset itself over the area. Eventually, she stopped at a series of cliffs towering over an empty pebbled beach below.

Curious and sensing an outlet for her frustration, she made her way down a set of rugged steps and onto the cobbles, as the cold and bitter North Sea roared in front of her. Upon seeing the sign at the side of the road marking 'Ryhope Beach' Sophie remembered the beach as somewhere visually appealing, where she'd visited when she was little, remembering that it was a great place to explore. As it wasn't somewhere people came to relax, she knew she could be alone there to express her emotions, especially amongst the beauty of the magnesian limestone cliffs, which being easily eroded by the sea, had produced many rocks and eerie gaping natural caves.

Having made her way down to the beach , Sophie stood still for a moment, before reaching into her pocket and pulling out a small crumpled photo. On it was a photo of a much younger girl, sitting with a woman who looked remarkably like Sophie. They seemed happy and fulfilled. As she clutched the photo, a tear dropped from her eye.

"I promise… one day I'll make you proud…" she muttered to herself out loud as the waves crashed in the background. She then sighed and put the photo back into her pocket, before proceeding to pick up pebbles from the beach and hurl them into the water in frustration. One after another, she continued to throw them, until suddenly she noticed a small stone of an unusual complexion nested within the others, which twinkled under the light of the moon.

Intrigued, she reached and picked it up carefully, to find that it had a star like inscription etched into it, which twinkled like crystal. Glancing at it, she then decided to put it in her pocket. Suddenly, she turned and saw a man standing nearby. Realising she was not alone, she startled and jumped back in shock. He had long brown hair and a beard, and his clothes resembled rags of sorts, as if he were homeless.

"Sorry, didn't mean to scare you!" he said attempting to calm her down on seeing her reaction. "Are you all right? You seem a bit upset" he then asked in a concerned voice.

"Oh… I'm fine," Sophie replied in a tense and uncomfortable voice.

"Good to know. Life's crap isn't it?" he then retorted, before taking a cigarette and puffing it into the cold night air.

Sophie continued to look at the man perplexed, and extremely uncomfortable.

"You're telling me…" she replied sarcastically.

"Well listen, things will get better trust me." The man then replied casually, with a care free look on his face. Sophie, continuing to be unsettled, decided to cut the conversation short.

"Okay then, I've got to go home now, see ya!" she said anxiously, before heading up off the cobbles and back up the steps to begin the very, very long walk home…

Chapter III: The Creature in the Night

Having calmed her nerves down somewhat, Sophie walked home. The time was very late, and certainly after midnight. Ryhope was a long, long way from Thorney Close. As she walked, she looked at the time on her phone.

"Should I call a taxi?" She thought to herself, feeling chronically tired. "No way, I can't afford that." She then chastised herself in her head as she continued onwards, heading up a long stretch of road which would lead continuously to her home suburb.

Sunderland, unlike London, was not a "city that never sleeps" and there was not a soul to be seen or heard amidst the blackness. As she passed an old industrial estate, she looked at a street sign reading 'Leechmere Road' before stopping suddenly. Looking around, she thought she had heard an unusual panting noise, which sounded aggressive and unsettling, as if a man was angry, and breathing deeply. Uncomfortable and startled, she looked over her shoulder, but there was no one to be seen.

"Maybe it was a dog." Sophie contemplated to herself, before continuing walking.

But then suddenly, a couple of streets later, the noise then continued again, as if it was following her. This made no sense, and she double checked around her again, but there was nobody to be seen.

"Perhaps it was just the cry of the wind," she reassured herself again, before carrying on. Finally, the sound seemed to disappear, and she thought nothing more of it.

Eventually, Sophie reached an open stretch of grass land within the urban jungle of houses.

"Ah, Barnes Park extension," she said in her head optimistically, knowing now she was close to home. The area was technically part of Barnes Park, which was the largest park within the urban core of Sunderland, with its extensions spanning westwards all the way to Thorney Close. Although the central area of the park was of a splendid Victorian Grandeur, the extension area was little more than open grassland with a path running through it.

Although Sophie knew she was near home, she entered the park vigilantly, knowing fine well it was often a place for anti-social behaviour and louts, leading her to look around again nervously. A small stream trickled through the middle of the open grass fields, which twinkled in the moonlight, and without street lights in the area itself offered the only solace of light for quite some distance.

Sophie entered the park footpath off the street, leaving behind the increasingly dimmer and distinct glow of the streetlamps, stepping deeper and deeper into the darkness. Soon, she was surrounded by the blackness to the point her only light now was the glimmer of house windows in the distance. Then suddenly, as she continued to walk, she heard the deep breathing noise again. This time, it seemed closer than the first time. Concerned, she took out her phone and turned on its torch feature, shining it around her surroundings to get a better view. But again, there was nobody to be seen.

She began walking again, slowly and nervously, but the

breathing sound continued. As she walked, the sound repeated itself and seemed to get louder and louder, as if it were getting closer. Increasingly scared, Sophie looked behind her and then suddenly, in the darkness, she then noticed the figure of what appeared to be a man at first glance. The figure was taller than normal, but its stature seemed rugged and feral. Its arms were long and in an unusual shape. It stood still, as if it were watching Sophie, with the breathing noise coming directly from it.

Sophie, increasingly scared, opted to ignore it and in a display of calmness, continued walking. However, she could not help herself but look back, for as she walked, the figure began to follow slowly and menacingly.

"Hello?" She raised her voice nervously, her will to ignore it breaking. "Can I help you?" she asked defensively, but the figure did not reply. "Please stop following me, or I'll have to call the police…" she said nervously, attempting to be brave. The figure simply grunted and then proceeded and at that moment began to start moving forwards. Sophie, panicking, put her phone towards it and shined a light on the figure.

However, as it came towards her and its appearance began to emerge, Sophie screamed. This was no normal man. Its skin was a dark greenish grey, Its eyes yellow and monstrous like that of a snake and pointy teeth were sticking out of its mouth, and it was dressed in a dirty set of rags, while wearing a red cloth hat on its head. Its arms were long and bony, with pointed fingers that more resembled claws. In its right hand, it wielded a large black axe that was black in colour, and flint like in texture.

Horrified, Sophie immediately began running as fast as she could, with no time to video or photograph her unhuman attacker. On seeing her flee, it then roared, and proceeded to chase after her. Its speed and acceleration seemed beyond anything a normal human was capable of, and it did not take much effort to catch up with Sophie. Pacing into the darkness and fearing for her life, she could not see which direction she was heading and subsequently slipped on the gap where the stream ran through, crashing head first down into it.

Unable to get up in time, the creature approached and stood over Sophie. It roared and raised its axe again, preparing to strike her. Sophie cowered in fear, believing she had met her fate to the unknown monster. Then suddenly, there was a flash of blinding white light. It seemed to blast from every direction. She questioned to herself if she had died, and this is what the afterlife looked like. The light then subsided to a pillar shape focused above her head, like the brightness of the sun. She then looked up and the monster had disappeared. As she shielded her eyes at the excruciating light, she then noticed within it the personage of a woman, one which seemed oddly familiar to her, who's brightness and glory defined all description.

"Sophie..." the woman called out from inside the light. Her voice sounded mystical, even electronic, yet otherwise one she had heard before.

"Mam... is that you?" Sophie asked in a fearful voice, trying to look up at the woman in the light.

"Sophie... you have been chosen," the voice then ushered. Then, all of a sudden, another blast of light filled the entire area. Sophie felt as if she was being lifted up, and then suddenly, everything started spinning around violently, to the point it became a blur which she could no longer comprehend. A loud ringing noise then seemed to permeate from every direction.

Sophie woke up in bed, shooting upright and gasping for breath. She looked around, everything was normal, and a prism of light edged into her bedroom through the curtains. She looked down at her body to find she was wearing her pyjamas, before then jumping on hearing a banging on her bedroom door.

"Oi! Gerrup! It's breakfast time, you've slept in too long! Ha'way!" the faint yell of Eddie sounded from behind the door.

"Huh... Yes, coming, Dad..." she replied in a more than relaxed voice, perhaps relieved that everything was okay, yet otherwise conflicted and confused.

"What had just happened?" she asked herself. Was it all a dream? Was she really attacked by a strange monster and then rescued by a figure that resembled her mother?

As it weighed on her mind, Sophie's only conclusion was to write it off, or question her sanity. She got up and nervously proceeded downstairs...

Chapter IV: The Rally

Sophie sat at the table awkwardly with her father while they ate breakfast. He did not seem happy.

"So where were you last night like? You were that late I ordered mesel a takeaway" He grunted as he chewed.

"Nothing... just – just overtime at work. That's all," she said nervously, clearly attempting to hide the unusual experience of the previous night from him and the fact she had no explanation of how she got home.

"Gerraway, what are yer hiding from me this time?" He reiterated. Sophie's calm broke quickly, still traumatised by the previous day's events, and raised her voice.

"Nothing means nothing! I was slaving at that bar to keep a roof over our heads! I went for a walk after, if you must know!"

"Sounds like yer were out on the drink more like. Now, what were ya doing?" Eddie asked again, steeped in distrust of his daughter.

"You know I never do that! But even if I wanted to, I can't, and the reason I can't is because of you!" she shouted back, emotional and in pain.

"Well if you tried tellin' the truth for once it might help!" he snapped, unwavering in his position.

"Why can't you just listen to me for once?" she pleaded emotionally.

"There's nowt to be listened to when it's just lies and whinging. I asked ya a question and ya didn't give me an answer." He snarled.

"Is it any wonder?" she hissed, before proceeding to get up and storm out of the room.

Aghast at her father's total inability to understand her, Sophie got ready, left the house and headed into town. Arriving at Park Lane Interchange that afternoon, Sunderland's central bus station, she got off and sat on a bench as people walked by, mesmerised into her phone sending messages as she waited for Millie.

"I'm on my way, won't be long!" a message from her read. Eventually, Sophie looked up and saw Millie get off a bus in the distance. Her face lit up as she approached. The two then quickly embraced.

"Oh Millie, so happy to see you again," Sophie said in relief.

"Again? It was only yesterday, Sophie, are you okay?" she responded in a concerned response.

"Yeah... just the usual you know..." she replied in an empty voice as the two started walking.

"I know, but you messaged me earlier saying there's something you really needed to talk about," Millie reiterated.

"Oh um... yeah... Just my mock exam feedback with Mr Marchant, it was crap... that's all," Sophie replied unconvincingly, struggling to express her true mind.

"You told me about that yesterday. Are you sure there's not something else?" Millie responded puzzled, observing that her friend was seemingly uncomfortable.

"I did? Sorry things have been so hectic I must have forgot I mentioned it... yeah... don't worry about it," Sophie added, awkwardly attempting to cover as she felt unable to discuss the events of the night previously.

"Okay then... let's go for a coffee," said Millie attempting to be positive, but still sensing something was wrong. Thoughts raced through Sophie's head as she walked, tearing her apart inside.

"Was that actually real? What if she thinks I'm crazy? There's no such thing as monsters and ghosts, mam is dead! It was just a dream snap out of it!" All of this was running through Sophie's head.

The girls walked down through the city and entered a shopping centre. With a big sign 'The Bridges', it was the only indoor shopping centre in central Sunderland. With a white painted interior, a series of bland pillars connected to the roof, and a cream tiled floor, it gave off a retro feel, reflecting the era of the 1980s it was built in. Still, it was bustling on a Saturday, as families and people of all walks of life descended upon the town. Sophie and Millie walked through before settling down in a popular coffee chain, where they ordered lattes and began chatting.

"So was work okay last night Sophie?" Millie asked, attempting to break the ice, on noticing Sophie still seemed uneasy.

"Oh tell me about it, that Micky lad I work with is absolute torture." She groaned in response. "He really wanted to meet me today actually and invited me to some rally or something." Her face cringing at the thought of it.

"What, you mean that awful William Parker-Fulton?" Millie said in horror.

"Oh yeah… that's his name I think, honestly I told him I could not be bothered with politics let alone boys." Sophie responded.

"Oh my god… Fulton is terrible. He's such a charlatan, really playing up people's anger about immigrants… I hate it!"

Millie said with revulsion. "You know, since the pandemic; it's been really tough being an Asian… in Sunderland. I remember my parent's takeaway was vandalised a couple of years back, so I wouldn't go near a boy who doesn't have the right values," she told Sophie.

"Oh… I mean I don't think Micky is awful. Just annoying, he's just trying to be overly nice when I don't want it you know, with everything going on in my life, he's not helping…" Sophie said with a tint of despair. "I just want to escape from everything… I actually think I'm seriously going mad," she said suddenly, leading to a pause between them both.

"See, I knew there was something…" Millie replied with concern.

"Yeah, there is… you're right, but it's hard for me to express because I don't even know if it's real or not." Sophie responded quietly.

"Let's go for a walk… my mind is racing so much that I can't sit still," she then said abruptly. The two finished their coffees and proceeded out of the café and the shopping centre. However, as they exited from the north entrance of The Bridges, they observed a large crowd gathering next to an open field of grass outside, where a man was addressing them.

"What is this?" Sophie asked cynically. "Are they still banging on about that old leisure centre?"

"No…" Millie paused, seemingly expressing dread. "It's the rally your mate was on about… Fulton," she groaned. "Come on, let's walk past quickly before someone says something to me…" she urged. At the centre of the crowd, a man stood dressed in a pristine suit. He spoke eloquently with a tremendously posh and well-spoken voice. However, his hair was messy and almost comical in appearance, with a jolly smirk on his face.

"People of Sunderland!" he proclaimed to the crowd, who cheered with enthusiasm as they listened. "I will stand up for ordinary people like you! We will make our country something to be proud of again! We will take on the Westminster elite and derail the gravy train! Stop the flow of immigrants taking our jobs and re-open the Sunderland Shipyards!"

He spoke with a hypnotising passion in his voice, so much so that Sophie stopped as her curiosity in it grew.

"We will be proud of our history, not ashamed of it! I give to Wearside my heart, and you may look upon it to see it is red, white and blue!" he said thunderously, being met with a round of applause.

"Come on Sophie… let's go…" Millie said anxiously, attempting to pull her away.

"I heard recently there has been a surge in delinquency throughout Sunderland! Strange stories of violent and aggressive young men attacking and chasing bystanders!" On hearing this, Sophie froze in shock, and shrugged off Millie's attempts to move her.

"Sophie, what's wrong?" she asked her in confusion.

"We have no idea who these strange men are, or what their motivations may be, but I promise you, I shall crack down on crime and anti-social behaviour with an iron fist! Tougher sentences! Get those yobs off our streets!" He roared, again to ecstasy from the crowd.

"Oh… nothing…" Sophie uttered. "Okay… let's go…" Millie then reiterated, finally convincing her to move, but then just as they turned around and started heading back into the shopping centre, who did they bump into? None other than Micky.

"Areet Sophie!" he said in a positive voice, emerging

suddenly.

"Oh man..." Sophie groaned quietly. "Yes, all right, Micky, long time no see." she replied sarcastically.

"So what are yer both doing here like? Don't tell me you came to the rally even though you said you wouldn't!" He laughed. "So must be Sophie's best marra, Millie, right?" he then said turning to Millie.

"Yeah... Hi..." she said awkwardly.

"I hear you're the one with the brains like" he said inconsiderately.

"Oi, what are you trying to say about Sophie?" she retorted defensively.

"Well aye, Sophie too but you knar, too smart to be working in that pub anyway I reckon," he chortled.

"Yeah that's it Micky, just keep rubbing it in..." Sophie replied sternly.

"So yers came to see Fulton?" he asked.

"Not in a million years mate... just an unfortunate coincidence," Millie replied in a tight voice.

"I love to hear what Fulton has to say. He says things how it is. I think he's class like personally." Micky continued cheerfully, but Millie wasn't impressed.

"Tell me, Micky, do you approve of his abrasive and xenophobic policies?" she then asked suddenly, attempting to put him on the defensive.

"That's one way of putting it like, but I just think he's what this town needs. Look at us, there's nowt going on for Sunderland. We desperately need change here. People are fed up." He responded, seeking not to engage in arguments or become antagonistic.

"And why do you think a toff, educated at Eton, would

understand a working man like yourself let alone help you?" she continued with an almost reporter-like style of interrogation.

"Well it's not where you're brought up, it's what's in the heart isn't it?" he responded, again attempting to play it down.

"Yeah, well isn't that the case for people like me?" she hit back again.

"No, don't get me wrong, I'm not racist or anything like that. But when there's weird blokes attacking people something has to be done." He responded, attempting to divert the topic.

On hearing that topic yet again, Sophie's discomfort shot up, and she actively sought to end the conversation.

"Okay that's enough… Micky it's good to see ya, but please don't get into this political muck with her… we're going for a walk, so I'll see yer at work later, okay?" she said in an urgent voice. Micky was taken back.

"All right then… I guess I'll see you for our shift, yeah? Keep out of trouble!" he replied awkwardly. "Ta ra then!" he said cheerfully, and walked off. Millie stood fuming.

"Ignorant prick…" she snarled.

"I'm sorry Millie… let's go," Sophie said in a quiet voice, and the two walked away from the rally and back into the Bridges.

Chapter V: A Holy Trinity

Frustrated and annoyed, the two girls walked through town.

"Why don't we walk down to the East End?" Sophie suddenly suggested. "Not many people around to bother us there, right?"

"Yeah, I guess we can, it's a bit dodgy though, no?" Millie then replied unsure.

"I know what you mean, but I get so nostalgic for it too. Somewhere I can really express my thoughts," Sophie replied.

The two girls soon walked down a long winding road which proceeded down the bank, with the vibrant scenes of the city centre disappearing behind them. The buildings surrounding them soon became older, with some of them even derelict and abandoned.

"Look at this place, it's like it's been lost in time." Millie commented, as she looked on at a closed down pub titled *The Eastender*.

"My life is lost in time…" Sophie then replied snarky. "I just know this place as 'Where Sunderland began' you know, there's a saying that 'everyone used to live here', before the town expanded outwards. I'm pretty sure my grandad, mam's dad, was born somewhere round here," she said as she pondered upon some of the older flats.

"Oh, and where is he now? Is he still alive?" Millie then asked curiously.

"He lives on Ford Estate I think, I didn't hear he died, but he fell out with my dad years ago. Not like that takes much doing…" she laughed.

"Oh I'm sorry to hear that," Millie replied sympathetically.

"Yeah I obviously don't come down here though, but you don't get the same feel of it when your family's never known it really. Sort of like going back to Hong Kong I guess…" She added. "I mean Sunderland is my home, but at the same time, not quite if you get what I mean."

"Yeah, I understand…" Sophie said softly as they continued to walk.

"Speaking of that, thanks for getting me out of the situation with Micky, some people here can be so ignorant, don't you think?" Millie replied as they continued to walk around the East End area.

"No problem, he's not ignorant, just insensitive. He thinks he's being cheerful but it comes across as rude," Sophie replied.

"So anyway, now that we're away from all that… isn't there something you still need to talk to me about?" Millie then asked with concern, changing the topic.

"Yeah there is…" Sophie replied ominously. "But honestly, I don't think you'd ever believe me," she added… "In fact, I don't even know if I believe myself, I don't know what's happening… Life is cracking me up…"

"Sophie…" Millie replied softly. "Don't worry, you know I will always stand by you. No matter what it is…" she attempted to reassure Sophie. "When you're ready, okay, I will listen." As the girls walked, they eventually reached an old church building accompanied by a green courtyard around it. It had a light red brickwork, with arched windows and a tower spanning from it with a clock embodied on the front. They stopped for a moment and looked at the church, with not a soul to be seen anywhere around them, even amidst the houses and tower blocks in the surroundings.

"It's the Holy Trinity Church... softly as they looked at it. This place was built in 1719; it was the first parish church for the town of Sunderland itself... Why don't we go and sit in the courtyard?" she suggested.

The two opened a rusty old gate, which had been painted black, and entered the green courtyard behind it, where two noticeable headstones stood in isolation across a flat grass field.

"You know, I read this place used to be a graveyard." Millie continued. "Over 100,000 people are buried beneath us here. Creepy isn't it?" she laughed, as the two sat on a worn and tattered bench next to the path, which was peppered with shards of broken glass from previous disorderly behaviour.

"Okay... are you able to share what is troubling you?" She asked, turning to Sophie. "No pressure obviously, but I'm here to help," she said, as Sophie's heart began to race with anxiety.

"So, last night, after I came home from work..." Sophie began. "... I was walking through the Barnes Park extension, when I was attacked..." she said struggling to find her words, Millie's face showing visible concern.

"... I thought it was a man at first, stalking me and chasing me, but it was actually like a monster. I don't know if he was wearing a costume or what, but it had grey skin, yellow eyes and big teeth, and it tried to kill me with a large axe. But then all of a sudden, I was rescued by some woman in a pillar of white light, who looked like my mam, only for me to wake up in bed," she said slowly and uncomfortably.

"Oh my gosh, Sophie..." Millie responded in a panic, as Sophie continued.

"I thought it was a dream, and it honestly seemed like it, that was until Fulton back there mentioned something that sounded similar to it, he spoke about news of strange attacks throughout the town. I just don't know…" she gasped.

"Sophie, don't bottle things up like that, I'm here to listen. I believe you. These experiences can be so traumatic it's hard to recall them properly so it's normal to have amnesia or a strange recollection, maybe you do need to talk to someone professional about it though."

"I know… I know, but it's weird about me mam, you know, because really doing her proud is the only thing I feel I have left to fight for, and that's why despite all the trouble with my dad, debt, work, I haven't given up. So what happened is scary, but it's weird too… maybe she is watching over me?" She pondered. "Or is life getting to me so much that I'm even hallucinating it all? Still, I don't know how I'm going to get out of this mess." The two then sat quietly, looking across the church and the graveyard.

Then, suddenly, Sophie felt something hit her head.

"Ow!" she yelled in surprise, looking to see the cap from a bottle of coke having landed in her lap. She then looked around frantically, to see Bertha standing near them, towering over them both.

"Well, well, well… look what we've got here, yet again. Sophie Stuck up and her little poodle. What are ya doing in this old dump? Ey?" she said antagonistically.

"Bertha, leave us alone please…" Sophie pleaded unconvincingly.

"Ha!" Bertha sniggered. "Leave you alone? I think you've forgot yesterday, unfinished business… luv" her voice turning nastier and meaner.

"Why? What have I even done to you?" Sophie said in a

distressed voice.

"I'm sick of your stuck up ways ya self-entitled cow, always whinging about your own life when you don't even know what you've got. Think yer so smart ey?" She then threw the plastic bottle at Sophie, who cowered and took the hit. Millie reacted furiously.

"Bertha, back off now!" she yelled, but Bertha merely laughed.

"What yer going to do like? Knock me out? I'd like to see you try. No teacher to protect ya now pet!" She scoffed.

"That's it, one more word out of you and I'm going to claw your eyes out!" Millie snarled, jumping up and squaring off with her again as she had previously.

But again, before either of them could land a single hit on each other, they were interrupted by the sound of a deep aggressive breathing and snarling from someone nearby.

"What's that? Someone trying to be funny like?" Bertha responded to the noise, with a hint of unsurety under her voice. On hearing the sound, the colour drained from Sophie's face.

"Millie, we have to get out of here now!" she screamed.

"Oi, you're not going anywhere love…" Bertha retorted, but with an underlying anxiety. She then looked around at the source of the noise, to observe a figure standing in the distance at the edge of the courtyard.

"Who's this divvy like?" She asked rhetorically. "Oi, think ya hard or something?" She shouted at the figure in the distance, which did not respond.

"Here man, knock it off!" She yelled again as the grunting continued, but again, it did not move. Bertha, getting angry, picked up the bottle cap she threw at Sophie, walked up to the figure and hurled it off its head, but again it did not react.

"Millie…" Sophie whispered as Bertha continued to antagonise the figure. "It's the thing that attacked me last night, it's real!" she panicked. But before the two girls could escape, it suddenly started moving and edged towards Bertha, grunting and snarling.

"Bloody hell man, look at this mong in a costume." Bertha laughed, trying to hide her anxiety as she continued to ridicule the figure as it approached her. As it came up to her, she then pushed it antagonistically, but it didn't move, as if she had no strength to do so.

Suddenly, before she could do anything else, the creature grabbed Bertha's wrists tight with its claws, demonstrating unmatchable strength, leading her to scream in agony. She tried to pull herself away from it in desperation, but she was powerless to move it under any circumstances.

"HELP!" she screamed in despair. Sophie and Millie looked on, frightened but unsympathetic, as the creature then proceeded to pick her up and hurl her across the courtyard as if she were a ball of sorts. She crash landed next to the gravestone of Jack Crawford, a 19th century Sunderland sailor known for his heroics, the impact knocking her unconscious.

"RUN!" Millie yelled as the creature turned its focus towards them, but it was too late.

As with the previous encounter, the figure moved faster than any capable human, and lunged on Millie like a jaguar, sending her tumbling to the ground. She squirmed in the attempt to shuffle away, as the creature then proceeded to grab her forcefully by the hair and pull her up to her knees.

Sophie looked on in horror, feeling extreme helplessness. The creature then brandished its axe as it clutched her hair painfully, wielding it as if it were about to decapitate her.

Panicking, Sophie screamed at it "Get away from her!" attempting to cause a distraction, but it didn't listen.

She then reached into her pocket and discovered the stone she had picked up on the beach the night previously. With no other time to think, she hurled it full force at the creature, hitting it on the head. While the impact did not hurt it, the distraction worked, leading it to drop Millie and turn its attention towards Sophie. It then paced forwards slowly towards her, holding its axe up high. Sophie stood still, in a panic, and without any other plan she decided to desperately shove the creature to stop its attack. Then, much to her surprise, the creature fell backwards and crashed to the ground like a bowling pin.

Sophie was stunned.

"How was this possible?" She thought to herself, before turning back to look at where the stone had landed, and could not believe her eyes. In place of where the rock had fallen now sat a sword. It was of a fine silver craftsmanship, and had a mystical purple hue around it which made it look surreal. As she looked upon it, a familiar voice sounded out of nowhere.

"Sophie, you have been chosen!" it echoed. At that moment, the monster proceeded to pick itself up from the ground and resume its attack.

The voice then called out to her again "Sophie, believe in yourself!" Without a pause, she then grabbed the sword and waved it against the monster with wariness.

Enraged, it swung its axe at Sophie, causing her to leap back anxiously, but on its second attempt she then hurled the sword in its way, blocking the attack. Inspired, she then swung her left fist and punched it in the face, which as with the first shove, knocked it backwards in pain. The creature roared and it swung its axe forwards again, but this time Sophie was ready and intercepted the blow with the sword, she then swung it at its hand and knocked the weapon out of its grip. Then, taking a chance, Sophie lunged herself forwards with the sword and impaled it clean through the creature's chest. The monster screamed in agony, before falling onto the ground. As it died, its body then suddenly crumbled to dust before her eyes as if it were made of burnt ash, which faded into the wind instantly as if it had never been there to begin with.

Sophie stood in both shock and awe, glancing at the sword in her hand and trying to get her head around what just happened. But before she could do anything else, it combusted into a beam of blue light and disappeared, leaving her holding the very stone that she had found to begin with.

"Sophie?" Millie said nervously, still sat on the ground, looking on in a sense of disbelief.

"Millie!" she shouted back with urgency running back over to her friend having remembered her situation. "Are you okay? I'm so sorry it's all my fault!" Sophie said emotionally as she helped her back up to her feet.

"Yes, I'm fine, don't worry, just a few grazes and a bit of dirt. Of course, it's not your fault, you saved my life!" she said tearfully, embracing Sophie in a hug. "Seriously, though, what happened? There was this… light then you produced a sword and killed it! Everything you told me was real!" She gasped.

"I can't get my head round it either, but maybe there is hope for me after all," Sophie replied, also still shaken. The two then glanced over to Bertha, who still lay unconscious next to Jack Crawford's Gravestone.

"What about Bertha?" Millie then asked, displaying conscience.

"Stuff her, would she have done the same if it were us? Let's get out of here!" Sophie urged, and the two left.

That evening, Sophie quietly opened her front door and stepped into her home. Without saying a word, she peaked into her living room where her father was watching television. Much to her alarm, a correspondent was giving a crime broadcast.

"Reports are spreading of strange attacks and intimidation occurring around Sunderland by strange looking men, described as wearing costumes. Police have urged the public not to panic, and vowed to tackle this anti-social behaviour. The public are urged to get in contact with any information they might have."

Detecting Sophie's presence, Eddie turned his head towards the door and shouted. "Sophie, is that you home?"

However, Sophie declined to respond and instead scuttled upstairs, leading him to shrug his shoulders as he continued on watching the television.

Chapter VI: No Turning Back

Confused and unsettled by the events of the past few days, Sophie had hoped the scene at Holy Trinity Church marked the end of it all, but the circulating reports of these monsters being witnessed by other people indicated there was possibly more than just one out there, and her hopes were wishful thinking. Despite this, her triumph over the beast encouraged her that she could eventually overcome the other challenges in her life.

"Maybe I'm no longer a weak and cowardly girl that people walk all over." Sophie thought to herself, pondering how she had now discovered in herself a new found strength and resolve in the form of a mysterious stone she once found on a beach.

"Is my mother watching over me?" She also wondered. However, despite the surmounting paranormal events, she was determined to carry on as normal with a new positive vibe.

After the weekend passed Sophie attended school on Monday. On looking round in the schoolyard, she soon noted that Bertha was absent, which despite making things peaceful, was an ominous sign.

Looking around in the yard, thoughts raced through her head, including "Is Bertha okay?" Also, "What if she decides to blame me and Millie for the attack against her?"

The two had left the girl unconscious in contempt for her behaviour against them, reasoning it was what she deserved after all, but that doesn't mean their minds were clear of it, and on Monday afternoon their worst fears were confirmed.

As the two sat in class working, there was a knock on Mr Marchant's door. It opened to a short and plump woman with long black hair and a stern look on her face, dressed in an equally uptight trouser suit. Her name was Joan Stoddart, the school headmistress. Almost immediately on entering, her eyes glared at Sophie and Millie sitting working.

"May I have a word with Sophie Scott and Millie Chen?" she asked in an intimidating voice. Mr Marchant said nothing and merely nodded, and the two girls got up and left the room, following her along a winding corridor to an office.

"Take a seat please!" She snapped, sitting herself down behind a small desk which her belly pressed against, barely fitting behind. On the wall around them were a slew of motivational posters.

One of them, featuring a funny-looking man with grey hair, highly energetic eyes and a black shirt, read "Always remember to be NOICE."

The two girls looked around curiously as there were a few moments of awkward silence, then Mrs Stoddart placed her hands authoritatively on the desk and began speaking.

"Bertha Bagshaw, what do you know about her?" she asked in an extremely menacing time, Sophie's complexion sinking in horror.

"No… what about her?" she asked, trying to play ignorant.

"On Saturday afternoon, she was found lying injured next to Holy Trinity Church in the East End. She's now in hospital recovering but she says you two were with her when a strange man attacked her. Is this true? Were you there?" She asked in an interrogating manner.

"No… we don't know anything about this." Sophie responded, feigning concern in her voice. "I hope she's okay…"

"Absolutely not. We don't know anything about this." Millie then seconded Sophie backing her up. "Neither of us were there. On Saturday we went to the library to study." She added. The headteacher gave them an unconvinced, yet ultimately defeated look.

"I see. You must understand we have to take this matter extremely seriously. The Police have been informed. We're not saying you've done anything, but we will continue to investigate this, do you understand?" She then reiterated seriously.

"Yes Miss, of course," they responded, nodding their heads.

"Okay then Millie, you're free to go. Sophie, stay here for a moment," she then said suddenly. As Millie awkwardly left the office, Sophie's heart trembled with fear. The moment it closed, she then turned to Sophie and spoke sharply.

"I'll keep this quick, but I'm well aware you have a conflict with Bertha, Sophie. I find it odd she'd lie about this experience, knowing her... so I'll be keeping an eye on you." Sophie's complexion turned from fear to resentment, but she chose to say nothing. "Okay, be away with you!" she snapped.

Later that day, Sophie and Millie had gym class, or how Britain liked to describe it, "Physical Education" (PE). The girls of the school had to dress in a navy blue polo shirt and shorts, along with white trainers. During this class they would exercise on the school field, which bordered a long stretch of road with terraced houses opposite. Today they were playing netball, while being led by their PE teacher Gemma Burlison, who while not being a mean spirited person like the headmistress, was also a no nonsense character who liked to push the girls.

On this day, they were playing Volleyball. Split into two teams divided by a net, the girls aimed to keep the ball in the air and land it on the other half of the court. Miss Burlison was eager to keep the rhythm going for as long as possible.

"That's it girls, keep it up!" She yelled enthusiastically as it bounced from side to side. While Sophie was never particularly bad at PE, even before she found herself gaining extraordinary powers, the events of the day were weighing on her mind and distracting her. As she played, she suddenly felt a dark feeling come over her, manifesting in a sudden burst of insecurity and uneasiness.

Losing focus on the game, she increasingly felt uncomfortable, as if someone was watching her. Then, looking over to the fence, she noticed a man dressed in a black cape from afar. His face was not visible, and nor did he seem similar to the monsters which had attacked earlier. He stood in front of the fence motionless, looking onwards to his direction. Then, all of a sudden, the ball crashed off Sophie's head and she lost her balance, falling over clumsily onto the grass. The girls on the other team laughed in unison.

"Sophie!" Miss Burlison snapped. "What's wrong? Eyes on the game!" She commanded.

"Sorry, yes, miss!" Sophie replied, picking herself up. She then glanced over to the fence again, but much to her surprise, there was nobody there. The mysterious figure had disappeared.

"Come on Sophie, let's beat them!" Millie then said supportively as they played on.

With no time to rest, that evening after school Sophie had a shift at the Dun Cow. Once again, Micky was again very much attentive to Sophie's withdrawn mood state, and as usual made an attempt to engage in conversation with her as they served customers and cleaned glasses.

"Sophie, you're looking very down again about yourself there." He commented. "Happy to hear you out." But as usual,

Sophie was determined to share as little as possible with Micky.

"Nothing... just a long day that's all!" she said abruptly, trying to shut down the conversation as usual.

But before either of them could say another word, Derek burst into the room carrying a newspaper, which he placed on the bar.

"Sophie! It seems you're better than usual today, keep it up!" He commented in an unusually cheerful voice. As Derek started assisting new customers, Sophie's eyes were drawn like magnets to the headline of the paper, which read:

"BOY SIXTEEN, MISSING AFTER ABDUCTION." Alarmed, she took a closer glance at it, which stated underneath "Farringdon Student Matthew James is missing after reportedly being abducted on Friday night by a strange figure. His disappearance adds to reports of strange men attacking and intimidating people around Sunderland."

Derek, on seeing Sophie glancing at the paper, then commented "Tell ya what, there's a lot of strange stuff going on recently. A girl attacked, and now they're saying a young lad's been abducted. Anyway, back to work!" He then ordered in his usual manner, before trotting off back upstairs. As soon as he was gone, Micky then grabbed the paper.

"Matthew James? Swear I've heard of that lad before, I think I know a mate of his," he said to Sophie.

"Seriously?" she then replied with unusual enthusiasm.

"Aye, proper chavs like, of course, always up to no good," he added.

"Okay, so what do you reckon happened here then? What's going on?" she then asked, surprising Micky who was not used to Sophie being so eager to chat, not least driving the conversation herself.

"God knows, but this is a bit different from you like. Do you know him too or something?" he asked.

"No, but those attacks… I need to know what's causing them, I'm worried," she then replied in a more anxious tone, letting her true emotions display to Micky for the first time.

"What? Did this happen to you as well or something?" he replied with a look of surprise on his face.

"That doesn't matter…" Sophie then responded, retreating and shutting things down, but Micky wasn't going to let it slip now.

"Ha'way Sophie, what is it then?" he asked impatiently.

"Honestly, you'd never believe me…" she said abruptly in a downer voice.

"Sophie…" he reiterated, remaining firm. "If you don't want to tell me then fair enough. But do you want to know more about this or not like?"

"Yeah… I do…" Sophie said softly, conceding.

"All right then, you can tell me the rest later, but in the meantime, I have a mate we can meet," he said softly. "Up for it?" he then asked positively.

"Yep," Sophie replied tensely.

It was at that very moment, coupled with the previous events of the day, that she came to the realisation that there was no turning back. The mysterious events at hand could no longer be ignored or wished away. They could only be investigated and confronted.

Chapter VII: Magical Narcotics

Backhouse Park was an odd kind of place. It was somewhere tranquil and beautiful, but also somewhere you didn't want to be caught in at night. That's because it acted as a bridge between one of the wealthiest areas of Sunderland, Ashbrooke, and one of the poorest, Hendon. The park itself was actually a scenic scoping valley which a small river, known as the Hendon Burn, carved its way through, surrounded by lush green banks and woodland.

Long ago, before the suburb of Hendon was built, the area was romanticised in local art as the "Valley of Love". As urbanisation spread, the park itself, once owned as a plot of land by the Backhouse Family, became the last holdout of the valley's former beauty. A popular place to walk dogs and take a stroll, it was also frequented by delinquents and troublemakers, originating from the suburb to its northern side.

And it was here in Backhouse Park that Micky had arranged with Sophie to meet his old friend, Liam Heskett, who he had known while growing up in Hendon. Liam led a very different kind of lifestyle to Micky and Sophie. While he wasn't a bad person, he had grown up in a rough environment without any guidance or direction in life, leading him to spend his days louting around associating with the wrong people, which often got him into trouble. But he didn't seem to care, because he felt he had nothing to fight for and nothing to lose. With short greasy looking hair and a few pimples, he often dressed in cheap tracksuits and was stereotypical of what some people liked to call a "chav".

The following afternoon after their conversation at the Dun Cow, after she finished school, Sophie met Micky and walked up towards Backhouse Park, which was only down the road from the school building. Sophie had urged Millie to come along, but she used studying as an excuse because she did not want to meet Micky again, and nor did she want to meet a random chav. So she braved it alone.

"So, how did you get to know this Liam?" Sophie asked curiously as she met Micky and walked up the street.

"I went to school with him, proper little toe rag but he's all right I guess," he replied, as the two pulled open a rigid metal gate and entered the park, which was surrounded by steep brick walls. The autumn leaves swirled in the wind as they proceeded up a small path, before they spotted a young man sitting on a park bench wearing a blue and white tracksuit, equipped in his left hand with a 50 energy drink.

"That's him," Micky said quietly as they approached.

"All right Micky," he said loudly as the two approached. "So is this yer lass then?" he scoffed, pointing towards Sophie.

"No way," she said very defensively. "He's just my work mate." Her face showed displeasure.

"Aye?" he laughed. "Well nice to meet ya anyway, Sophie is it? Ya very bonny like," he added, leading her to scorn with displeasure again.

"Okay, I'm meeting you because we need information," she then said sharply, firmly setting the agenda.

"So Micky said, about young Matthew?" he then asked, not seeming to be bothered by Sophie's harsh and reserved tone.

"Yes, so I was wondering, who took him and why? And

where do you think he's gone?" she asked.

"Pushy this one isn't she?" Liam laughed to Micky, who stayed silent. "Well, if I knew that we'd have already found him. But if you want to know a bit more, ya have to promise to keep it to yourselves and not tell the coppers. I'm not going to cooperate with no police investigation like," he said, striking a more worried and quieter tone.

"Nah, it's not about that mate, don't worry." Micky intervened on behalf of Sophie.

"Alreet then, so first, have yers seen these Radgie fellas appearing around town?" Liam asked.

"Yep... more than seen them" Sophie replied tensely.

"Aye, they're involved with it," Liam replied. "They've got something to do with this new ket that they call Lava. It's red and shiny and you drink it. I haven't tried it meself like, but apparently it lets ya vent all your anger and feel so good."

"So, they're making this?" Sophie asked, now engaged and more comfortable.

"I don't know like, but word is it's coming from Tony Radcliff's gang from up Southwick. No idea how they're making it like. So, this lad Matthew starts trying it, he couldn't get enough of it, so he ended up owing Tony's lot money and, of course, he couldn't pay it. He got into an argument on Friday night up Foxy Island then one of those blokes abducted him in front of his mates."

"Tony Radcliff, are you kidding me?" Sophie reacted loudly.

"What? You know him like?" Micky reacted with surprise.

"Heard of him? My stupid dad owes him money, Radcliff's been extorting us for months," she said with an angry tone under her voice.

"Explains a lot like..." Micky commented.

"So are you telling me this bloke is the one behind all this? And he's now kidnapped this lad in this "Foxy Island?" she asked passionately.

"Aye, as far as I can tell yer aye…" he replied softly.

"Where is that place anyway?" she asked.

"It's a nickname for those woods and grassland between Doxford Park and Farra, opposite Gilley Law as well. Plenty of wrong'uns like to go for a session there," Micky replied.

"Aye that's right. Apparently, they've got a base there. But the coppers searched the whole area and found nowt. If you're gonna go find him, remember we didn't have this conversation, right? Tony is a nasty piece of work ," he then said in a quiet and more serious tone.

"You don't need to tell me…" Sophie replied sharply.

"Right, okay then!" Sophie said authoritatively. "You've been a great help Liam, but we've got more to do.' She clasped her hands together and stood up.

"It's only been five minutes man," he laughed. "Nee bother though, if you want to come for a sesh one day just let me knar okay? Now, take care and like I said, dinnit mention my name," he replied as Sophie and Micky then made their way back to outside the park. As soon as they passed the gate, Micky then turned to Sophie sternly.

"All right then Sophie, I'm gonna ask again, based on what you said up there, what's this about? Tony Radcliff is after you and your dad?" he asked in a serious tone. Sophie hesitated, but did not close herself off.

"I wish I knew myself, weird things are happening…" she replied.

"What kind of weird things? These gadgies seen around town? You need to tell me Sophie if I'm going to help you."

She looked at him for a moment in the eyes, before unleashing everything off her chest.

"Well, where should we start? I keep being attacked by monsters, one of them just nearly killed a bitch from school before trying to kill Millie too... oh and this was all before I received a magical sword and special powers by a woman who looks like my mam!" She took a deep breath after unloading.

"What?" Micky replied, confused. "Are you kidding me?" he then asked more cynically.

"See! This is why I don't talk about it." She then responded in a frustrated and angry voice.

"Well, what am I supposed to do when I hear about magic swords and superpowers like?" he asked, showing his palms in a defensive gesture.

"What you could do is try listening for once. See ya!" Sophie snapped, before proceeding to storm off down the street.

Micky looked on as Sophie walked off in a huff, before proceeding to have a change of heart.

"Sophie! All right then, I'll hear you out." He shouted. "I'm sorry!" Sophie then stopped and turned around.

Chapter VIII: Making Sunderland Great Again

"So you want to go to the police?" Micky asked cynically as they walked, after Sophie had explained to him the events of the past few days.

"Yes, I do," Sophie replied uncompromisingly. "Tony Radcliff is at the root of every single problem in my life, and based on what I've heard we have an angle to report him that isn't about the trouble with my dad!" She continued in a stressed voice, but Micky disagreed.

"Liam just told yer not to do that in exchange for telling you!"

"Yeah, well I'm not intending to rat him out, but I've got a lot to lose if I don't do something!" She argued back.

"Aye I know, but listen, coppers are self-serving and they don't deal with something if they have to get off their backside to do it," he replied.

"Yeah? But it's their duty to help and protect people isn't it? I mean people keep being attacked. How can they ignore it?" she continued to insist.

"Sophie, you're so innocent. Nee offence, but you have no idea. The police have no reason to believe you, let alone help you. It wouldn't surprise me if they're literally on Radcliff's payroll man," Micky said insistently as they got out of his car and walked through Sunderland City Centre towards the police office.

"Then what do we do?" Sophie asked defensively. "Look if I don't deal with this, then my future is going down the pan. I have no choice! So yes, we're going to the police station." She continued, getting angry again.

The two continued to walk into Sunderland City Centre, before approaching a small police building situated on the corner of the street, which looked no different from your average shop unit. Despite being a big city, Sunderland unusually did not have a large central police station. It did once, but funding cuts from the government forced it to close down, much to the dismay of the local population. Upon entering, they sat down in a small waiting room as they waited for an officer to attend to them, a process which proved to be long and tedious.

Finally, a slightly overweight police officer wearing a crumpled shirt and tie entered the room and called them in. He had a serious look on his face which did not express any emotions. He led them into a dark and intimidating interrogation room which had no windows and limited light. The desk was messy and filled with various papers. As he sat down on his comfy office chair, a map of Sunderland and the wider area hung on the wider wall behind them, with little red pins dotted throughout depicting various locations and addresses.

"Okay, what can I do for you?" The officer said in a very cold, yet seemingly disinterested voice. Sophie gulped, before nervously starting to speak.

"I'm here to give some information about Tony Radcliff, a criminal causing trouble throughout town," she said with great unease.

"Okay, what sort of trouble?" The officer asked sharply.

"His gang is behind all these strange attacks and occurrences throughout town, including against me a few days ago, Bertha

Bagshaw in the East End on Saturday, and kidnapping schoolboy Matthew James," she explained.

"Okay, so you were attacked too?" he responded in an interrogative tone. "And how do you know this Tony Radcliff is responsible? Was it him directly, or these strange men that's been reported?" he then asked critically.

"Well, um… I heard from a source that it's connected to a drug ring linked to him," she then responded.

"Okay, then who is your source?" the officer then asked.

"I can't say, they wanted to be confidential… but I heard they captured Matthew up near the woods next to Farringdon," Sophie said a less confident voice, realising she wasn't convincing the officer.

"Right, so if you can't name your source how can we possibly help you? You haven't provided any evidence here whatsoever that Tony Radcliff is involved. Unless you show proof, it's all hearsay," he grunted.

"But surely you can investigate it?" Sophie then asked in a disappointing voice.

"We are always investigating. We can file a report for you that you were attacked and mentioned this, but there's not much we can do right now," he said, shutting down the conversation. "Please, write your name and details here, please," he said as he handed Sophie a purple form and a pen. She filled it out hastily, writing excessive detail on it in a last gasp attempt to try and convince someone in the unlikely scenario it would be read later. She then returned it to him promptly.

"Okay then, thank you very much," the officer said unenthusiastically as Sophie left with Micky, wearing a disappointed look on her face.

"See, I told you going there was a waste of time man," Micky said the instant they stepped out of the door.

"Then what should we do?" Sophie yelled in frustration. "Radcliff is messing up my life in every direction, I'm probably going to get blamed for Bertha and now, to top it all off, there's a lad missing!" she groaned. "What's your idea then, Micky?" she asked sarcastically.

"Sophie man, as hard to believe as it was, you told me something about having special powers and a sword. If that's true, why don't you just go and deal with it yourself? What would your mam have wanted you to do?"

Sophie stopped for a moment, taking out the stone she had found out of her pocket. She paused and looked at it for a moment, thinking deeply.

"The voice told me to believe in myself. You're right I guess, she would have wanted me to be strong, not to cower away, to look after others…" she said thoughtfully.

"Exactly, so if what you have told me is true Sophie, why don't you go and rescue this lad yourself and then deal with Tony? Stop him trampling on you and your dad, find out what's going on with all this and end it all," he said enthusiastically. Sophie's face lit up with inspiration.

"Okay then, yep, let's do it. Tonight after work, let's go and investigate that area, but I'd like to invite Millie too," she then added in a more serious tone.

"All right, we can do that, tonight's going to be busy mind. Fulton's holding an election event and speech in the function room." Micky added, Sophie's face quickly turned to dread on hearing this.

"Oh man, you're kidding me?" She reacted with disdain.

"Derek didn't tell you? It's tonight at eight p.m. Aye it will be hectic but I'm dead excited, we're expecting a big crowd as well," Micky responded.

That evening, crowds flocked to the Dun Cow Pub in anticipation for William Parker-Fulton's election speech. Fulton was running to be the mayor of Northumbria, or the "North East Combined Authority" which consisted of Sunderland and all the surrounding towns and cities spanning from the River Tweed on the Scottish Border down the River Tees, and the election was now just days away. In running for Mayor, he was the candidate of a party known as the "People's Democratic Party" (PDP) which was a populist organisation with highly right wing overtones.

Although the city of Sunderland was known for its historical overt loyalty to the Labour Party, with its links to its industrial past, the decline of the city's industries and the rise of widespread disillusionment and cynicism had given rise to a backlash against politicians and fuelled movements that vented public anger and discontent against the elite.

In 2016, Sunderland after all had made national headlines for being the first place in Britain to deliver a decisive victory in favour of "leave" in the European Union referendum, a moment which set the mood of the night ahead. It also made it a prime target for politicians such as Parker-Fulton, who despite having nothing in common with such a place and being from a very different sort of background, saw political gain amongst the anger of local people, and subsequently framed himself as a Messiah like figure.

And unsurprisingly, the Dun Cow upper function room was heaving. Sophie and Micky were soon run off their feet pouring drinks, collecting payments and serving people. When they got a moment to pause, Micky, wondering about the night's plans, turned to Sophie.

"So, did Millie agree to come?" seeming a bit anxious.

"She said it's late and she has to study, so it's not looking likely…" Sophie replied in a less than enthusiastic voice. "I think she's still uneasy after the attack, and of course, her argument with you," she added.

"Just us then? Shame but areet then…" Micky added, as he picked up a glass and started wiping it. Suddenly, as they carried on working, pub manager Derek entered the room and raised his voice, which bellowed across the room.

"Ladies and Gentlemen, please give a round of applause for William Parker-Fulton!" And at that moment, an explosion of clapping filled the air as Fulton entered from the staircase, smiling and waving superficially at the crowd as he passed, with television cameramen following him.

However, instead of heading to the makeshift stage, he first came over to the bar. Approaching Sophie, he said in an overtly charming voice:

"Excuse me, dear, if I may!" As he politely moved Sophie out of the way and then proceeded to pull himself a pint, before raising it up in the air and giving a "Cheers" to the crowd.

"A toast to our country, a toast to our people!" He proclaimed, which was met with a roaring cheer from the crowd. He then took a sip of the pint, before walking over to the stage still clutching it.

"Good evening, ladies and gentlemen! I'd say good evening "everyone" but as you know I'm not one of those gender-neutral types after all." He opened his speech, prompting laughter from the crowd. "Don't you just love our great English pubs? You don't get many places better than the Dun Cow! It's what makes our country great if you ask me! And I'm here in Sunderland to keep it great!" He then emphasised with passion, stopping for a moment as the crowd cleared and clapped.

"That's because if you know me well enough, I fight for a normal world, a common-sense world, the old world we used to know, and being here in Sunderland tonight I'm as close to that world I can get! AND WE'RE GOING TO FIGHT FOR IT!" The crowd cheered again as he took a deep breath and another sip of his pint.

"So, do we have any woke warriors in here then? I bet you won't find any of those goons in here. As I said on GB News last week, these people are eating themselves with self-hatred. They want to erase our history, tear down our statues and make you feel bad about who you are! They might talk of justice and equality, but where is it for people like us? Let me tell you this, they don't care about ordinary folk like you and me!"

Micky sat watching Fulton in awe, while Sophie showed little interest and pressed on with her work. "They are middle class, metropolitan lefties, they sit posturing in their fancy restaurants eating their lentils and luxury food. They think they're better than ordinary folk yet they haven't worked a normal job in their lives! That's why I'm proud to be here in Sunderland, I look upon you all, the sons of miners, shipbuilders, hardworking men who built our country with their bare hands who are now having it taken away from them! Well NOT ANY MORE!" This is followed by further roaring and cheers from the crowd.

"I pledge to you that the People's Democratic Party will restore Sunderland and the North East to its former glory! Out with the socialists, in with the real people! As Mayor of our region, I will stand up to the gravy train in Westminster and make sure that they take us seriously! First, no more asylum seekers! The London metropolitan luvvies are sending these third world rejects to our town and taking up our housing, driving up prices and bringing in crime. Sorry folks, but Sunderland is FULL UP, Britain is FULL UP and it's time to put our own people first!"

"Fulton is absolutely class like!" Micky said passionately to Sophie as the crowd cheered.

"I can't wait until this is over…" She groaned.

Fulton then continued "I heard recently a lovely young man was taken! We must be honest, Sunderland has a problem with youth disobedience and delinquency. It's leading our children astray. We have too many parasites in our society! They're taking benefits from your taxes, living idle lives and contributing nothing to your area! Whoever these yobs are, they must be crushed! And that's why I will be tough on crime and tough on the causes of crime! There will be no more chavs or lost boys on my watch!"

"See, Sophie!" Micky said pointing over to him. "This is why you should support him, he might even be able to help you with this situation." Sophie shrugged her shoulders in apathy.

"He's pushing this issue really hard. Can't wait until we get to the bottom of it all. When's the election anyway?" she asked.

"Next week!" he replied.

"Right, no wonder it's in my face so much. But don't you think he knows more than he should about this?" Sophie then asked puzzled, but before Micky could respond, Derek spotted the two talking and he was not impressed.

"Oi, what did I tell you two? NO slacking!" He barked, forcing them to return to work.

Fulton continued "So yes my friends, a vote for me is a vote for Sunderland's future. Let's save this town, let's save our region, and save our people! Let's make Sunderland great again and make the North East the driving seat of the great British renaissance! A hub of our identity, heritage and culture! The left have ruined this town and you all deserve so much better! I promise you, no longer will you be left behind! Thank you very much everyone and goodnight!" He proclaimed, ending his speech.

At this point, the crowd combusted into euphoria.

"Fulton! Fulton! Fulton!" They chanted in an almost hypnotic fashion.

"I've never seen a politician receive a reception like this in Sunderland all my life like." Micky remarked as the two began collecting empty glasses. "Fulton is a big name, and this is a big moment for our city. Is there hope for us? I'd like to think there is." He smiled.

But Sophie, still unsure, said nothing.

Chapter IX: The Terror of Foxy Island

The clock struck eleven p.m. After having cleaned and washed up the litany of pint glasses, gathered up all the litter and vacuumed the carpet, Sophie and Micky were finally finished for the night. But they weren't going home, because they had other plans. Eager to get to the bottom of the disturbing events happening to her, and to begin a resistance to the problems undermining her life, she and Micky had decided to investigate the aforementioned place commonly known as "Foxy Island".

Despite its name, Foxy Island wasn't actually an island at all. It was a span of open moorland and forest wedged between four south western suburbs of Farringdon, Doxford Park, Gilley Law and Silksworth. With the appearance of a pure wilderness, it was an isolated location, where people could hide in the trees and very tall grass, often getting up to no good. It was also used for cross country runs by the school which bordered onto it, making it a much loathed location amongst students.

After finishing their shifts, Sophie and Micky stepped out of the Dun Cow and into the night. The autumn air was cold and bitter. They then proceeded to walk down the street to where Micky had parked his car. Suddenly, they were interrupted by a voice shouting in the distance.

"Sophie! Sophie!" They yelled, sounding familiar. Sophie turned around surprised to discover Millie belting down the street towards her anxiously, quickly running up and embracing Sophie, who reacted by surprise.

"Millie, what are you doing here?" she asked in a surprised voice. "I thought you said you were studying?"

Millie smiled. "I studied all evening, it's eleven p.m. now! I've sneaked out," she said cheerfully. "I didn't think I could do it after what happened, but it was weighing on my mind and I realised I had to support you, no matter what. We're in this together, through thick and thin." Sophie's face lit up.

"Areet then, let's do it," Micky said enthusiastically.

The trio got into Micky's small red car and drove off into the night, winding through the streets of Sunderland, which were dimly lit with orange street lamps illuminating the silent roads.

"Right Sophie, what exactly is our goal here tonight? Are we actually going to try and find that lad?" he asked, with his eyes focused on the road.

"Yep, we want to try and find out Tony's role in all this and try and save this lad, both ideally. If we don't find anything, we keep looking," she then said passionately.

"Aye aye captain. Anyway, I had a question, Sophie, if you don't mind me asking. Have you actually told your dad about any of this? You know, being attacked and all that…" he then asked curiously.

"Nope, not a single word of it. Waste of time and oxygen because he'll never believe me. I'd rather stick pins in my eyes than try to explain it to that old tosser," Sophie replied, barely concealing her contempt. "He would absolutely find some way to blame me, even though this whole situation is his fault."

"I'm sure there's still good in him," Millie then added softly "Don't give up on him," she added. Sophie said nothing, and the car then fell silent. As he drove, a number of large imposing tower blocks appeared on the horizon, standing over the housing estates around them. They were coloured completely white, although they had become a bit stained with age. This was the suburb known as Gilley Law, famous for those very iconic towers which had been built in the 1960s.

"Right, I'm going to park here in Gilley Law and we can walk over to Foxy Island from there," Micky said as they approached. He parked the car in a small car park outside one of the tours and the trio got out and walked upwards towards the fields in the distance, which was covered by the blackness of the night. They then cautiously veered off the road and onto a dirt track path, leaving the estate further and further behind them as they ventured into the forest, with the light withering away. There was also no sound around them to be heard other than the gushing of the wind.

"Well... here we are, Foxy Island, Sunderland's very own area of outstanding natural beauty!" Micky said sarcastically, as he gazed out from the trees across the sloping blackness of the hills around them. "Nah, it's minging..." he then added sharply, as he looked upon the litter around him and attempted to avoid the mud.

"Okay, so where and what do we start looking for?" Millie then asked. "I mean it's so muddy, how do you even begin to do this?" she asked.

"Ha'way man." Micky then urged. "This is nowt compared to when I played footy. If I didn't get stuck in me dad would ratify me," he said in a tough voice, attempting to be encouraging.

"Yeah, well I don't play football do I? I mean mud is mud... pigs can play in mud too." Millie then said, showing displeasure. "It stinks too..." she said uncomfortably, her face wrinkling in discomfort.

Micky, perhaps without thinking, decided to speak his full mind and bit back.

"Well, I'll tell you what else stinks too, your attitude. We're doing this to support Sophie but ya just keep whinging on. I mean you chose to come, you didn't have to!" he said in an angry voice.

"Excuse me! I've known her for longer than you have, you're just jumping on the bandwagon. And I actually have valuable time I am sacrificing coming to this hole." she then snapped back.

"What a load of twaddle!" Micky then reacted angrily. Hurt and emotional, Millie then turned to Sophie and wept.

"I'm really sorry, but I can't take any more of this idiot Sophie! I'll go to another part of the area and investigate on my own. I'll catch up with you after." She then stormed off into the blackness.

"Millie, wait!" Sophie then shouted anxiously, but she didn't listen.

Sophie then quickly became angry.

"Micky man, you idiot! She came along despite the fact she felt unsure, and you just had to mess it up!" Micky wasn't sympathetic and shrugged his shoulders in indifference.

"Stuff her man, just let her be." But Sophie only grew more aggravated at his response.

"She's my best friend! And she's a young girl, alone at night at a dodgy place like this! We have to go and find her, NOW!" she snapped. The two then began urgently heading in the direction she left, walking through the trees down beside a small riverside. "Millie? Millie?" Sophie called out in despair, but she got no answer.

Then, all of a sudden, before they could make another move,

a female scream rattled through the trees in the distance.

"Well done Micky!" She seethed, "Come on!" She snapped quietly, running forwards towards the source of the noise, Micky hurrying after her frantically.

"Bloody hell man I've never known anyone to move as fast as you!" He panted "Maybe I do need to get back to footy after all." He panted, gasping for breath.

"Will you just shut up man?" Sophie responded, still distressed and angry.

"Here, look at this?" Micky then suddenly said in an urgent voice, pointing towards a tree.

"What is it?" Sophie asked. She walked over to see him looking over at a series of symbols that had been carved into the side of the tree. Curious, she shined her phone light over them. They were a deep crimson red in colour, and represented a mysterious set of runes. Underneath, a slogan had been carved out in English, of the same colour, which read *"The Lord will rise again"*.

"Christ..." Micky then said suddenly.

"What, it's about Jesus?" Sophie then asked in confusion.

"No... Christ, someone's coming, hide!" he snapped quietly, before proceeding to drag her behind some bushes. As soon as they hid, the silhouettes of two men suddenly appeared in the distance, the leaves crushing under their feet. They were large in stature.

"Swear I heard someone scream around here just now... But nobody's found anything right?" one of them grunted with a voice that was very familiar to Sophie.

"You are joking... it's Tony Radcliff," Sophie replied very quietly.

"So it is all true..." Micky then added. The two watched him carefully as Tony, standing with another man large in stature, glanced around the area.

"Aye he's still there, and not a thing. It's not like the coppers will be looking any more is it?" the other man grunted back, his voice deeper and far less sophisticated than Tony's.

"Aye, excellent, Kev," Tony then responded. "I think we can make many of them out of him like. The angrier they are, the more radge they are, the more energy they emit. The boss will be delighted," he said in a menacing voice, grinning deviously.

"Aye, but he still wants that big prize aye?" Kev then asked, sounding unsure.

"Who knows where that might be like. I'm a lad for hire, not bloody Indiana Jones," Tony then scoffed.

"Well anyway, the den's fine. Sweet and sound," Kev replied.

"Right, let's get out of here before some knacker sees us. Come back for the supplies tomorrow. The Redcaps will be taking guard," Tony then replied, as the two men subsequently vanished into the night. As soon as they were gone, Sophie then sneaked back out cautiously.

"They must have a hideout round here somewhere, but we need to rescue Millie first, and I don't think they were the ones who took her…" She whispered.

"Aye, they have a hidden den somewhere here. Sounds like wherever she is, Matthew might be there too." Micky added as he followed.

The two then walked in the direction Tony and Kev came from, searching the area frantically. Then suddenly, Sophie spotted something on the ground amidst the leaves, running over to it panicking.

"Oh my… it's Millie's backpack," Sophie said sorrowfully,

picking up a two strapped backpack from the ground. But Micky wasn't paying attention.

"Um... Sophie" he said, looking over at something else, seemingly paralysed with fear.

"What? What is it? I've found her bag..." she said, turning back to Micky unaware.

It was at that moment that Sophie also stopped in fear, noticing that there were a number of dark figures now surrounding them in the woods, who edged closer menacingly.

"Oh no..." she said ominously as they emerged, revealing themselves to be not just one, but three of the same monsters that attacked previously, all of them armed with similar black axes. Their yellow reptilian eyes glistened in the darkness, striking terror into the pair as they stood, unable to contemplate what to do next. As the monsters emerged, one of them then threw Millie down onto the ground forcefully, tied up with ropes and her mouth taped over. She muffled as she attempted to scream. At this moment, Sophie's fear turned to anger.

"LET HER GO, NOW!" She roared at them. But the creatures did not budge. "Who are you? What do you want?" she then asked sternly. It was at that moment, one of the creatures, seemingly identifying itself as the leader, walked forward and demonstrated an ability to speak, going beyond the mere growling and grunting they had only shown so far.

"We are the Redcaps. We serve the lord and await his return." It hissed.

"Okay, who is your lord? And what is this all about?" Sophie then demanded.

"He is the Lord and Father of the nation. We have been blessed by his tender mercy to serve him. He sleeps, but when he awakes, we will rise and reclaim what is ours. All shall greet him, as flesh or dust." Unsatisfied, Sophie then gave him a confused look and asked again.

"So why do you keep targeting me? What did I do to you?" The Redcap then replied menacingly.

"The lord greets you as the chosen heir of Oswald. As our lord soon will, you have returned to this world. And now, you must submit or die."

"Oswald? What are you talking about?" Sophie then asked in frustration. "Let Millie go, leave us alone!" She shouted.

The Redcap showed no emotion or interest to her response,

"Submit or die," reiterated the Redcap. Sophie, taken back, then looked at Micky, before earnestly making her choice.

"Okay... Ha'way then!" She yelled courageously. Remembering her first encounter, at that moment she then took the star marked stone from her pocket and looked at it as the Redcap lunged at her to make an attack, when suddenly it again transformed into a sword with a purple hue in a blue flash of light. She then swung it at the leading Redcap, blocking his attack.

But at that very same moment, the other two Redcaps, who had stood in the background, also dived forwards, growling and roaring and proceeded to attack. Sophie did not waver, but managed to manoeuvre quickly to block all of their attacks concurrently. She then paced backwards in a bid to find space, as Micky and Millie watched on helplessly. The Redcap leader then charged forwards and led a new attack on her. Sophie blocked his attack before locking her sword with his axe. Seeing her occupied, the other two approached, leading her to kick the Redcap leader to the ground to break the deadlock. She then quickly engaged the other two again.

Despite Sophie having successfully defeated the first Redcap at Holy Trinity Church, to deal with three at once was a whole new ballgame, not least because she was outnumbered. She may have acquired newly found powers, but this wasn't so easy against monsters who not only showed little trace of humanity, but seemingly did not get tired either. She quickly began to be worn down by the endless attacks by the trio, which soon overwhelmed her. In that moment, one of the Redcaps successfully swung their axe at her full throttle, and although she blocked the attack, the sheer force sent her sword flying across the forest, as she fell to her knees on the ground.

Unusually, instead of just killing her there and then, the two lesser Redcaps stopped, and their leader walked over to her, speaking once again.

"Our lord is a merciful lord. He will readily accept you. Once again, you can serve him, or die." Sophie looked up at him in a sense of disbelief, thoughts pressing on her mind.

"What do I do?" Her mind then flashed back to the moment she defeated the first Redcap, and how her ability to overcome it came not just through a miracle of sorts, but also by renewed faith in herself, the unwillingness against all odds to accept her or her friend's fate.

And it was at that moment that the voice of the woman, she attributed to her mother, sounded out again to her.

"Sophie, believe in yourself. Push past your limits!" It proclaimed. The Redcap, not able to hear the words, looked at Sophie patiently, as if to anticipate an answer.

"Then what will it be?" It asked calmly.

"NO!" Sophie then roared defiantly, and in a burst of inspiration she reached out her arm to the sword's location, stood several metres away and as if by total magic it suddenly shot up through the air towards her, landing firmly back in her grip. She then leaped forwards, and before it could make another move she slashed the Redcap leader down in one strike.

Seeing this, the other Redcaps charged at her mindlessly, but Sophie was ready for them. Fending off their attacks, she then struck the second Redcap so hard its axe broke in two, before again dealing a chronic blow across its chest. The third, enraged, then tried to decapitate her in a last gasp reckless gamble. Sophie ducked down, before springing back up and impaling it in one clean blow to the stomach. It fell to the ground groaning in agony as Sophie yanked her sword out of it unapologetically. As with the one she had defeated earlier, the bodies of the three slain Redcaps quickly crumbled to dust.

"Well, shoot me sideways, that was absolutely class!" Micky cheered loudly, but Sophie showed little interest in celebrating, rushing over to Millie frantically and cutting the ropes off her.

"Millie, are you okay?' Sophie gasped emotionally as she set her free.

"I'm fine... but I'm so sorry Sophie," she then said joyfully as she got up.

"No, it's me who should be sorry." Sophie then added.

"No, it's actually me..." Micky then interrupted in a humble voice as Millie glared at him in disapproval.

"Okay, we have no time to relax, we need to find that lad! We know now he's around here somewhere," Sophie said in a restless voice, assuming leadership again. The group then began frantically searching around the area. As they walked, Sophie shined her phone light on every space possible, while Millie searched in bushes, as Micky absently looked around in an unhelpful manner.

"We've searched everywhere," he moaned. "It's like we're going round and round in circles... At what point do we call it a day?" he then asked.

"Micky, you encouraged this in the first place," Sophie replied with displeasure. "I don't have the privilege of calling it a day, we solve this now or never," she snapped.

"I know Sophie, I know…" he replied, trying to calm her down. "It just seems like we're getting nowhere with this, they've hid it really, really well." At that moment, Micky then proceeded to kick a large pile of leaves in frustration, revealing underneath it an unusual rusty manhole lid, as if it had been deliberately concealed.

"Had on a minute like, what's this?" he then said with curiousity, leaning over the lid. Sophie then dashed over and peered at it.

"This has to be it, we should open it and see where it leads to," she said in a serious tone.

"Right, let me try and open it." Micky boasted, grabbing the sides of the iron lid and pulling it strenuously. He gasped, but was unable to move it. Sophie tutted.

"What are you like? Here let me try!" She then placed her hands on it and pulled back forcefully, groaning as she strained. The lid then creaked loudly, before almost rocketing off into her hands.

"God it's weird seeing a lass as strong as this," Micky then said jokingly, with Millie again giving him a look of disapproval, Sophie looked carefully at the deep black hole that had now appeared underneath where the lid sat. She then shined her phone torch down it, partially revealing a jagged and seemingly unreassuring rusted iron ladder running down it.

"Looks like it's a shaft to somewhere," she said. "Tell you what, as you've been the most unhelpful tonight, why don't you go down first Micky?" she then asked, striking a harsher down.

"Cheeky get," he mocked. "You're the one with the special

powers to fight monsters, but aye I'll be a gentleman and take this one for the team," he then replied cheerfully. He then got onto his knees and dipped himself in the hole slowly, gripping the uneven ladders nervously. He then slowly edged further and further downwards, gradually disappearing from sight.

"You all right?" Sophie then shouted down the hole, her voice echoing into the blackness.

"Aye, I'm fine, reached the bottom. It's a bit wet down here and I can't see a thing!" Micky's voice then echoed back upwards.

"Okay then!" Sophie said, turning to Millie. "Let's go, not a moment to waste!" And they quickly followed him down into the mysterious dark hole…

Chapter X: The Legend of King Oswald

Having reached the bottom of the ladder, they stuck out their phone lights into the almost impermeable darkness, revealing a mineshaft like cavern with walls that had been carved out and the ceiling held up with wooden posts. It was barely tall enough for them to stand, forcing them to crouch down uncomfortably. The surface of the walls were black and dusty, containing the essence of coal.

The same red runic inscriptions, as seen on the trees above ground, had also been carved into the walls.

"It looks like this place was once a former mining shaft," Millie whispered curiously, shining her light around the cave.

"Aye, this was probably part of Silksworth Colliery. Me Granda worked at this pit, but now I'm guessing Tony's made this into some kind of den. This is creepy like," Micky replied.

"I get the impression it's more than just Tony though," Sophie replied. "I mean I just don't get it, how does your run of the mill drug dealer and loan shark create magical monsters. He's in on it… but there has to be something more, obviously…" She contemplated. As they walked, the loud sound of water dripping echoed through the chamber.

"You don't think there's anyone else keeping guard do you?" Millie asked nervously as they moved slowly, their feet getting wet and uncomfortable amidst the puddles that had accumulated between the uneven rocky surface.

As they walked through the winding shaft, an ambient red glow appeared on the horizon.

"There's something at the end of the tunnel!" Micky pointed, as they hastened their pace. The light grew larger and larger, soon revealing itself to be coming from a larger cavern. As they approached the entrance, they saw a number of digging tools and wheelbarrows lying around the floor, as well as piles of rocks left in the midst, as if this new area had been cut into from the existing mineshaft with a wall having been brought down. They entered the room to discover a dome shaped facility, with its hue stemming from a number of blood red candles that had been lit in a distinct circular pattern around the floor, where a raised platform filled with ash was situated.

"Look, over there!" Millie then pointed with shock. At the back of the room sat a young boy, wearing a black school uniform, tied up in rope with an unusual hospital-like drip device wired into his right arm. The drip had a bag filled with a strange red liquid in it, which shined like a glittery colour. To the other side of the room sat dozens of plastic bottle holding crates, which were filled with vials containing the same liquid.

With little time to analyse the rest, the trio ran over to the boy, who seemed to be in a partially conscious state, and began freeing him.

"He seems like he's been tranquilised or something..." Sophie said as she pulled back the ropes and very carefully uncoupled the drip from his arm. The boy groaned as they helped him free, but did not seem to talk or acknowledge awareness of his surroundings.

"What have they done to him? What is this place even?" Millie said in revulsion as she began to look around.

"I think this is the lava drug Liam mentioned earlier, and they're force feeding him it," Micky said observantly.

"But why exactly?" Millie asked, puzzled.

"Listening to Tony earlier, it has something to do with those monsters," Micky replied. He then looked round to Sophie, who was helping the boy up.

"He's starting to come around," she said softly.

"Okay, what's our plan now then?" Micky asked.

"Help him out of here, destroy the drugs and call the police," she said authoritatively.

"Destroy the drugs? But isn't this evidence against whoever's responsible?" Millie asked in a concerned voice.

"Stopping these attacks, the monsters and Tony has to be our priority. My life depends on it" she replied in an uncompromising voice.

"Ugh, where am I?" The boy, Matthew, asked suddenly, as he slowly regained consciousness, with a dreary and completely drained look on his face.

"It's okay, we're here to rescue you," Sophie said in a comforting voice. "Get him out of here, I'm going to use these candles to burn down the supply!" She yelled, as Millie and Micky then put their arms around the boy's shoulders and guided him out through the darkness. Then, without any further thought, Sophie plucked out the candle from the holder and held it to the plastic crates carrying the lava drug, melting them until it started a fire. As thick black smoke began to permeate the unventilated shaft, she then quickly followed her friends back through the tunnel to the exit.

Once back on the surface, the trio slowly guided the boy through the woods back to the Gilley Law estate where they had started off.

"Do you remember anything? Matthew?" Sophie asked him softly as they walked.

"Uhh, not a thing…" he mumbled, tired, drained and lacking awareness.

"Not anything about the person who took you?" she then asked.

"I honestly can't remember," he groaned.

"He's completely out of it. We need an ambulance not just cops like." Micky stated in a serious tone, observing his frayed state.

Having got back to Gilley Law, the trio sat him in Micky's car to rest while they called 999.

"Hopefully, they better not take the mickey this time like," Micky said begrudgingly as they waited. Eventually, a series of blue lights beamed in on the estate as an ambulance, combined with several police cars, descended on their vicinity. As paramedics rushed to the boy with urgency, a number of police officers got out and confronted the trio. Amongst them was a senior officer.

Despite the fact a high profile case had seemingly been solved, he did not look pleased, approaching them with a scowl on his face and cold, empty eyes. His countenance seemed as far from a hero's welcome or congratulations as you could possibly get.

"Well, well, well what do we have here then?" he said in a frosty voice. "My name's police chief David Simm, and it's my understanding you have, in extraordinary circumstances, happened to stumble across this missing young man, in this location, at…" He then demonstratively looked at his watch "…one a.m. How exactly did that happen?" he asked in an interrogative voice.

Sophie was the first to speak up.

"We rescued him..." she said nervously. "He was trapped in an old mine shaft down in those woods, where he was being force fed a drug of some kind," she said slowly and calmly.

"All right, and how did you know exactly where this place was? And why are you the ones who went to rescue him?" he then asked in an interrogative tone.

"We found it, and we did it as we received a tip off about him, but when we filed the initial police report the officer was disinterested." She attempted to explain.

"And where are these drugs he was being given then?" he then asked suddenly. At this moment, Sophie realised her mistake.

"We... destroyed them... but you can still go and see the shaft yourself. It's down there we can show you, come on" she then urged, but Officer Simm seemed unconvinced and rebuffed her attempts to lead him there.

"Look, after he went missing earlier this week we searched this area like a tooth comb, I'm absolutely certain no such mineshaft exists, and here you three are, telling me you supposedly went straight to him," he then responded abruptly, shutting Sophie down. "But not only that, you're now telling me the evidence of your supposed claim doesn't exist because you destroyed it!" he then said in an intimidating undertone, as if he were attempting to insinuate the group as being responsible.

Micky, who had up to this point remained silent, could no longer contain his anger, and immediately came to Sophie's defence.

"Look, we received a tip off that Tony Radcliff's gang were responsible for this, the source doesn't want to reveal itself. And if you bloody coppers seriously couldn't find the place we found then maybe you just aren't doing your jobs properly!" He said in an angry voice. "We have just helped you resolve a serious situation you couldn't get to the bottom of and here's you now trying to implicate us in it. You should be happy, not bloody radgey," he continued.

"Oi! That's enough sonny!" Officer Simm then hit back. "We're trying to get to the bottom of this. This young lad disappears without any explanation, and then here you three are, springing up that you saved him in absurd circumstances as some kind of premeditated rescue. Clearly, this is not the first report you've made about Tony, and it stinks to high heaven. You were on the scene, not him."

"Don't talk crap copper. We'd never even as much as been near this area before tonight. Me and Sophie were working at the Dun Cow on Friday and Saturday night during the time he disappeared, as well as tonight before this. We came because we had information and wanted to help, not because we're implicated, but if you want to play those games just arrest me and see how far you get." Micky snapped, continuing to be confrontational.

"Yes, and I was with them too before this. Sophie works hard at a pub while studying at school." Millie then butted in, offering a second alibi. On hearing this, Simm appeared to relent on attempting to accuse them for the time being, especially as for some unclear reason, he seemed unwilling to investigate the scene himself.

"Right, okay, that's enough! We have a job and an investigation to do. I would like to express my thanks for you happening to find this young man, and you've certainly made a family very happy tonight. However, my questions remain and we shall be in touch. Now away with ya." He barked.

Disgruntled, the group then got back into Micky's car and they drove away.

"What a prick. You save a lad's life and he tries to blame you for it. There's something not right about him like." He moaned as he navigated the roads.

"Yeah, especially as you'd already tried reporting it before…" Millie replied.

"They've shown no interest in it whatsoever, I get the impression the police can't protect us, and that's why we've taken this path." Sophie then added.

"But besides that like, I'm still trying to get me head round all of it. So these Redcaps or whatever they're called think you're this Oswald or summit? Who's that?" Micky asked, confused.

"He was an Anglo Saxon King of Northumbria, from about 1400 years ago. We're learning about him in school." Millie answered.

"Right, a bit random like, but why would they think it's you Sophie?" he continued to ask.

"I don't know, it makes as little sense to me as it does to you. But I'm doing this, because I feel I have to," she replied in a tired voice.

"And that little stone you have, it just transforms into a sword whenever? How exactly do you even do that like?" He continued quizzing.

"I wish I knew. Just seems to happen when the timing is right. Like magic…" Sophie responded, taking it out of her pocket and looking at it.

"You know what, if it really has some link to historical Northumbria, I think there's one person we could try to ask about it tomorrow," Millie then said with an exciting voice.

"Who's that then?" Sophie then asked.

"Mr Marchant, of course! It's connected to our class! We need answers, especially if you're going to stop Tony," she then urged.

"I suppose… never going to get up in the morning after this mind." She laughed.

"Right, let me get you both home, and I want to hear what you find out about this," Micky then said in a positive tone.

"Hold on, you're taking me home? When did I agree to that?" Millie then snarked in response to him.

"Well, unless yer fancy walking home you've got no other way like at this time." Micky smiled.

The next morning, the school bell blasted as the girls sat in their classroom. Sophie and Millie were slightly tired, but nonetheless very eager for the lesson ahead. Noticeably, Bertha was now back in attendance, but she now appeared shaken, as if she had suffered a massive loss of confidence. She sat behind the two girls in silence, daring not to look at them or utter a word, as Mr Marchant waltzed into the classroom jovially.

"Good morning! It's time for another spiffing history lesson! Now, today we're covering the second module, which is Thatcher era Britain! So just a quick survey around the class, what do we know about Mrs Thatcher then?" Almost instantly, a girl shouted out from the back of the classroom.

"She's an evil cow who destroyed this city!" The class then burst into laughter, Marchant, who kept his cool, simply responded saying

"Thank you, Marta, anyone else?" He then probed the classroom for hands raised until he spotted Sophie.

"Ah, Sophie!" He then responded.

"Good morning, sir, sorry I know it's not about this module, but just before we start the lesson. I have several questions I'd like to ask. First, what's a Redcap? And what does King Oswald have to do with them?" she asked randomly, some of the other girls giving her confused looks.

"Nice to see you more enthusiastic and in better spirits Sophie! A bit random, of course, but ok, sure!" As Mr Marchant began to formulate his answer, Bertha looked on in resentment from behind.

"A Redcap is, of course, linked to our first module about Northumbria, but only in the folk or legendary sense, as opposed to actual history... in such folklore a Redcap is described as a murderous creature. They're often depicted as being like a goblin, so named for the red hats or garments which they characteristically wear. Legend says they rejoice in violence and have incredible strength. They are said to be created from the negative energy of men, often through tyranny, despair or wicked deeds. But it's such a curious question... where did this thought come from exactly?" he asked.

"Oh, well, I've just been more interested in local history and legends recently. So do they have a connection with Oswald?" Sophie replied, reiterating her first question.

"Intriguing! Not what I had in mind today, but ok I guess to add to that, there is a strong supernatural aspect to the life of King Oswald, owing to the religious and superstitious nature of the time. It is said he was given a set of mythical powers, bestowed to him by a "lady of the lake" as in Arthurian legend. These powers were said to be given to him because of the purity of his heart, having stayed true to his faith in Christianity as opposed to the temptation to return to the paganism of his ancestors. In the pre-Christian era, the kings of Northumbria's predecessor kingdom, Bernicia, had professed themselves to be descendants of Germanic god Odin through his demi-god son Baldur. Because of this, some deemed Northumbria's conversion to Christendom was an act of treachery. Having refused to contemplate a return to paganism, a sorcerer named Glanfeoil by legend stood against King Oswald, and with dark magic created the monsters known as the Redcaps. Siding with Celtic invaders led by the Welsh King Cadwallon, Oswald defeated Glanfeoil and his followers at the Battle of Heavensfield in Hexham, banishing them from the mortal world. However, as the legend goes, Glanfeoil may one day return, and likewise, as will the spirit of King Oswald through anointed heir, once again with the mission of saving his people from the ancient evil. Okay, does that answer your questions?" he then said, taking a gasp of breath, wiping the sweat off his forehead.

"Yes sir, thank you," Sophie said humbly, as the class continued to give her odd looks.

That lunchtime, Sophie sat with Millie in the cafeteria, discussing what they had heard earlier.

"I still don't get it..." Sophie asked as she bit into a sandwich. "How does a local gangster access the magic of a legendary dark sorcerer to make monsters, who then thinks I'm an heir to a long dead Northumbrian king?" She continued, feigning frustration. "I mean with the sword and everything else, it's hard to believe it's not true, but just why me?" she then asked rhetorically.

"Yeah it just all seems so surreal, but this is reality, and I think the truth is we're sort of locked in a race to stop him now anyway," Millie commented in response.

"You can only imagine what's going to happen if he gets away with all this, and I just don't mean to your dad, but to everyone. No matter what anyone says, you're doing the right thing Sophie," she said, attempting to comfort her. "I'm with you," she added. It was at that moment, the doors of the cafeteria swung upon and Mrs Stoddart the Headmistress trundled in. Her face was so red with indignation it represented a swollen balloon.

"Sophie Scott!" she then said with a raised voice, drawing everyone's attention. At that moment the hustle and bustle of the cafeteria flatlined into an eerie silence, and everyone looked round at her. "Come with me please!" she then snapped. Sophie's face drained in horror. She looked at Millie awkwardly, before slowly getting up and following her.

At that moment, Bertha, who had been sitting watching from the other side of the cafeteria, grinned with amusement as Sophie was escorted out of the room.

"Ha, you're done for now princess!" She sniggered to her friends…

Chapter XI: The Reckoning

"You have some explaining to do... Miss." The headmistress snapped as she reclined into her squeezed spot behind her desk.

"What is it?" Sophie then asked nervously, attempting to feign ignorance.

"We've had a call from the police. You were on Farringdon very late last night with that missing boy, claiming you found him. They are very concerned about what you were actually doing there, seen as this has turned out to be the second incident you have claimed to have been on the scene of." She snapped

"What?" Sophie asked in disbelief. "What incidents? No, we went to rescue him after we received a tip off about where he was, I didn't do anything wrong! Would you have preferred I did nothing and he was just left there to die?" She then responded with indignation.

"That isn't the point, the point is this has revealed to me that you've been lying to us." She then added abruptly.

"About what?" Sophie asked defensively.

"Bertha..." Mrs Stoddart replied. "Having spoken with the police, you had filed a report to them that you had witnessed that Bertha incident, but you and Millie told me you hadn't seen anything!" She then barked.

"I didn't do anything!" Sophie yelled.

"You're very lucky the police haven't got enough evidence yet to arrest you..." she then responded coldly. "But there's an involvement in all this stuff happening around town that you are not disclosing. You've been on the scene of several crimes now, this is very serious."

Sophie then responded angrily again.

"I haven't done anything! I've been trying to tell the police it's a local gangster called Tony Radcliff, but they won't listen to me!" She yelled.

"SILENCE!" She then shouted back at Sophie. "I'm afraid I can't comment, that's not my problem, but when my students are involved, my hands are tied. As a result, I'm afraid Sophie Scott that until all investigations into this matter are completed, both inside and outside of school, I have no option but to suspend you, effective immediately. We'll be keeping a close eye on Millie too."

Sophie looked at her blankly, aghast, before suddenly, unleashing an outburst against her.

"Taking away my future because I did the right thing? Have it your way then you witch!" She then thumped her hands down on the table violently and proceeded to storm out of the room, slamming the door in her wake, before immediately walking out of the school. Enraged and heart broken, she stormed down the street at an angry pace, barely able to hold back her tears.

"My dreams and life have been ruined..." she snarled to herself. "Why me? I never asked for this situation, and I only tried to defend myself through all of the chaos." She thought to herself. "Monster attacks, magical swords, abusive gangsters, why should I take the fall out for it all?" She continued to think to herself as she walked aimlessly through Sunderland in a bid to cool her emotions down, desperately contemplating what she needed to do next.

Upon leaving the school area, she crossed Backhouse Park, where she had previously met Liam Heskett with Micky. After walking over the bridge and the trickling stream, she exited on the north gate, taking her out into the suburb of Hendon, before proceeding to head down a long road dotted with various shops and businesses. This road, known as Villette Road, was the main street of Hendon. Emotionally worn out, she stopped for a moment and decided to treat herself to a drink, having contemplated that she never did anything for herself, so something small might be a token of much needed self-appreciation. She then entered a small shop on the corner of the road.

In no rush whatsoever, Sophie took her time looking upon the drinks fridge deciding what to buy. As it wasn't something she did often, and because she cared about her weight and appearance, she was never a huge fan of sugary drinks. Monster Energy? "Minging", Fanta? "Too sweet!", but maybe a Diet Coke, "yeah, go on…" She thought to herself, but just at the moment she was startled by sudden yelling behind her.

She turned round to see a rugged man, wearing a woolly hat and a cheap puffy plastic coat, as well as a medical face mask, holding a knife up to the shopkeeper, who was of South Asian origin.

"Do you hear me? Empty the register now!" the man shouted viciously. The shopkeeper, in a state of panic, was scrambling to remove money from the cashier amidst the threat.

Sophie, hardly in a mood to tolerate bad behaviour from anyone else, scowled before walking over calmly to stand in front of the shop door.

"Cheers mate!" the robber said sarcastically as he grabbed the money from the terrified clerk. He then turned round to discover Sophie standing in his way.

"Where do you think you're going?" she asked in a cold

voice, unphased by the criminal.

The robber was, of course, taken back by the fact a schoolgirl was seemingly challenging him.

"Is this a joke? Get out of my way little girl!" He laughed, not taking it too seriously.

"Give him the money back then," she said calmly, refusing to move. Despite having seen her as non-threatening, the criminal was soon spooked by her resistance to him, and quickly turned nasty.

"Or what? Move lass, or I'll stick this right through ya!" He then barked, brandishing the knife towards her. Again, Sophie did not budge. "I'm warning ya!" he then snarled.

Running out of patience, the criminal then lunged his knife towards Sophie, but much to his surprise she then swerved the attack with a speed he might not have deemed possible. Before he could react, she then proceeded to kick him with full force, sending him flying across the store. He crashed into a display of chocolates, sending them everywhere. He pulled himself up, now even angrier, and charged at Sophie again.

"You'll pay for that you little cow!" he roared, only for Sophie to effortlessly punch him in the face, knocking him to the ground unconscious in an instant.

She then picked up the stolen money and handed it back to the shopkeeper, and without wanting to cause a fuss, ran out of the store.

"Thank you! Hey… Wait, wait!" The shopkeeper shouted out in a friendly voice, bewildered at what he had just witnessed in front of him. Sophie then paced down the street and out of sight. That evening, however, Sophie knew she had to face the music again, realising that on arriving home her dad would have certainly been informed that she had been suspended from school, and unsurprisingly, that he would have little sympathy for her situation and point of view.

And as she entered her front door, it was exactly how she expected it.

"Sophie!" an angry voice grunted the moment she put her foot in. "What have you been up to?" He barked as she entered the living room, standing in front of him as he stood with his arms folded.

"I've had a call from the school, said you've been suspended after you went to Gilley Law last night with that missin lad! Like a told yer the other day, you've been up to no good and keep lying to me about it!" Sophie grinded her teeth in frustration, struggling to keep her cool.

"No, you don't understand! I saved that lad, and I can tell you right now that it's that parasite Tony and his gang that are responsible!"

"Haddaway and crap" He responded dismissively.

"See, what's the point of even telling you, if you don't believe a word I say man. But one thing you do need to know: this is all happening because of the situation you got us into with him!" She yelled. "All I want to do, is to try and stop Tony, so we can live a normal life, so I can focus on school…" She then pleaded, her voice becoming softer. "Is it that hard to understand?" She then asked in a considerate tone.

For a moment, Eddie's face appeared to twitch as he contemplated her words, as if she had gotten through to him, but then he quickly reinforced his barrier and simply replied.

"Haddaway man, what can a girl like you do to stop someone like him? You haven't lived pet, thinking you're a smart alec as usual and getting into trouble. You know nowt," he said belittlingly.

Before the two could argue any further, suddenly there was a loud thumping knock at that door.

"That will be him now actually... I'll go and hide, tell 'im am not home!" He whispered, before rushing out the back. Sophie's eyes rolled in frustration, as she walked over nervously to open the door, and sure enough there was Tony Radcliff standing beneath her on the step, his two thugs standing shoulder to shoulder. She stuttered for a moment, wondering if Tony had cottoned on to the fact he ransacked his base the previous night and killed the Redcaps, or if for that matter, he was sending them in the first place. None of that seemed clear, but oddly enough, he didn't incline to mention any of it on seeing Sophie.

"Well hello again Sophie... may I speak with your father?" he asked, putting on a glaringly fake polite voice.

"Oh... hello Tony. No he's not home. He's staying at his brother's down in Fence Houses," she then replied without enthusiasm.

"Seems as if he's never home when I call these days! Fancy that? Care to pass on a message to him, as he doesn't pick up his phone either?" he then asked menacingly.

"Okay..." Sophie replied uncomfortably.

"It's payday in ten days' time, and your Dad still owes me an outstanding ten grand. And if he doesn't cough up the dough, then everything in this little house is gonna foot the bill, including his kneecaps! Understood?" He then snarled, the fake undertone of his voice disappearing.

"Whatever you say Tony, but ok I'll let him know, cheers." Sophie responded, attempting to conceal her anger and contempt, before slamming quickly.

She then walked back into the living room, where Eddie was now standing having come out of hiding. She glared at him without speaking a word.

"What?" he said in a helpless voice, shrugging his shoulders as if there was no problem at hand. Disappointed and infuriated, with nothing more she felt she could say, Sophie then walked off and upstairs.

Chapter XII: Politics & Propaganda

The next day, Sophie made use of her new "free time" by studying furiously at home. If every cloud has a silver lining, in this case it was that she now had more of her own free time to manage, with her schedule consisting only of work in the evening. With little interest in talking to her father, she locked herself in her room all day long reading and practising essays, at least living in the tentative hope that the situation might be resolved before her exams later that school year.

But that, of course, didn't mean she was free from the mounting stress and anxiety of the deteriorating situation around her.

"How could I possibly deliver £10,000 into his hands?" She panicked to herself. "I can't believe I didn't just beat him up at the doorstep there and then!" She also bemoaned to herself, realising that she now had the physical powers to do so, before eventually reasoning a more nuanced scheme was needed.

Suddenly, as Sophie sat studying, a knock on the door came from downstairs. Assuming it was Tony again, or some annoying hawker, as nobody ever came to visit their house, she vowed to ignore it and get on with her work. However, Eddie soon shouted up the stairs.

"Sophie!" He barked. "There's someone at the door for you. A reporter she says!" Putting her head into her hands with dismay, she then worked her way downstairs, with Eddie quickly veering off into the living room, disinterested. Sophie approached the door to find a young woman standing there. Dressed smartly in a formal jacket with a long skirt on, she had long red hair with freckles across her face, along with a nosey impression.

"Hi, I'm Katie Clough, I'm a reporter for the Sunderland Shine! You're Sophie Scott, right?" She spoke very fast in a formal, but enthusiastic voice.

"Yeah… that's me," Sophie replied awkwardly, feeling immediate discomfort at the prospect of the media. "How can I help you…" she then asked.

"Nice to meet you! Okay, I'd like to ask you a few questions about the attempted robbery yesterday. I imagine you've heard of it? May I come in?" she then blurted out like a machine.

"No… I'm busy" Sophie replied hesitantly, "I have to study, you see," she said, holding her hand to the door as a defensive gesture signalling a desire to close it, but the journalist was not deterred.

"Yesterday I heard you beat up an armed robber with your bare hands? All after being suspended from school due to an attack on your classmate and involvement with that missing young Matthew. Some say you're a hero, others say you're a troublemaker. What do you say?" she then continued at a hurried pace.

Sophie quickly became angry on hearing this, and decided to engage.

"No, those allegations are totally false! It's all originating from a criminal gang who has been targeting me and my family. The impact of it all is why I can no longer be silent. Now, please, I'm busy trying to study!" She said, raising her voice.

"So you see yourself as a hero? Is that right?" Katie then asked in a more interrogative voice.

"No, I see myself as someone who wants to get their life back on track. Now please, leave me alone!" Sophie yelled, and before the reporter could go any further she slammed the door in her face, before dashing back upstairs.

Several days then passed without incident. Hopefully, Katie's story wouldn't be published, Sophie reasoned with herself as she continued to lock herself away like a hermit and proceed with her studies, besides when she was working. Finally, Saturday morning came, and she welcomed the opportunity to spend some hard earned free time with Millie. She woke up and got ready, only to head downstairs to find her father with his arms crossed waiting for her, scowling.

"Okay... what is it now?" Sophie said in an aggravated voice on seeing him.

"This!" he snapped, before producing a newspaper from his side and thumping it on the table.

"Read!" he growled. Sophie nervously picked the paper up, titled the "Sunderland Shine", its headline read: "Super Sophie? Local Hero or Loony?" complete with a distorted unflattering photo of her, which appeared to have been taken from a secret camera attached to Katie's jacket.

Sophie then proceeded to read the article:

"*Schoolgirl Sophie Scott is dividing opinions throughout Sunderland. Linked to the mysterious spree of attacks throughout the city, Sophie was suspended from school after being allegedly present on the scene of Bertha Bagshaw's attack at Holy Trinity Church, in the East End, last week.*

Despite that, Sophie has denied any involvement with the attacks, telling reporters that she is a hero fighting local gangsters who are attacking her family. In that same week, she had also claimed with her friends to have rescued local schoolboy Matthew James from up in Farringdon, leading to claims she may have been linked to his disappearance.

Then, she appeared to foil an attempted burglary in Hendon and beat up a man in the store. Her spree of stunts throughout Sunderland have been met with criticism from police, who have described her deeds as reckless vigilante activities endangering the safety of the public, who have questioned the motivations behind it...

"Anything to say for yourself?" Eddie then said sternly as she put the paper down. "You've even revealed to that bloody paper the situation with Tony!" He raged.

"Well, be thankful you have a daughter willing to defend you despite all the crap you got us into... see ya later Eddie." Sophie then huffed, before grabbing her bag and coat and departing.

"Oi Sophie, hear you've been a hero!" A voice then sounded from outside as she walked down the street. She looked back to see her neighbour, Joe Goya, wearing his signature hat as ever, waving to her. He stuck up his thumb in an act of appreciation for her.

"Don't listen to the press man, it's all a load of horse plop, keep up the good work!" he urged.

"Thanks Goya, I appreciate that!" Sophie smiled before walking off.

She then proceeded to get on the bus and travel to Roker beach, where she had planned to meet Millie today, having messaged her earlier. In a sharp contrast to the isolated and rocky Ryhope beach, Roker Beach was one of the most popular and pristine places in Sunderland. Having emerged as a Victorian resort, Roker was known for its wavy golden sand, crystal blue water and its famous pier, not least its growing assortment of cafes and restaurants.

Of course, the unfavourable British weather made it too cold to be a tourist resort, with seaside areas in the country having declined since the 1960s. So while Roker had been experiencing a mini revival of sorts, it was local at best, and its glory days, with photos depicting it as having bustling beaches, circuses, a fairground, parades and even a zoo in neighbouring Seaburn, being well behind it.

As Sophie got off the bus, the weather wasn't really ripe for a day at the beach, being grey and murky. The waves were also choppy and restless, lashing themselves off the famous Pier and crashing into the sand and pebbles. She then walked down a small path which cut down through the cliffside smoothly onto what was known as the promenade, or "Marine Walk". This area, recently renovated, had a row of small, brightly painted wooden huts, all home to various eateries and other establishments. Sophie looked around, searching for Millie, before turning to her phone and texting: "I've arrived, are you here yet?"

Soon enough, a reply came in, reading:

"Yes, just round the corner two minutes, sorry!" So she sat herself on a wooden bench and waited until Millie arrived not long after.

"Sophie!" She cried out.

"So good to see you, it feels like forever because of that stupid suspension," Sophie replied joyfully, hugging her. "So yeah… about that article." Sophie then added in a more ominous tone.

"Yeah you mentioned… I read the online version and it was terrible," Millie said sympathetically.

"Apparently, this is what passes for journalism these days," she continued as they began walking along the promenade. "It's all so frustrating, because how can I even tell them the full story let alone explain it? They'd probably section me," Sophie groaned.

"Yeah, newspapers these days are sensationalist and outright misleading," Millie said in frustration. "Journalism in this country has become toxic, they only care about appealing to people's worst prejudices, as opposed to telling us the truth, because when did the truth ever sell?" she asked rhetorically.

"Yeah exactly, especially when I'm being smeared like this just for trying to help people..." Sophie moaned.

"But if journalists will not stand up for the truth, then who will?" she asked. It was at that moment they passed a William Parker-Fulton poster pasted onto a nearby lamp post, which read in caps: "VOTE FULTON: BRINGING POWER AND TRUTH TO PEOPLE."

"Well, definitely not him..." Millie scoffed on seeing the poster. "The lies by the media are the only reason people would even consider voting for anyone like that." She added, with Sophie looking on at it silently.

"Or maybe they just don't know what to believe in any more..." she then added. "But then again, neither do I."

It was at that moment, as they walked, that suddenly Sophie's phone began to buzz. She pulled it out of her pocket urgently, to see that the caller was from an unknown number.

Anxious, Sophie picked it up nervously and uttered a cold "Hello?" into the handset.

"Hello there? Is this Sophie Scott?" an oddly familiar voice then suddenly spoke jovially through the phone.

"Um yeah... that's me," Sophie replied uncomfortably. "Who is this? Do I know you?" she asked, having recognised the voice from somewhere but not being able to pinpoint it.

"This is Mayor candidate William Parker-Fulton speaking!

I know it might be a surprise, but I've heard some good things about you Sophie and I'd love to have a chat!" He said suddenly, prompting her to react with shock. Millie, listening next to hear, made a confused expression.

"Um... okay... hi," Sophie responded, not knowing what to say. "What do you want? And how did you get my number?" she then asked.

"Too much to discuss over the phone, but are you available to pop into my office and have a chat sometime? I'd love to meet you," Fulton then replied cryptically. Sophie, unconvinced by such a random cold call, then reacted defensively.

"Sorry, but I couldn't care less about politics so why do I need to meet you? How about you tell me what you want and get to the point of this creepy call?" she snapped.

Fulton, unshaken by her comments, then replied with a touching, sincere voice, as if he was trying to connect with her emotionally.

"Sophie..." He pleaded. "Listen to me, this will help you. Don't you want to clear your name and get back to school? No? I read your story. I too am sick of the media spreading lies, and I want to help you."

Sophie's guard dropped, as if something clicked in her mind. "... okay, so what do you want exactly?" she then asked.

"Like I said, come to my office, we can talk about it there in person. If you're free at four p.m. today, please drop by. Trust me." He then iterated at the end. Before she could say another word, the call then suddenly dropped. She then turned to look at Millie, who appeared shocked.

"What in the world? Are you kidding me?" she then said with a loud voice.

"I know... its crazy..." Sophie replied. "But who am I to

reject it? Maybe he can help me…" she said with a tint of doubt.

"What have we just discussed? Don't do it!" Millie urged in a serious voice. "He's a charlatan and an opportunist. The fact a famous politician just cold called you like that asking you to meet him is one of the creepiest and most bizarre things I've ever seen." She stressed to her. Sophie looked at her for a moment, unconvinced.

"I know… but when you have nothing, you have nothing to lose, right?" Sophie replied coldly. "I need to get my life back. The Redcaps attacked us, the police won't believe our story, and I'm being accused of attacking Bertha and I got suspended from school… only to get smeared by the gutter press. Tell me Millie, if a politician won't vouch for me, who will? My dad?" she then said, acting defensively.

"No Sophie… listen, I don't disagree about your situation, but he's not the person you need, not now, not ever!" she pleaded.

"Millie, it could mean the difference between me going to Durham or not, and stopping Tony. Just be thankful you haven't been suspended as well, despite the fact you were there both times!" she then hit back, argumentatively.

"Yeah, but at what cost?" Millie then asked, becoming increasingly agitated.

"I don't have a choice, you don't have to slave at a pub for a halfwit lazy dad who got in debt to some gangster, who if he cannot pay ten grand in less than a week, hinted at something terrible! You have good parents, you'd never have to fight for anything in your life!" Sophie snapped, emotional at the situation.

"Okay then Sophie… if that's you want, have it your way. You forget I almost died twice for you… and stuck up for you long before your special powers came along, maybe it's best given that I don't stick around!" Millie shouted, angry and emotional, before storming off. Sophie, seemingly feeling cold towards her, stayed put and simply let her walk off without intervening.

"Stuff her then…" Sophie muttered to herself in a grumpy voice, before turning back and looking at the waves crashing off Roker Pier in the distance. She had made her choice, she would indeed take a gamble on the controversial, highly unpredictable and distrust worthy nature of William Parker-Fulton, in the desperate bid to cling on to her own dreams.

Chapter XIII: A Working Class Traitor Is Something to Be

Sophie, with no hesitation, decided to immediately take the trip to Fulton's office. When her mind was set on something, she was never the kind of person to mess around. It was precisely this diehard attitude which had allowed her to make it this far against all odds, even if at times she had been overly submissive to others in the past.

As she walked to the City Centre, she blasted a song from John Lennon over her air pods to reflect her mood, and the discussions of that day about the media and politics, "*A working class hero is something to be.*" Surrounded by betrayal and people perceived to be keeping her down, she deemed the song to personify her own anger, especially the lyrics

"*They hurt you at home and they hit you at school. They hate you if you're clever and they despise a fool, 'til, you're so bloody crazy you can't follow their rules.*"

Crossing Wearmouth Bridge, she entered the city centre and headed up to High Street, where Fulton had situated his campaign office. Although the mayoral election was for most of the North East region, he had calculated that the campaign would be won or lost by voters in Sunderland, County Durham and surrounding towns such as South Shields, giving little heed to the more liberal and cosmopolitan constituents of Newcastle Upon Tyne, who he deemed antithetical to his cause.

Despite this, opinion polls remained on a knife edge, because widespread disillusionment and cynicism worked both ways, as getting people in Sunderland to vote at all remained a tremendous challenge for any politician seeking to break the historical monopoly of the Labour Party, let alone someone from a very different background such as Parker Fulton, who despite claiming to represent ordinary people, had been educated in Eton and Oxford, which, of course, could be very off-putting in somewhere like Wearside.

Still, that wasn't stopping him, and in the case of Sophie, who was politically apathetic for the most part, the question boiled down to "What other choices do I have?" Sophie, of course, did not hate immigrants or buy into the mantra of right wing populism, but she did feel desperate enough to the point that concerning her own life circumstances, nobody else was listening to her or understanding, and on a broader scale, this was how Fulton's politics was so effective, despite the fact it was morally flawed in the eyes of some.

She soon approached the outside of his office nervously, glancing at a sign which read "Vote Fulton, just common sense." Before she headed in the door. Upon entering and walking up a series of steps, she was then greeted by a slender looking young man with a smug look on his face, with big ears and well-groomed hair.

"Hi!" he said enthusiastically as Sophie walked in, who reacted awkwardly.

"Oh hi…" she responded.

"I'm Tom, pleased to meet you, how can we help you today? Do you have any questions?" she asked with overloading enthusiasm.

"I'm actually here to see William himself, if he's around. My name's Sophie, he actually invited me to meet him," she explained awkwardly.

"Oh! Sophie Scott! Nice to meet you, yes he told me to look out for you!" Just a moment please, he then scuttled into a back room quickly, leaving her standing awkwardly. Sophie then waited idly for several minutes, before suddenly he raced back out excited.

"Yep, he's all ready, you can go on in and see him!" He smiled.

Sophie then slowly walked through the doorway and into a long dark corridor, before spotting an office door at the end of the passage which was painted bright red. Approaching it, she then tapped on it lightly with her knuckles.

"Come in!" A cheerful voice called out from inside, and she pulled the handle and pressed forward lightly. As she peered inside, there was Fulton sitting comfortably on a padded leather chair behind a desk. A large bookcase towering behind him.

Noticeably, on his desk sat a little metallic sculpture of Pinocchio.

"Oh, hello Sophie! What a pleasure to finally meet you!" he then said jovially as she entered. "Do take a seat, you know I think I recognised you from my speech at the Dun Cow last week actually!" he said cheerfully as she sat down. "I appreciate you coming, you have no idea what that means to me!" he then stressed.

Sophie looked at him blankly.

"Okay, what can I do for you? And how can I help you?" she then asked in a cold undertone.

"Well, Sophie, I think you're a hero, congratulations!" he then spoke out with gusto.

"Oh… thanks," Sophie replied, unsure what to say.

"I've read about your good deeds recently! Don't listen to that fake media! I need you to know, you have my full support for what you're going through right now," he then said empathetically.

"You mean my suspension right?" she asked.

"Yes, Sophie, your suspension and everything else about those gangsters. The reason I asked for you to come here is because I believe you, and as I mentioned, I want to help you." Sophie then smiled awkwardly.

"Okay, but how exactly can you help me? What's your plan?" she then asked.

"Look, Sophie…" he then said, lowering his voice in an ominous way. "I'm aware that things are not right in this town, reports of strange attacks and goings on. None of it makes sense, does it?" he then asked rhetorically.

Sophie became more engaged on hearing this.

"That girl, she got attacked and the school blamed you didn't they?" he then asked in a very convincing way.

"That's right…" She followed carefully.

"And you know who is really responsible for it all, don't you?" he then asked.

"Yes I… do…" she then replied nervously.

"Well you know what, I do too, and I know they're up to no good," he said quietly again.

"You mean Tony Radcliff and his gang right?" she then asked casually.

"Precisely… listen Sophie, they are terrorising this town with these strange individuals and we need to act. I don't trust the police to solve the problem. In fact, I think there's a big cover up involved. Didn't you get that impression when you spoke to them?" he asked.

"Yes, they just seemed so unhelpful, almost an obstruction…" she said, pondering her experiences.

"And so you want to clear your name, don't you? Get back to school? And stop whatever he's doing to your family?" he then asked, looking her in the eyes.

"I do…" she followed.

"Well, this is why I need your help Sophie. You help me, and I will help you," he then said in a serious tone. "We need to stop them, because the plans they have are quite scary…" he then said, attempting to give the impression of fear in his own voice.

"Okay… what plans?" she then asked, a bit confused.

"I have it on a good source Sophie, their ultimate goal is to look for an ancient artefact of some kind. I'm not sure of its name, but it's from the Anglo-Saxon times, a thing of legend apparently, and it's hidden somewhere in the North East," he then said, standing up and looking out of the window down on the street below. "These strange men, their ultimate goal is to hunt and steal this item, under the supervision of Tony, attacking anyone who stands in their way."

"So, what is this item?" Sophie then asked.

"A staff I believe, some say it is magic, but I don't believe in that piffle. If they find it, it will be a devastating loss, a crime against this region. I know it sounds odd, but I think this can be your solution. If you can help me foil their little plot, as well as ending their drug ring in the process, we can stop them, clear your name and get you back to school." He reasoned with her, and seemingly, the proposal clicked in her mind.

"Okay, but where do you even begin to find something like that? If they don't know where it is, how can I?" she then asked.

"Good point, I mean given the circumstances we can barely establish if it exists at all, but that's not the point. They are making heists everywhere too, and this will continue. That's why, with the police disinterested, I need the help of a hero such as yourself! This can be your moment Sophie," he then said enthusiastically. "Find it first if you can, and if not, foil them in the act," he then said an encouraging voice.

"Okay then, I'll do it," Sophie then replied, albeit in a reluctant voice.

"You are a star Sophie!" he then said loudly, placing his hand on her shoulder. "Now listen to me, we didn't have this conversation, okay? I need to get back to work now. If you need me again, here's my business card. Until you find the staff, make sure you keep your eyes and ears open!" He then handed her a small white and blue card with his details on it, before ushering her out towards the door.

Sophie then promptly left the office, heading back out in the street. As she walked, she glanced at the business card she had been given obsessively. Was this now her answer? Did she get the answers she wanted? And more importantly, did she establish her pathway out of the chaotic situation around her? It all, of course, boiled down to the very same conclusion she had previously arrived at, to stop Tony Radcliff, but now seemingly she had a means to do so. She smiled, encouraged, convinced and brushed off the scepticism Millie had urged about him. Nobody was going to get between her and achieving her dreams after all, not even her best friend.

That evening, Sophie started work at the Dun Cow, with Micky also being present. Thankfully, because it was a weekday, the pub was quieter than usual and work was much less strenuous, meaning they didn't face a berating from Derek every five minutes either. This gave Sophie the opportunity to discuss the Fulton situation with Micky.

"So you actually got to meet with Fulton, and he called you a hero? That's class that," Micky said as he wiped the bar, hearing Sophie's story. "Sorry about Millie though honestly. I knar, of course, she's been your best mate, but she's hard work, especially when she sets on a disagreement with yer over something."

"I know right? But it's less class when it happens on the back of you getting suspended from school and demonised by the press. Today has been a rollercoaster," Sophie then replied.

"True. But I tell you what, he's spot on about those coppers like." Micky then noted. "I couldn't believe it the other night. You can tell Simm is bent. They did nowt to save that lad and actually seemed angry that you found him," he commented bluntly.

"Do you reckon he's in with Radcliff or something?" Sophie then asked.

"I wouldn't be surprised, I said it mesel, but a legendary staff? I mean if I hadn't seen all that stuff the other night I wouldn't believe it, but nowt seems off limits now!" he then replied, rinsing the cloth over a sink.

"But do you think I should trust him? Fulton?" Sophie then asked suddenly, in an expression of doubt.

"Ha'way man, of course, you should. This is your best chance to get out of this mess. Rather than you trusting him, you should be confident he's putting his trust in you!" He then said optimistically. "Get Millie out of ya head man she'll come round eventually. I'm confident he's not like the rest, and says things how they are. But this isn't about him, it's about you." He added. "Anyway, how do you plan to stop Tony?" he then asked abruptly.

"Well, according to Fulton, he and the Redcaps are robbing

places, so we need to be able to foil a break in and catch them on the scene, whether it's him or his hit men," Sophie replied.

"Aye but where would they even go man for some weird artefact?" he then asked.

"Beats me… it could be anywhere in the North East, we just need to be ready for it when it happens," she replied, shrugging her shoulders.

The two of them then fell silent, and continued to work idly into the night, hoping that perhaps the opportunity to stop Tony might present itself sooner rather than later, and the need to play a hero might end relatively quickly and allow Sophie to get her life back…

Chapter XIV: The Schoolgirl Fugitive

"I fancy fish and chips for tea t'night." Eddie announced in a more positive voice as he watched television, as Sophie stared at him from the other side of the living room.

"Yep, I know, you want me to go down..." Sophie then groaned compliantly.

"Aye, if you can stay out of trouble for just a minute," he then said snidely. "It's your lucky day though, won a cheeky tenner this morning on the horses, take that with ya."

He then pulled out a ten pound note out of his pocket and handed it to her. Sophie didn't know whether to react with gratitude or disdain, because such "gifts" didn't come often.

"All right then, won't be long..." Sophie then said enthusiastically, as she took the note and grabbed her jacket. Leaving the house, she proceeded to walk through the streets of Thorney Close and down towards the Central Shopping Arcade.

Although the streets were calm, her mind wasn't.

"What am I going to do?" She panicked to herself as she walked. A number of days had gone by, and the deadline for Tony's payday had been drawing ever closer.

"Although he's been horrible to me, I have to save my dad, get my life back and end this, but how?" She pondered as she continued to walk, turning off into a large loop-like street.

Heading down the road, she then passed by a pub. Creamy

and red in colour, it was a long rectangular shape with a pointed roof with a banner on it reading "*The Thorney Close Inn.*" Being Friday night, it was quite busy and Sophie could hear the chatter radiating from the inside.

"Grandad used to go there, I wonder if he still does," Sophie then said to herself, stopping for a moment and gazing at the club. But just as she was about to continue, she then noticed a certain car parked up outside, which seemed familiar to her.

It was deep blue in colour, and a much more expensive brand than usual, as if someone with a lot of money owned it. She moved closer, and then upon seeing its registration plate, which read: "*R9DCL1F*" she soon recognised who it belonged to. Sparing no other thought, she then quickly walked up the steps and quietly opened the club door.

Nervously walking in onto a red and grey retro carpet, her nose was met with the familiar waft of beer she knew from the Dun Cow. As she stood awkwardly, the place was bustling, with the sound of chatter and laughing so loud that her presence could scarcely be noticed. Her eyes immediately began scanning the tables and bar area like radars, before they latched onto Tony in the lower area of the room down some steps, sitting with a Cola in his hand amongst several men, including Big Kev, who were drinking alcohol.

"Bet that's not the only coke he deals in the fat prick." Sophie scoffed to herself as she slowly positioned herself on a chair near to the staircase, aiming to eavesdrop on their conversation without being seen.

"So recently you know I've been loving me history." Tony chuckled to the men, taking a sip from his coke. "You could even say I'm going to collect a few old things." He then added, his voice sounding almost cryptic.

"What kind of old things like? Dinosaur bones?" Big Kev then asked him gormlessly.

"Well there's nee need for that because we've already got a bloody neanderthal in you man!" Tony then mocked him.

"Ha'way, you know what it is, do I need to remind yer again?" he then said scornfully.

"Oh... that thing," Kev then remembered.

"Aye, well tonight, you might say we're going to be shopping for antiques, browsing a few collections, aye?" Tony then hinted to the men.

"Going fishing anarl," he then added, laughing with the men around him.

Sophie fixated on Tony's words, realising that she was listening in on a plan. It puzzled her for a moment that he was being so open about it, yet the anticipation of the moment sent her spinning with excitement. Suddenly, Tony stopped and looked upwards to where Sophie was for a moment, causing her to freeze in shock. However, he then returned to his drink and conversation as if he hadn't seen anything, leading her to sigh with relief.

Sophie then proceeded to dash to the exit of the pub without thought. However, on getting outside, she then put her hand over her pocket and her heart convulsed; she had left her phone back inside. Anxious and unsettled, she turned round and scuttled back inside, hurrying back towards where she had sat, and surely enough there was her phone on the table. Breathing deeply to relax, she then pulled herself together and picked it up, before turning again to exit again a second time. However, just as she was heading for the door she then felt a hand come over her shoulder firmly. Surprised, she turned round to see Tony standing behind her.

"Well, well, Sophie Scott, fancy seeing you in here!" he then said menacingly, grinning as he looked her in the eyes. "And what are you up to?" he asked. Sophie panicked, before scrambling to come up with an excuse.

"Oh... hi Tony, I was here for a job interview, just before I go to get our tea from the chip shop... just easier because it's closer to home, you know."

"Reet, well it's my money anyway so I'll wish you luck." He smirked. "But remember, payday is soon pet..." He then added in a much sinister voice. "You'll be hearing from me!" he then said ominously, before brushing past her rudely and exiting alone. Sophie stood for a moment, wondering if he realised she overheard his conversation.

"I don't think he did..." she then thought to herself. "He fell for the lie." She contemplated, before she darted out of the pub and back down the street to the local fish and chip shop.

While waiting for her order to come through, she then pulled out her phone and frantically began hammering out a message with her fingers.

"MICKY!" She then sent off with enthusiasm.

"Sophie, are you all right?" he then replied almost instantly, voicing concern.

"You'll never believe this, I spotted Tony in the local pub, they have plans to rob somewhere tonight!" She sent back quickly.

"You're joking me, right?" he then asked in shock.

"Deadly serious man..." she replied.

"All right, where is it then?" he asked.

"They were talking about seeing old collections, I think it's the museum," she then retorted.

"All right then, want to meet up asap?" Micky then asked.

"Yep, straight after I've given that prick his tea." Sophie then responded, smiling.

"Let's get him!" She then added. Not long after, Sophie's order was ready, and she raced to the counter and picked up the greasy paper bags with the cod and chips wrapped in them, before darting out and racing up the street back home.

Sophie soon burst through the front door back into the house, prompting a confused reaction from Eddie, who also noted she was gasping for breath.

"Yer took longer than unusual and looks like ya've been doing a runner, Christ I only sent ya to the chippy and yer still managing to get up to god knows what," he said in a cynical voice as they sat down at the table.

After a very awkward tea with Eddie, Sophie, not eating a great deal, then sped outside again offering little explanation to him before sprinting down the street and hopping on a bus to the city centre, at this point the darkness of night had fallen across Sunderland. As she travelled, she texted Micky again.

"Meet up at John Street, okay?" she confirmed with him.

"Aye, will be coming on foot," he replied.

Arriving in the City Centre, Sophie got off and began walking. There was not a soul to be seen anywhere. Eventually, she reached a large multi storey building that looked like it had once been a department store of sorts. On the face of the building it read in red and black text: "*Jopling House.*" Glancing at it for a moment, she then walked up before waiting quietly in the shelter of the building next to the road.

"I'm here, outside Joplings." She then texted Micky.

"Two mins away, coming," he then replied, as she waited patiently. Eventually, Micky appeared quickly running from up the top end of the street, smiling as he spotted Sophie.

"Sophie, all right?" he said cheerfully.

"Yep, just doing me thing..." she replied in a more sober voice.

"God, I hate John Street like, reminder of everything this town has lost man." He then commented on his surroundings as they started walking down towards the museum area. "Love the museum and winter gardens though, can't lie," he then added on a positive note, as they caught a glimpse of a classically designed building, finely sculpted with arches and pillars. Accompanying the Museum building to its left hand side stood an equally impressive giant glass dome like structure, resembling a supermassive greenhouse. This was known as the Winter Gardens, which contained exotic trees and plants from all over the world.

"So, you definitely think Tony is going to strike here tonight?" Micky then asked as they walked.

"Positive, that's pretty much what he said..." Sophie replied, reassuring herself.

"All right then, let's find a safe distance and keep watch." Micky then suggested. "How about in Mowbray Park, aye?" He added, as the two continued to walk.

Walking to the back of the Museum and Winter Gardens, the pair then entered a large encased park connected to it. With a large pond bordering the facility, it had an abundance of trees, with their autumn leaves rustling in the evening wind, as well as pristinely cut green lawns and beautiful flower arrangements. Amongst it all were a series of sculptures and items heralding a foregone era, including stone lions, beautiful encased drinking fountains and an antique Victorian bandstand.

"You know, I've always wondered what this walrus is all about." Sophie then pondered as she looked at a life-like metal sculpture of a Walrus situated by the pond.

"Thought it was just a place for the seagulls to crap all over," Micky replied cynically, noting the colourful white coatings all over the top of it. "Anyway, so we're just going to sit and keep watch?" he asked.

"Yep, for as long as it takes," Sophie then responded in a determined voice.

The two then sat on a nearby bench which had a good view of the building, observing it closely. They then waited, and waited, twiddling their thumbs idly in the anticipation something might happen, but it didn't.

"It's freezing like," Micky then commented, shivering as they sat, continuing to wait patiently as the night ticked on. "Should we get going then?" he then asked her, leaning towards giving up.

"Micky man you have no patience. We can't afford to miss this. Just five more minutes…" Sophie then urged, eager not to give up and firmly staying put on the bench. But it was at that very moment Micky was on the verge of giving up, that Sophie noticed something suspicious towards the winter gardens. Although it was difficult to make out in the darkness of night, she spotted the shadowy figure of a large man seemingly breaking part of the glass discreetly, before sneaking inside.

"Micky, do you see that?" Sophie asked suddenly, pointing at the direction of the Winter Gardens. "Someone's breaking in!" she snapped.

"Oh man… it's actually happening…" Micky then replied.

"Ha'way, let's get him!" She then urged sharply, before belting across the park at a blistering pace.

"Aw man, got to keep up again…" Micky then moaned as he jogged after her.

Sophie approached the Winter Gardens to find a ground level glass panel shattered into pieces, creating a space which allowed easy entrance of the premises. Waiting until Micky caught up, she then proceeded to enter without hesitation.

"Follow me!" She whispered, stepping into the thick blackness, brushing away the thick and tangling leaves of the various plants from her midst, and jumping down onto the cobbled walkway.

"It looks like they've gone into the museum building," Micky then said quietly, as the two proceeded through a door and into the main hallway. They looked around, but all was silent. Suddenly, they then heard a bump from the ceiling upstairs.

"Quick, to the staircase." She urged, as the two slowly sneaked upstairs, determined to avoid detection and not make a sound. Reaching the second floor, Sophie then cautiously looked down the dark hallway, while urging Micky to stay hidden on the staircase.

"Stay here, I don't want you to get hurt." She then whispered.

"You'd think I'm the lass here..." Micky then groaned quietly as he held back.

Then suddenly, a dark figure raced out of the shadows and shot through the corridor near to them, disappearing into an exhibition room. It looked too short to be a Redcap, yet too crafty to be the sort of mindless blundering idiot sort of robber Sophie confronted in the store a week earlier. Having spotted him, she followed him quietly into the exhibition room, which was dedicated to a study of geological history and dinosaurs.

Unusually, as she approached, the figure stood idly in the middle of the room with its back turned, as if it were waiting for her. It made no attempt to hide or avoid detection. As she grew closer, she deciphered the figure of a man, wearing a large black leather coat with a hoodie underneath, concealing the back of his head. Sophie stood observing him for a moment, before breaking her silence confidently.

"Who are you? Show yourself!" She snapped in an authoritative voice. The figure then pulled back his hood, before turning around slowly. Suddenly, Sophie felt a familiar feeling, as if she recognised the man. It was none other than Tony Radcliff, he smirked menacingly as he looked her in the eyes.

"No Sophie, the question is… who are you?" he then asked in an intimidating voice. "Destroying me stash, thinking you could grass me up to the police, pulling your slimy publicity stunts and thinking I didn't see you spying on me back in the Inn earlier. Thought you were going to catch me out?" he then snarled. "Trying to pull your father out of the brown stuff? Or is there something more?" he then asked suddenly.

"Well you should have thought about that before trying to ruin our lives, sending monsters after me, and take away what is dear to us!" She then screamed at him, unleashing all of her frustration. Tony reacted by laughing psychopathically at her.

"Sophie dear, I think there's been a misunderstanding… " he then said slowly. "Maybe I'll just settle for you for payment instead." He then grinned.

"What did you just say to me?" Sophie replied in a sense of disbelief.

"Your body, of course… THAT MEANING YOUR WHOLE DEAD CORPSE! You're mine!" he then shouted at the top of his voice, before whipping a gun out of his right pocket.

Without a second to pause he then fired it at Sophie's direction instantly, displaying his utter ruthlessness. Sensing the attack, Sophie dodged the shot instantly before ripping off a large crystal from a display and hurling it at him, hitting him on the abdomen with such a force it knocked him to the ground, disarming him. Before he could recuperate Sophie then promptly picked up the gun, holding it over his head as he laid on the ground winded.

"You mate, are in for a long stretch inside!" she then said harshly and smugly, believing she had finally avenged herself. But Tony, despite being hurt, smiled and laughed on the ground.

"Sorry, who is it? Who's in for a long stretch inside?" he then asked in a teasing voice.

"What?" Sophie responded confused. Tony said nothing, and then just moments later hoards of police barged into the display room.

"Here he is, I've got him!" Sophie yelled confidently.

But much to her surprise, they weren't in fact after Tony.

"Drop your weapon!" they then shouted, turning towards Sophie. She stood still, confused for a moment.

"What? No, this bloke is the criminal! I came to stop him. He's behind everything." She then responded, assuming they'd made a mistake.

"I said drop your weapon!" An officer then barked, as a familiar voice then sounded from the corridor.

"You must be joking if you think we're going to fall for this one again! Let me kindly explain what's happening. Sophie Scott, you're under arrest for burglary, kidnapping and possessing an illegal firearm! Put the gun down and surrender!" The voice snapped, revealing itself to be police chief David Simm. Sophie's only stroke of luck in this scenario was that none of the police had guns, as they were not expecting her to have such. Noticeably, they were also oblivious to the presence of Tony.

Sophie then looked past the officers out into the corridor, where Micky, who had not been spotted, looked on with a sense of despair. As the officers proceeded to move in on her, Sophie then tactfully fired the gun up to the ceiling, causing all of them to fall to the floor in terror, before belting past them out of the room and down the staircase, with Micky following.

"GET HER!" David Simm was heard barking as the officers gave chase.

Unfortunately for the officers, having anticipated to set up a "gotcha" moment, nobody was guarding the break in entry point of the museum, allowing them to charge past and out into the street. In a bid to shake off the police and confuse them of their presence, Sophie and Micky then ran back into Mowbray Park, racing through the trees and up its banks, before emerging from the south exit and into the streets of Hendon. But it wasn't over yet, with police cars now operational and chasing them up the road.

In the bid to escape them, Sophie and Micky quickly shot into the narrow back alleys of the Hendon terraced Streets, pulling over wheelie bins to the ground to obstruct their path. Before any police could reach them, they then fled into a very dark and run down looking industrial estate, where they hid inside of a giant metal warehouse. But the officers had not given up yet, and exiting their vehicles, they then began probing the area with torches.

"Tony really is in with the police... He led me into a trap, I can't believe it..." Sophie whispered to Micky in a tearful voice. "What am I going to do?" Micky, too focused on monitoring the police, didn't respond. As they grew closer, he then quickly ushered her away, taking the lead.

"They're coming, this way," he whispered, attempting to

sneak out of the warehouse. However, an officer spotted them in the process.

"Stop right there!" He shouted, leading the two to start running again.

The chase continued around the industrial estate, like a game of cat and mouse, before they then shot out down a narrow road heading towards the port of Sunderland. With the police out of sight completely, they then dived into a small gap present in some thick bushes.

"Stay here, don't move, don't make a sound." Micky whispered as he peered out, but struck with fear and shock, Sophie could barely control her heavy breathing.

The police then reappeared in the area, getting closer, and closer. They stopped next to the bushes for a few moments, wondering where to look next, and without shining their torches on them, they glanced over at the location for a moment. Sophie gasped quietly, fearing the worst and even readying the gun, her stone having unusually not emerged into its sword form during this whole confrontation.

However, the police did not seem to register the gap in the bushes they climbed through, and the officer then shook his head to signal denial to his colleagues, before walking off further down the road they had run up, assuming they had gone in that direction. Sophie then gave a sigh of relief and looked over to Micky.

"Well, there's nee turning back now like," he then said in a serious tone.

"You're not kidding," Sophie then said, regaining some calm. "Everything is screwed but one thing has been clear all along anyway," she added.

"What's that like?" Micky then asked.

"We have to win, and that is that," she then said boldly.

"Aye, you've got to stop him. But honestly, Sophie, I need you to know I'm with ya in this," he then said in an emotional tone.

"Cheers, Micky, I was wrong about you. I will do this and as you said, I will do it for my Mam, if she is the one guiding me after all. It still doesn't make sense, but if it's leading me to something, I have to live up to it," she contemplated.

"Well, Sophie, I'm here," he then replied, before sticking out his hand to shake Sophie's. But instead of shaking it, she then wrapped her arms around him, hugging him. But before the embrace could turn into anything more intimate, Micky then awkwardly asked.

"By the way, since you've got that sword and all that, do you mind giving me that gun?" Sophie smiled and giggled, before handing it to him.

"Okay..." she then broke the mood, turning to seriousness again. "I'm on the run, I can't go home, I need somewhere to hide." She spoke sharply, dashing Micky's hopes.

"And I know just the place! Coast is clear! Ha'way..." He then urged, and the two sneaked out of the bushes and quietly dashed off into the night.

Sometime later, Eddie sat glued watching the television screen in the darkness of his sitting room, the only light beaming out from the screen. He glared at it emotionless as police chief David Simm undertook a press conference in front of news reporters, sitting at a desk with a blue cloth draped over it, complete with a glass of water to his left hand side.

"Today we are naming a suspect wanted in connection with the break in at Sunderland Museum, her name is Sophie Scott, 17 from Thorney Close. Her whereabouts are currently unknown, but she is believed to be actively on the run now. She is also wanted for questioning in relation to kidnapping and linked to a series of violent attacks around the city. If you see her, do not approach her as she is armed and dangerous. Call the police on 999 immediately. If you have any other information, please get in touch dialling 101," he said in a serious and formal tone.

Eddie said nothing, his face expressionless. He then turned off the TV and abruptly exited the room.

Chapter XV: Playing Hard Ball

Darkness covered the forest, as a cold and empty wind howled down and around the trees. Sophie, lost and panicking, seemed to run aimlessly as a dark hooded figure stood within her midst, his face not visible. In his left hand, he held a long, wooden and crooked staff with a purple orb embedded into a slot at the top, with smaller branches wrapped around on the outside.

As she ran, desperate and short of breath, the figure hissed into the air, projecting an omnipresent voice that sent shivers through her.

"Sophie, submit or die... submit or die." He called out in a cold and empty voice. At that moment, Sophie was pierced by a ringing of inhuman-like high pitched screaming all around her, dragging her to her knees in agony.

Sophie then woke up in a sense of terror, gasping for breath. She looked around frantically at her surroundings, sighing with relief as she comprehended the untidy bedroom and mattress she was situated on.

"Phew... it was all a dream." She muttered to herself, still reeling from the terror.

"Sophie! Sophie! Are you all right?" Micky said suddenly rushing into the room, having heard her waking up in fright.

"We have to find the staff! We have to find it first!" Sophie then panicked suddenly, leaping up with urgency.

"Woah, Sophie calm down man, everything's fine..." he said, reassuring her. Sophie then took a deep breath.

"Sorry... just a bad dream. What time is it anyway?" she then asked.

"Eight a.m., you were out of it last night after everything," he then smiled.

"Yeah, and where exactly are we again?" she then asked awkwardly, the dream having brought on amnesia of the time just before she slept.

"Liam's, don't worry... we're safe here," Micky then replied, assuring her. Sophie's face crumbled in dismay for a moment before recuperating, as she looked around to observe the room, which had no carpet and the walls were stripped bare of paper, with a lightbulb dangling from the ceiling without a shade around it, and the window boarded up with black plastic bin liner in the absence of curtains.

"So, if you don't mind me asking, what happened in the nightmare?" Micky then asked curiously.

"It's always the same dream on and off for years, and it always feels so real to the point it freaks me out, I don't often talk about it. I see a cloaked man in the forest, and he calls my name, as I try to run away from him..." she said in a fearful voice. "It feels like they're linked to everything that's happening of late. But this time it was different, he was holding a staff."

"Creepy that like..." Micky replied in a worried tone. "Could be a sign." Before they could discuss further, the door then swung open suddenly and Liam Heskett casually walked in, with a carefree look on his face.

"Morning, Sleeping Beauty!" he said cheerfully. "So, the bizys are after ya then? Knew it wasn't a good idea to be poking your nose into that sort of stuff like. The Police have even put out an appeal for ya."

"Oh man..." Sophie responded with dismay, putting her face

in her hands.

"Aye, was on the telly earlier this morning. They called ya a critical threat to Sunderland and a psycho to boot. All a load of crap, of course, but like I said, ya can never trust the coppers. Did you honestly think they'd help ya with Tony?" he then asked.

"Yep, they literally worked with him man to frame her. I still can't get owa it." Micky then butted in. "God knows what we're going to do now like."

"I told you, get the staff and expose Tony!" she snapped.

"Aye, so you're just gonna go up to his base in Southwick and knack him or summit?" Liam then scoffed.

"Sure is looking that way." Sophie responded in a serious voice.

"Well, now stopping yer then doing it right now," he replied, attempting to be witty, but at that very moment there was a sudden, loud and abrupt knock at the front door. "It's the coppers, you two garn hide now!" He then whispered. Sophie and Micky then hid in the kitchen at the back of the house, listening closely as Liam walked slowly to the front, before opening the front door in a relaxed manner, and sure enough there stood a police officer, the same one that Sophie and Micky had met at the station earlier, now wearing a signature police hat and a bright green and blue jacket.

"Good morning. We're conducting neighbourhood searches for the fugitive girl Sophie Scott. You haven't seen her by any chance, have you?" he asked in a serious but non menacing voice.

"Nah man, course not I haven't seen owt. There's no-one here but me," Liam replied, skilfully hiding any impression of anxiety from the officer.

"Well, then you'd be fine with me searching your property?" the officer then replied suddenly, cornering Liam.

"Well I like to keep meself to meself really. I dinnit want to waste yer time," he then replied, attempting to stall the inevitable. The officer then reacted with anger.

"That wasn't a request, it was an order. If you don't comply, we'll have to arrest you," he replied.

Sophie, upon hearing the conversation at the door and realising he was going to end up coming in, turned and whispered to Micky.

"I've got an idea…" At that moment, Liam relented, but moved out of the way very slowly in a bid to further stall the policeman's advance, who quickly barged past him into the house, and began looking around in a disrespectful and aggressive manner.

But just as the Policeman approached the Kitchen, Sophie jumped out from hiding in front of them and shouted at him in a provocative tone.

"Oi! Copper, over here! Come and get me!" His face turned to fury and he rocketed forwards instantly, but the second he passed the door suddenly Micky stuck his foot out in front of the officer, tripping him and sending him crashing down to the floor with a thud. As he fell, Micky and Sophie then dived onto him, grabbing his arms, seizing his handcuffs and tying him up.

"You devious little pricks!" the officer roared, kicking his legs aimlessly like a toddler. Micky then quickly seized the rest of his equipment, including his handheld radio, truncheon and pepper spray. Liam, returning from the front door, walked into the kitchen and grinned to Sophie.

"Bloody hell man, class work that like." He then turned to the officer and scoffed. "You have the right to remain silent."

The three of them then proceeded to tie up the officer's legs with tape, before dragging him across the floor into the bedroom and plonking him onto a wooden chair. Micky's face seemed to beam with delight at the prospect of getting his own back against the police.

"All right plod, we need information, you're gonna talk and tell us everything we need to know," he said to the policeman in a menacing voice.

But the officer, despite his situation, wasn't convinced.

"Fat chance of that son, if you don't let me go now I promise you this will end with you spending the rest of your life in prison!" He barked. Micky simply laughed.

"Well you couldn't be bothered with Tony Radcliff, so I wouldn't expect much now either. Tell me now, why are you targeting this lass? What's going on?" he then asked, upholding his intimidating voice.

"Because she's an attempted murderer and child kidnapper you idiot!" The officer snarled back, resisting his overtures.

"Bull!" Micky then shouted back in his face. "Tell me the truth, or I'll spray this right in your ugly mug," he then said nastily, holding the pepper spray he had taken from him earlier.

"You wouldn't dare you little scroat! You'll go away for a long time for this!" He yelled back.

"Oh, you wanna bet?" Micky then said angrily as he held the spray up to the officer's face, tapping it lightly and allowing a small amount to come out. Hit with it, the officer coughed and spluttered in discomfort.

"My eyes! AHHH" he yelled.

"Want some more? Then tell us the truth!" Micky then yelled at him. He then readied the can, preparing to spray again.

"Please… please stop, don't do it again, I'll talk" the officer then relented, lowering the aggression in his voice.

"Okay, talk then." Sophie then butted in.

"From what I know it's Simm." The officer began, as he coughed. "He's made a deal with Tony Radcliff to hide the drug linked to those strange attacks, all the while they look for a staff or something, they say it's magic... It was all planned to set you up in the Museum."

"But why target me?" Sophie then asked.

"Well you put yourself in the situation by deciding to rescue that lad and naming Tony to me when you made that report... He personally didn't care about you before that, but besides him, those blokes seen all over town kept going on about some legend known as the "North Star", believing you were the one sent to stop them or something... some superstitious crap if you ask me."

"Okay then, so why are they after a staff?" Sophie then asked, taking control over the interrogation.

"I honestly don't know much about that, only that Tony, with those men, was doing it as a job for someone else. I've no idea if it is even real, apparently it's hidden in some sacred place around here, I don't know!"

"Right, but seen as you coppers are covering it up, where do they plan to look for it?" Micky then intervened with his 'bad cop' posture.

"Apparently there's a riddle hidden somewhere with a route to it. They searched everywhere but couldn't find it!" The officer then spluttered.

"So where do they think it is? Where have they searched?" Micky then barked.

"They will go to Durham Cathedral! That's all I know! Now can you please let me go?" The policeman pleaded.

"What? For knowing all this and then being an accomplice to it all? For covering up corruption and wrongdoing in your work ranks? You look after yourself, you selfish grifter." Micky then ranted. "You can get stuffed, we're not letting you go until Radcliff, and your boss, are behind bars. Nice prisoner exchange."

The policeman looked at Micky helplessly with horror.

"Ha'way let's go Sophie. Liam, keep a watch on this one," Micky then said, proceeding to kick the officer's chair over, sending him crashing back to the floor, as they left the room.

"I'll happily keep ya company copper…" Liam then grinned, as he stood over him dangling the handcuff keys.

"You little scroats! Help!" The officer was heard yelling in vain as they left the room.

Unsatisfied with her appearance, having slept relatively rough overnight in her current clothes, Sophie quickly tidied herself up in Liam's very humble bathroom, rinsing her face and combing her hair, before donning a pair of cheap sunglasses and a cheap woolly hat she found lying around in order to disguise herself to the public, before heading outside with Micky.

Thankfully, the officer had travelled to the house on foot from the city centre, and had not brought a car with him which would cause additional complications. As they opened the door, they looked around carefully in case any of his counterparts were nearby, before quickly traversing through the terraced streets of Hendon to where Micky's own home was located a few streets away, where his car was parked outside.

"It's a good job they haven't named you as a suspect too…" Sophie said as they walked up another street of terraced houses towards where Micky's car was parked.

"Aye, that never made sense to me. Could happen mind, but I reckon it shows how bent they are that they only want you. Saying that, they'll get me now if they get the chance like, after what happened back there."

"So this is where you live?" Sophie asked, looking up at the two storey terraced home. In the suburb of Hendon, all houses had been built in a traditional inner city "terrace" style, with not an inch of space between them. The style was sort of similar to that which spanned the inner suburbs of London, but not as nice or luxurious, of course. Although some streets also consisted of smaller, one storey-cottages.

"Aye, this is home. I still live with me parents, saving up for my own place, of course, but that's going to take a long time if the Dun Cow is anything to go by." He laughed. "Tell yer what, do you want to come in for some breakfast?" He then offered kindly. "Me parents know you're a good lass and probably don't believe it, they won't turn you over anyhow. I would have offered you to stay here instead of Liam's, but as you can see being there too long will lead the coppers to turn up." He then said assuringly. "Just wait a moment, let me pop in and explain." He then added. He then disappeared through a cream white front door.

Sophie waited in the street awkwardly, then eventually Micky emerged again signalling positively.

"Aye, it's okay, ha'way in." Sophie quickly hurried inside. Removing her shoes as she entered, suddenly a white fluffy ball of fur raced towards her, jumping up and panting excitedly at the new guest.

"Oi, Spank! Down!" Micky then snapped at the dog.

"You call your dog Spank?" Sophie said, making a bizarre look on her face.

"Aye, might look adorable as a toy poodle, but honestly he's a little monster because Mam spoils him. Don't go anywhere near him when he's got food." Gently brushing aside the dog, Sophie then made her way through on a soft carpet. The house smelled overtly perfumy, and far better for that matter than her own. The walls were clean, and lined neatly with various family pictures, as well as football related memorabilia, including a photo of Sunderland's Stadium of Light.

They then made their way into the living room, which was also immensely tidy, with several leather chairs and a sofa, an exotic Persian style rug laid across the carpet, an ornate white fireplace dotted with a series of ornaments, as well as a multi-pronged series of decorative lights hanging from the ceiling.

"Make yerself at home," Micky then said politely, offering a seat. "Not much I know, but world class compared to the rest of Hendon." He laughed.

"Don't worry, it's lovely," Sophie then commented politely. "Far better than my home," she added. At that moment, a burly middle aged man wearing a tight t-shirt and jeans waddled into the room. His hair was grey and curly, with his face puffy and wrinkly.

"Areet then, what do we have here?" he then asked, on seeing Sophie. "It's only Sunderland's most wanted," He then laughed. "Nah, nice to meet yer," he then extended his hand out to Sophie, literally yanking her up in the process as she stood up to greet him.

"Nice to meet you as well Mr White," she said politely.

"Nah, call me Steve," he then added. "Micky here has been telling me all about you. Clever girl I hear!" he said, raising his eyebrows.

"Oh yes..." another voice then echoed from the hallway, before a slender middle aged woman wearing a flowery shirt and black trousers entered the room. She had shoulder length dark brown hair and a relatively kind look about her face.

"I'm Jayne by the way, but fancy having you visiting us today!" she commented. "Hopefully they won't be coming banging our door down..." she then added nervously.

"Well, thank you for letting me in, despite that..." Sophie said awkwardly.

"That's okay, don't worry." Jayne then reassured her, as she took a seat opposite. "I seen it and I think it's disgusting how the police are attempting to frame a young girl like you for all those crimes. Making you out to be some kind of Ronnie Cray. Eee I don't know what the matter is with them." She commented.

"I'll tell yer it's because they're corrupt." Steve then butted in abruptly. "Boys club looking after their own." He then commented.

"Aye that's right actually, working in league with Tony Radcliff to get her." Micky then added.

"Okay! Shall we head for a spot of breakfast?" Jayne then asked enthusiastically.

The group moved out of the living room and gathered round a broad wooden table in the Dining Room, as Mrs White quickly began cooking.

"So besides your little trouble, you're studying to go to University?" she asked, as she pondered over the stove.

"That's right, well I was... but I haven't given up hope yet." Sophie then replied uncomfortably, having still not felt the ice was broken under the pressure of being in someone else's home.

"Our Micky didn't go to Uni." Steve suddenly commented rudely. "Didn't stick in at footy, or school did ya lad?" he then asked in a demeaning way.

"Dad man..." Micky then responded in an embarrassed voice.

"Aye well, what's done is done but you need to aspire to

better things than that bloody pub like," Steve then said in a scornful way. "So keep sticking in Sophie if you don't want to be like him," he then said in a more joking voice.

"Honestly, he's a good lad," Sophie then said lightly in his defence. "Not sure what I'd be doing without him right now," she then added in a more serious tone.

"Aye, he's nee bother, but he's too easy going and doesn't aim high." Steve then hit back.

"Oh Steve, don't embarrass him in front of his friend," Jayne then responded from the stove in a caring voice. "He's still got his whole life ahead of him."

Sophie, feeling guilty for a second as they sat, sprang up from the table.

"Do you need any help with that? I don't just want to sit here," she asked. "I literally make breakfast for my own dad every day, or I did," she added.

"No, don't you worry!" Jayne then responded politely, refusing.

"Sounds like a lazy prick." Steve then commented abruptly.

"Eee well I don't see you helping here either." Jayne then joked back.

"Eeesh..." Steve then groaned, before getting up and preparing some dishes, knives and forks.

"Your parents are canny." Sophie then commented to Micky. "Makes me wonder how him up there is taking all this news... if he cares at all," she then replied with a doubtful voice, as Jayne then placed several plates of sausages, bacon, eggs and toast on the table.

"Thank you so much!" Sophie then said in a very enthusiastic tone, as if she'd never been given such a breakfast before.

"So if you don't mind me askin?" Steve then said shortly in a similar manner to Micky, as he held his fork. "What's your plan? You just gonna hide out there with Liam Heskett and stay on the run?" he then asked abruptly. "Bet his house stinks anarl, always off his head that one." He then commented rudely.

"Nah, Dad... she's going to take them on and win," Micky then said in her support.

"Aye, and how's she going to do that like?" His dad then replied confused. "She's smart, but no offence Sophie, she's just a girl."

"Ah well yer see," Micky smiled as they ate. "Sophie is very special. Special enough to overcome an army of monsters and rescue that lad on Farringdon," he then said proudly. "She's going to find that Tony Radcliff, and that David Simm, and give them a reet kicking. I kid you not," he added. At that moment, the poodle, Spank began hovering around the table, panting and salivating. He then dashed under Sophie's legs in the hope he might recover scraps of food.

"Oi Spank, knock it off!" Steve then snapped to it. "Tell yer what, vicious this little thing like."

"Oh, he's lovely, just give him a bit man," Jayne replied playfully and lovingly, before throwing him part of a sausage which he immediately seized upon and wolfed down quickly. At that moment, Steve callously moved his foot in the dog's direction, leading it to snarl and snap aggressively.

"See what I mean?" he then said smugly, "Vicious."

"So Micky mentioned you have a Chinese friend from school you've been going around with, where's she in all this?" Jayne then inputted suddenly.

"Oh... you mean Millie," Sophie replied nervously. "We kind of, fell out," she then said in a downing voice.

"Over what? What happened?" Jayne asked.

"Well, it's over William Parker-Fulton" she then uttered very nervously. "Fulton contacted me after the story appeared in the newspaper and offered his support… and she disagreed."

Suddenly, Steve put his hand up symbolically drawing attention to himself.

"Am voting for him! Wouldn't for anyone else!" he said proudly. "If your little friend doesn't like him she can go back home for all I care," he then added very rudely.

"Steve!" Jayne then nagged. "Don't say that, she was probably born here!" Casting an awkward silence over the group.

"Yeah, she was born here… but the thing is, it's not about politics for me, it's about survival. My hopes, my dreams… you know, " she then said thoughtfully. "I don't have a choice…"

"Exactly dear, but if she truly is your friend and if she cares about you, I'm sure she'll come to understand the choices you face, and realise what she's lost," Jayne then replied comfortably. "Steve here, as you can tell, is very vocal about his politics. He reminds me about it every day, and I don't agree with it. But I don't forget what he means to me as my husband, because there's always more to a person than that," she explained.

"Tell yer what, after we're done here why don't we go and check up on her?" Micky then proposed.

"Where does she live like?" Steve then asked curiously.

"Seaburn Dene," Sophie replied.

"Posh SR6 snobs then," He laughed. "But sayin' that like, one good thing about those Chinese is that they study hard, like you should have Micky!" Metaphorically sticking the boot into him again.

"Oh dad man…" he groaned, as they continued to eat at the table.

Sophie paused for a moment as she contemplated Jayne's words carefully, before firmly announcing to the table.

"Okay then, let's go and find Millie after this. You're right, I can't abandon her. She's been a part of this journey, and we need to make sure she's okay."

Chapter XVI: A Chinese Mackem

"In 1962, the Conservative government of Harold MacMillan implemented the Commonwealth Immigrants Act, which imposed restrictions on the migration of those from the Commonwealth countries, or Empire as it was once known, into Britain." Mr Marchant waffled to his class, as Millie sat alone at her table with an empty seat next to her. "The act was a reaction of sorts, to anti-Immigration sentiment that had emerged in the country following the intake of post-war migrants, including those from the West Indies, India, Pakistan, Bangladesh, Africa and Hong Kong, of course," he then said with emphasis, looking over to Millie who reacted with discomfort. "Despite the fact that the Empire once saw Britishness as something to be universalized, opening the gates in the 1940s to those who were part of this empire, what changed exactly? Or did anything change?" he then asked the class provocatively, attempting to spur debate.

"Well the Empire came to an end, didn't it? Britain was reassessing its role in the world," one girl then answered.

"Very good! And what evidence do we have of that?" He continued, pushing on the discussion.

"Britain's empire was declining, and they wanted to join Europe," another girl responded.

"Very good... but what do you think this change in attitude meant to those who came here, who were promised they could be British?" he then asked. "Millie, if you don't mind me asking, what are your thoughts on this? Seen as your parents, of course, are from Hong Kong."

Millie stared at him for a moment, clearly uncomfortable to talk, an awkwardness also falling across the classroom amidst the other students.

"Um, well they came in the 1990s so it's a long time after this, but yeah even for me being born here, you wonder sometimes where you really belong. I mean I'm British, but sometimes I don't feel it if you get what I mean..." she replied nervously.

"Don't kidnap him for it!" Bertha then sniped at her across the classroom quietly, with Marchant failing to hear it. The rest of the class nonetheless giggled, leading her to feel deeply agitated.

"So yes, thank you Millie, that leads us to our next question, what this course, of course, wants us to explore in the historical context, what exactly does it mean to be British? And to what extent does the decline of the Empire change that?" He then continued as the class went on...

After school finished, Millie walked out of the school alone and towards the bus stop, feeling frustrated and downtrodden. As she walked, she spotted election posters for William Parker-Fulton peppered across the lampposts, making her think of Sophie, but also the fundamental question, where did she belong? As the bus arrived, she stepped on board, where a bald middle aged driver sat behind the wheel and screen.

"One single to Seaburn Dene please," she then asked unenthusiastically, placing her debit card on the machine.

"No problem..." the driver replied, before suddenly commenting. "Tell yer what, your English is good, you almost sound like a local." On hearing this, Millie looked at him with shock and confusion.

"I beg your pardon?" she replied. "Thanks, but I was born here mate… please," she groaned, before walking up the bus and sitting down.

After a brief journey, Millie got off the bus at the Seaburn Dene estate, where her family lived. This neighbourhood was one of the nicer areas of the city, especially due to its proximity to the Seafront and beach. Styled "SR6" by its residents due to its postcode, people from here typically asserted a tongue in cheek superiority over those living elsewhere in the city.

She walked up the street and headed to her home, which was a semi-detached house with a garage and driveway, one which neither Micky or Sophie ever had the privilege of living in. Entering through a neatly arranged porchway, she then shouted:

"Mum I'm home!" in a friendly voice, using English. The interior of her home was pristine and modern in style, with linen wood flooring and smooth white painted walls.

In the living room, several small red banners were hung on the wall symbolising wealth, and prosperity in Chinese characters, as well as a wide arrangement of photos of Millie growing up. On the right hand side, stood a gaping bookshelf. Besides the use of calligraphy, there was nothing in the minds of an outsider to make the judgement that the home was "alien" or "exotic" as one might misjudge, and looked like any other well to do family home.

"Millie!" A woman then said urgently, emerging from the corridor, with an accent completely different to her daughter's. The woman was thin and short in stature and had short black hair. A pair of glasses were perched on her nose, while she was dressed in a red sweater and jeans. She responded however, in Cantonese, saying.

"I've told you, you need to remember your Cantonese! There's no reason to greet me in English, try again please." She then snapped.

"Okay then..." Millie groaned as she entered the living room. "Hi Mum... I'm home," she replied, using Cantonese.

"Good..." her mother then responded, also in Cantonese. "There we go, I know you're busy with your studies, but I don't want you to forget your roots! Even for the most simple things at least!" She then nagged. "You're a native Cantonese speaker, not a Mackem speaker." She then scolded, stressing the word "mackem" in English.

"But mum, I'm a Mackem, I'm from Sunderland, this is my home." Millie then responded.

"So are you like the Gweilou out there?" Her mother then responded, using a pejorative word in Cantonese.

"Is it really about skin colour? Mum, I know...we've had this conversation many times before. I just try so hard to fit in it's easy to forget my roots." She then groaned. "And today isn't a day for fitting in, especially with everything happening over Sophie. Everyone is awkward at school." She then expressed herself.

"Don't worry about them, they aren't your concern." Her Mum then proceeded to lecture. "This is a big year for you, and I want you to make us proud and set a good example for your sister!"

"Yes, I know..." Millie replied, accepting of her mother's advice, but seemingly tired of hearing it.

"Many people in this country do not care about their future, or their commitment to society. If they reject you as different, you must show them that you are better." She continued.

"Well if you feel that way, why did you even come here in

the first place? Why not stay in Hong Kong?" Millie then scorned. Her mother was not impressed.

"Well, if you fancy paying millions to own a tiny high rise box as opposed to a house like this, feel free to go back there." She then scorned.

"Okay, Okay... sorry," Millie then said, respecting her mother.

"Dad will be home later, we will eat then. Sorry, I know you've just come in, but can you do me a favour and go to the shops and get me some milk before you start your evening studies? I just realised we ran out just as you came," she then asked politely.

"Yes, Mum..." Millie got up, groaning.

"Okay then, see you soon. Love you Millie," she then said softly, as she approached the door.

Millie then, not in the best of moods, walked back down the street she came up and towards the shops she passed.

"Why didn't she just text me before I came in?" She muttered to herself as she pondered the rest of her words, which only for her sharpened the contradictions between her own family background and the reality she lived in. She then entered a small convenience store at the bottom of the road.

On entering the shop, she noticed a big burly man looking at the crisps. His head was largely shaven, and he was accompanied by a younger, scrawny boy who had glasses, short blonde hair and a rat-like complexion on his face. As Millie moved past to head to the milk fridge, the boy almost seemed amused at her presence. Millie, of course, was not a stranger to this kind of racist mockery in her life at times, not least because she had even had to face it at school in the past.

Although the majority of people she encountered were kind,

tolerant and polite, she reasoned that everywhere had its idiots, and as such Millie opted to simply ignore such idiots, as opposed to reacting. She attempted to avoid looking at them, before picking up the milk and heading over to the cashier.

As they continued to loaf around without buying anything the cashier was not impressed and began to get frustrated with their presence.

"Please buy something or get out, please," he said sternly, giving Millie the pretext to escape. As she left the shop, something then clicked in the mind of the larger man, and he turned to the younger boy asking.

"Ow, isn't that Sophie Scott's little mate?" he said quietly.

"I've nee idea like Kev," the boy replied, revealing the man to be 'Big Kev' the accomplice of Tony Radcliff.

"Tony said she had a Chinese friend and ah swear it's her from what I've heard… she might knar where she is, cos her dad hasn't got a clue like." Big Kev then grunted.

"Let's get her then, think of the cash we'll get for catching this one man it will lead her right to us." The boy whispered to him. The two then left the shop without paying for anything, helping themselves to a chocolate bar or two along the way.

"Oi! Get back here!" The shopkeeper screamed, his cries falling on deaf ears.

At this point, Millie was about to walk up the street back to home when suddenly, Big Kev came out and shouted behind her.

"Ow you! Come here now!" Millie opted to ignore it again and kept walking. In response, Kev then walked up and grabbed her by the shoulder, causing her to scream.

"You're Sophie's mate! You're coming with us!"

Despite it being broad daylight, he then proceeded to try and drag Millie by one arm to where he had parked his car as the other boy watched, leading her to scream louder.

"HELP! I'm being kidnapped!" But nobody seemed to hear.

"It's areet, just helping a friend." Big Kev then grunted in a very unconvincing fake voice to anyone who might be listening.

Millie continued to struggle as he dragged her to the car, but he was too strong to break free from or kick away. With the milk in her left hand, she then had an idea. Uncomfortably screwing it with her mouth, she then ripped the seal off the bottle with her teeth before forcibly hurling its contents in Kev's face, landing in his eyes and mouth, causing him to let go in shock.

"Aw me bugs a'jarra!" he then moaned. "Well don't just stand there man get'a!" He then barked at the other boy, who having stood gormlessly, then charged at her. Millie, furious at his previous comments, took a chance and swung a punch at his nose, hitting him so hard it started bleeding and sending his glasses flying off his face, which then landed and cracked on the ground.

But it wasn't over yet, realising she would be eventually overpowered, Millie darted over the road and into the next street, having known revealing the location of her home to them would be a mistake, especially with the police being effectively broken. Kev, having recuperated, then jumped into his car and then began chasing Millie, the boy, injured but not defeated, jumped in for the ride. Both of them now seemed angrier than ever.

The car made a ferocious noise as he blasted the accelerator, quickly approaching where Millie was running. As she ran, she took out her phone and desperately tried to call her Mother, but for some reason she just wasn't picking up. So she then tried her Dad, but he was busy and likewise, missed the call.

"Crap, I'm out of my monthly data and texts quota..." she hissed to herself as she desperately attempted to use her

WhatsApp, leaving her only with calling minutes as the two men chased after her at an obsessive and frightening pace.

Needing somewhere to hide off-road, she then spotted a cemetery ahead of her, which was surrounded by massive bushes. The metal entrance sign read "Mere Knolls Cemetery." Without any other direction to take, she darted inside and fled from the main road, amidst the many gravestones, forcing Kev and his counterpart to stop the car, get out, and look for her.

But before he started searching, he then walked round to the boot of the car and opened it, retrieving a large wooden baseball bat. He then tapped it several times on his palm as a show of aggressive intent, before walking across to scour the gravestones for Millie.

Nestling herself behind a large gravestone, large enough to conceal her, Millie then attempted to phone home again, but again nobody was picking up. If her Mam and Dad weren't answering, then she wondered who could possibly help her?

"Should I call Sophie?" She then panicked to herself as she hid uncomfortably. "No way, how selfish, rude and inconsiderate that must be, and why should she ever save me after that?"

But Millie's time and options were running thin, the two attackers grew closer and closer in a bloodthirsty manner and her phone battery dwindled.

"Come, come, come out little mouse!" The boy scoffed out loud, leading her to shiver with fear as she desperately attempted to text for help, then suddenly, her phone died. She was on her own. She quivered, trying not to cry, as they circled around her periphery like predatory birds, determined to hunt and close down on their prey.

Millie looked around for somewhere else to hide, but there weren't any other options available to her than to keep running, but maybe, she thought to herself if she could make it to the shops and restaurants on the seafront, someone could maybe intervene and save her.

Then, suddenly, a looming shadow came over where she was cowering. She looked up and there was Big Kev, armed with a baseball bat and furious.

"Aha, no escape now you little rat!" He then snarled, raising up the baseball bat with the intention of hitting her over the head. Millie stumbled backwards on the ground in shock as she attempted to escape, but just as that very moment he seemed certain to strike, suddenly, a whooshing sound came from behind him and cut the bat clean in half.

Confused, Big Kev looked at the bottom half of the bat in his hand with horror, and slowly turned round perplexed, only to find Sophie Scott standing with her sword in front of him, with Micky by her side.

"Oh no," he said out loud, before Sophie proceeded to symbolically tut and shake her head calmly, before suddenly punching him in the face like a rocket, sending him crashing to the ground.

She then turned sternly to lock on to the other boy, who proceeded to run away in terror. Sophie chased after him through the cemetery, catching up with him effortlessly. She then proceeded to push him over to the ground aggressively. He then trembled in terror as Sophie pointed her sword towards him.

"Please don't hurt me…" he wailed helplessly.

Sophie then proceeded to pick him up forcefully and single handedly by the scruff of his neck.

"You work for Tony, right?" she then asked him menacingly…

"Aye… that's right." He gulped.

"Well hear this, don't you ever pick on my friends ever again you little divvy." She snarled at him before throwing him by his hoodie back to the ground, leaving him quivering in fear.

Dropping her tough posture, Sophie then ran over to Millie and helped her up off the ground, embracing her in a hug.

"I'm so sorry... this time it was me" Sophie weeped immediately on hugging her.

"No, I'm sorry, this time it is actually me!" Millie then replied emotionally. "I won't abandon you again, I promise," she cried.

"It's all right, friends forever? Okay?" Sophie then said emotionally, as Micky stood looking a bit isolated.

Before leaving the cemetery, Sophie and Micky proceeded to slash the tires on Big Kev's car, before walking out of the cemetery with Millie and back towards her home.

"So how did you find me in time, I don't get it?" Millie then asked curiously.

"After speaking with Micky's Mam earlier, we already made the decision to come find you and work things out, just as well isn't it?" Sophie then explained. "Suddenly I had this strange feeling, an urge even, to come to this spot and find you. As soon as my sword then activated, I knew there was trouble, and there you were, about to be caught by Tony's goons, so just in the nick of time." She smiled.

"I can't thank you enough, is that three times now?" Millie then asked in a humble voice. "I also can't apologise enough, I realise because it was never really about politics, it was always about supporting you..." she then said in a sorrowful voice, as they continued walking. "I just guess, it feels so hard to fit in sometimes, given my background, and it is easy to become upset because of the political situation." She then explained.

"I know, don't worry. Let's do this together, no matter what." Sophie then smiled.

Chapter XVII: The Promise

The short gain of relief from having saved Millie did not last long. As Millie, Sophie and Micky walked back up the streets towards her home, her Mother stood outside in a sense of disbelief, wielding her phone in a panic. Upon seeing Millie arrive, she breathed a sigh of relief, but was far from reassured.

"Millie? What's going on," she said in a worried voice. "I've been worried sick! What happened?" she continued, before looking over to Sophie. "And what are you doing here with my daughter? The police are after you!" She then hissed in a more aggressive tone.

"No Mum, it's okay... she saved me." Millie then reacted defensively, attempting to calm her down. "I was attacked by two thugs while at the shop, they wanted to kidnap me."

"And Sophie comes to save you? I don't believe it, they attacked you because of her, didn't they? Right?" Mrs Chen then correctly guessed. "I thought you told me you fell out with her because of everything that happened!" She shouted "We agreed after we heard the news that you'd stay away from her because of the danger it would cause you, but then here she is! It's causing nothing but trouble!"

"No, she wasn't there, she came to save me," Millie then replied.

"No Millie, I just don't know what to say..." her mother then iterated in a voice of grief. "Even her standing here is putting us in more danger right now!" she continued, emotionally.

"No Mum, that's not true!" Millie then retorted. "Sophie saved me, and it's not the first time she saved me either." She added, then stuttering on realising her mistake.

"What?" Mrs Chen replied in shock "You mean there are other incidents of this kind you never told me about?" she said, feeling horrified.

"Yes," Millie then acknowledged in a remorseful voice.

"You didn't tell her about any of it?" Sophie then turned to Millie surprised.

"No, I didn't, because I didn't want to upset my Mum and make her think you were a bad influence," she then replied sorrowfully.

"So what else have you lied to me about?" Mrs Chen then screeched at her. "She wouldn't need to save you, if she wasn't the cause of the problem!" She then snapped, in a mix of anger and grief. "You haven't been studying with her, you've been going on these wild adventures and that's why they're now targeting you too!" She wept. "It's the most important time of your life and you've put yourself in extreme danger! What will your father say when he gets here?"

"You two should go, NOW!" She then yelled at them, but Sophie hesitated.

"Mrs Chen…" She intervened softly. "Please… listen." As she held out her hand attempting to calm her down. "I need you to know that Millie is the most dedicated, loyal and caring daughter you could ever wish for." She began to explain. "You should be proud of her. I know obviously as her mother, you care about her and seek her safety and wellbeing, but all she ever wanted to do is support me." She spoke softly. "And in this world, as I face a dad who is crushing my future with his debt, a gangster who is targeting me, a crooked police chief, monsters known as Redcaps and dishonest journalists and even bullies at school like Bertha, there's been nobody who's been a greater rock for me throughout it all than Millie." She continued emotionally, as Micky gave her a funny look as if to imply he was left out. "I don't know what I'd do without her. We've already been through so much together, and we owe so much to each other."

Millie's Mother seemed to calm as she listened carefully. "So yes Mrs Chen, strange things are happening, and her association with me is involving her in ways that she can't avoid now. The only way out is for us to win, to find a legendary staff and bring to an end whatever evil these people are planning. After this, we will soon go to Durham, and we will take a stand. But I need you to know, I will do everything in my power to keep Millie safe, no matter what. That is my promise to you. Be proud of Millie, and believe in your daughter." She then pleaded, holding onto Millie's Mother's hands for empathetic value. Mrs Chen said nothing for a moment, but then looked at her daughter and began to cry.

"Millie, do you want to support and help Sophie?" she then asked sorrowfully.

"Yes Mum, I do." The two then hugged each other. "Millie, you are our precious daughter. We have such high hopes for your future, and I couldn't live with it if anything had happened to you. Do you trust Sophie in this? And do you believe it is the right path to take?" she then asked her.

"I do," Millie then said softly.

After having embraced, Millie then rushed upstairs to her bedroom, got changed, packed a bag chaotically and came back down to tearfully wave her mother goodbye.

"How do I even begin to explain this to your father and

sister?" She then wept as Millie came back out.

"Just be honest with them…" She then said softly.

"And please…" her Mother then interrupted. "Keep in touch with me, let me know everything, no matter what!" she then added, as the two hugged one more time and they tearfully waved goodbye to each other as she walked down the street with Micky and Sophie, getting into his car and driving off.

"That was touching like…" Micky said in a very solemn voice as he drove away, which was met with silence. "So we're off to Durham tonight, aye?" he then asked.

"That's right," Sophie then replied coldly. "We have to beat them to whatever they're trying to find, before it's too late," she added. "We then need to get back to my home for my Dad's payment deadline tomorrow…" she continued in a more ominous tone.

"You know, I've often wondered why don't you just go up to Tony's base and do him in there and then." Micky then wondered bluntly. "I mean after what I've seen, it wouldn't take much from you," he commented.

"I think about that all of the time man," she replied in an unfriendly tone. "And we will when the time is right. But the thing is, we're not just up against him. There's a bigger scheme at hand…" She then said with an underlying fear in her voice. "There's not only Simm, but I can't get over that dream. We have to find the staff, first by getting hold of the riddle."

"Right, and this riddle is at Durham Cathedral right? Based on what the copper said." Micky said.

"Well we know they're going to search there, that's all," Sophie replied. "But at the least, I think we can sabotage their plans, provided it's not a trap or anything…" she then said less optimistically.

The car then fell silent as Micky's car winded its way through the openings of the city, crossing the River Wear and heading southwest through the route known as the Durham Road, a road which had connected Sunderland and the City of Durham for over a millennium.

The City of Durham, of course, was the jewel in the crown of North East England, with its mighty cathedral and Norman stone castle, its beauty and glory shone over the rest of the region as a wonder to behold. It had, as mentioned, been founded upon the legend of a Dun Cow, which had acted as a guide marker to the Community of St Cuthbert, who then built their sanctuary upon a bending meander of the River Wear.

Their settlement subsequently grew up as an educational, political and religious centre, a centre of pilgrimage and homage to the great Northern Saints, with the Venerable Bede of Sunderland and King Oswald himself being interred there. It was subsequently little wonder that both sides to this struggle now homed in on this cathedral in the sense of what it ultimately represented regarding the region's history and the legends which surrounded it.

The time was now five p.m. Autumn darkness had long already fallen over the land, and as Micky's car approached the city the two towers of the cathedral gleamed out in the night like beacons, projecting light on the city which stood below. After having found a place to park the car, the trio got out, Sophie having donned her disguise, and slowly walked into the city.

On entering the city limits, they first crossed a mediaeval style stone bridge, which arched itself over the River. A sign was marked, saying "Framwellgate Bridge, 1400".

"Hopefully, this is where we'll be studying if everything works out." Sophie then commented bleakly as she looked upon the beauty of the city as they crossed over it.

Although a lot of modern construction was nonetheless visible around the Riverside, because Durham had never grew up as an industrialised city, such as Sunderland had. The shape and integrity of the inner city inside of the river had been beautifully preserved, with narrow sloping streets on the hillside still arranged in a medieval fashion.

"So we know they've been looking here, but do we have any actual idea where in the Cathedral we need to look? Or what form this so-called riddle might come in? It's not like it's a small building." Millie then commented as they walked upwards to the market square.

"First, I want to follow my inspiration…" Sophie then replied softly. "I have a gut feeling we should go and see where King Oswald's head was buried. It was in our class reading that it was put there with St Cuthbert, and I thought, if the Redcaps claimed I was chosen to follow in his footsteps, don't you think there could be a sign? Or some kind of miracle?" she asked.

She then took out her stone from her hand and looked at it as they walked. "I mean voices telling me I've been chosen, stones which become swords spontaneously… All this magical stuff is happening around us, so we should look for inspiration, as well as clues." She pondered.

"True, trust your instincts." Micky then agreed.

The three then walked up past the historic Durham market square, and up another winding narrow street as they homed in the two towers of the Cathedral. Although it was evening time, the streets were largely bustling as young people pursued their university lives, eating, drinking and moving to and from classes, leading Sophie to continually contemplate her own future as they watched them.

Reaching the top of the hill, they then looked at the building which stood before them in front of a square courtyard and a long stretch of perfectly maintained lawn.

"It's sometimes hard to believe there are such wonders close to home..." Millie reflected as she marvelled at it. The entire Cathedral was a gothic architectural masterpiece, with every intrinsic detail, nook and cranny of the exterior having been chiselled with such majestic perfection.

Heading towards the Cathedral, they then approached its giant wooden arched door, with its famous cast iron lion sanctuary knocker embedded on the front.

"Don't you get let off your crimes if you touch this?" Micky then asked curiously, remembering a spot of local history. "You should cling onto it Sophie and clear your name" he then joked as they made their way through a makeshift glass visitor entrance built into the exterior.

"Hello there!" a voice suddenly proclaimed as they entered. They turned around to see a priest dressed in a black and white robe greeting them. He had short grey hair and glasses.

"We're closing at six, so I would advise you to be very quick in looking around," he then said in an overtly friendly voice.

"Thank you," Sophie then responded politely. "We'll try not to be long!"

The three of them then proceeded down the gigantic nave, which was equally as majestic as the exterior. With gigantic finely carved pillars and arches spanning forwards, the feeling of being amongst it all was simply mystifying, as the echoes and sounds from around the area echoed throughout the building in a spooky way.

"Okay, let's go and visit Cuthbert's grave." Sophie then urged. "Keep your eyes open for any kind of clues or hidden messages..." As the three of them walked up the Cathedral, the priest then began watching them carefully from a distance, his polite and friendly countenance having vanished into a serious, if not sinister look. Sophie, Micky and Millie then proceeded to walk up a small staircase, leading to a cut away elevated room near the top of the Cathedral, which housed the shrine and top of St Cuthbert.

"Well, here we are." Sophie said softly, as they began to look around. The tomb was decorated with an array of candles, of which surrounded a large stone tombstone embedded into the ground. Directly up above it, suspended from the ceiling, sat a religious painting of St Cuthbert, depicting him sitting in blue and red robes, as an aurora of golden light shone behind him, with a halo around his head. On each corner of it was an entity with wings, including a bill, an eagle, a lion and an angel.

"Okay, let's have a look around very quietly, or see if you feel or sense anything." Millie then whispered, as they observed the contents of the tomb and thought deeply. Sophie sat down, meditating, in the hope that something mysterious or miraculous might manifest itself.

After a few minutes, Micky turned and asked "do you feel anything, Sophie?"

She then paused for a moment, before shaking her head and answering.

"No, nothing."

"Well that was just one idea. Let's keep looking," Micky urged, and after another minute or so, they quietly walked back down into the foyer. As they reappeared, the same priest stood watching them incessantly.

"We could look around the back rooms," Sophie then suggested. "Or there's even a library, we could give it a try I guess" she said, attempting to keep herself and them encouraged.

But it was at that moment they headed towards the Cloisters and inner courtyard of the Cathedral, that the priest, who had watched them with suspicion from the door, turned around and ushered some additional "visitors" into the premises. Holding open the door for them, a group of armed police officers entered the nave, followed up by none other than Police Chief David Simm. As they entered, he then pointed towards the direction of Sophie, Micky and Millie.

As they wandered around the Cloisters, they had little inclination as to what was coming.

"You know," Sophie asked. "Wasn't something filmed here?" she then asked curiously. "I'm trying to remember what it was." Micky then gave her a confused look.

"Nee idea like personally, probably many things," he replied, as they peered through a stained glass window into the dome shaped Chapter Room.

"The library is up here I think, if we can sneak up who knows what we could find." Millie then suggested, pointing to a staircase. However at that moment, Sophie felt a strange tingling sensation in her pocket. She piled her hand in urgently and pulled out her stone, which was now glowing.

"Sophie, what's gannin on?" Micky then asked as he noticed, with a hint of surprise.

"There's something," she replied. "This might be a sign…" she expressed with excitement, assuming it was an answer.

"So we're getting closer?" he asked.

"Seems like it!" She responded positively. But then suddenly, a dark feeling fell upon her, and she looked round to spot a horde of police officers bursting through the door.

"RUN!" She screamed, dragging Millie and Micky forwards

as the officers gave chase. Simm, behind the officers, then barked.

"You have permission to shoot them on sight!" And at that moment, as they darted through a doorway, bullets flickered and sparked off the walls as the officers opened fire.

Following Sophie's lead, the three of them darted through the cafe and bookshop, racing out of the back door and into the streets, heading down a hill towards the river, south of the Cathedral. The police continued to fire almost mercilessly, damaging cars and windows in the process, but failing to land a hit on the trio.

Having reached the bottom of the street and charging towards the valley, they approached another stone bridge crossing the River Wear, which led to an assortment of trees and houses on the other side. But just as they started running across the bridge, in easy range of the officers standing above Millie then tripped over on a large stone on the ground, sending her crashing onto the cobbles.

"MILLIE!" Sophie then yelled, as the officers seeing her immobilised, proceeded without hesitation to take aim at them and prepare to fire. It was at that moment Sophie's conversation with Millie's Mother flashed before her eyes. She had vowed to protect her, no matter what, and in her own words, to do "everything in her power".

While Sophie had, of course, saved Millie on three successive occasions, these incidents, which included Redcaps and gangsters, were an extension of Millie's own selfless devotion to Sophie, in situations she had control of, where these adversaries could be readily disposed of. But this time was different, as the stakes were much higher, and Sophie now realised she had to make a clear choice between her own life, or her friend's.

And she made her decision. Just as the officers pulled the trigger, Sophie dived selflessly on top of Millie, shielding her, as the loud bang of gunshots echoed in the distance. Millie, unharmed, got up on her knees to find Sophie lying on the floor next to her, a red line of blood trickling from her as she still clutched onto the stone in her other hand.

"SOPHIE, NO!" She screamed, kneeling over her body.

The officers didn't fire any further, but stood and watched. With Sophie down and others helpless, Simm then commanded them.

"The primary target is eliminated, arrest the other two." He snapped, and then began to walk towards them slowly, holding their guns forward as they moved. Micky, not a man to show great sorrow, shed a tear as he looked on in despair.

Sophie woke up in a room which was completely white. She looked around, confused, yet painless. She was no longer on the bridge, and was wearing a blank white robe from head to toe. Suddenly, she saw the figure of a woman standing in front of her, the same woman for that matter, which had appeared to her during that first incident at the Barnes Burn. She was wearing a white dress, and her hair was long and blonde.

"Mam, is that you?" Sophie then asked, identifying the woman's face.

"Sophie…" the woman then said suddenly in a mystical voice. "You have done me proud. I am with you, always. This is not the end, but the beginning. It is through sacrifice, that we become anew." The woman spoke mysteriously. "You stayed true to your promise to your friend and laid down your life, and thus I confer upon a blessing."

But before Sophie could respond, the entire room she stood

in burst into a flash of white light. But it was not just there, as the police approached Micky and Millie, standing over her body, that same flash of light permeated the bridge, shocking David Simm. The voice of the same woman then echoed through their surroundings, of which everyone could hear.

"Sophie, you have passed the test and accepted your path, accepting your path as the chosen hero. The spirit of King Oswald dwells within you. You have proven yourself worthy to become his new champion and as such I bestow you the title of the North Star, who stands as the guardian and protector of this sacred land. This shall be your destiny. Arise Sophie, and do what needs to be done!"

There was then another flash of light, as the police looked on bewildered. Suddenly, Sophie was no longer lying on the ground, and as if by magic, the blood had all disappeared. Instead, she stood facing them, and as the light faded she was now wearing, minus a helmet, a purple tinted set of mystical armour which twinkled in the light of the night. On the front of it next to her chest was embodied a symbol of the North Star, Polaris. Her sword firmly gripped in her left hand.

Her eyes were glowing mysteriously, while her long blonde hair waved in the wind.

"Sophie?" Micky then gasped, looking at her with shock and awe. The officers, now confused and panicked, staggered as she walked towards them.

"I am the North Star!" she then proclaimed boldly. David Simm, horrified and in a panic, then shouted at his officers.

"Well what are you waiting for? SHOOT HER!"

The police then open fired on Sophie from several directions, but the rounds seemed to harmlessly bounce off her armour, while she easily deflected any intended headshots with her sword. As the officers paused for a moment, stumped on what to do, she then jumped forwards at a lightspeed space and began slicing their guns in half before their eyes.

Their attacks having failed, several other officers then tumbled towards her with their batons, trying to beat and wrestle her down, but Sophie overpowered and disarmed them instantly, hurling them to the ground. Horrified and distraught as she battled the officers effortlessly, David Simm then fled the scene in a cowardly manner and dashed back up the street, disappearing. Choosing not to chase him at this point, she then calmly walked back towards Micky and Millie, who were so stunned they were lost for words.

Another flash of white light then radiated across the area, and the voice of Viviane sounded once again.

"My champion shall prevail. I now confer upon you a riddle. Lo and hear. "*I come and go, but I'm always here. I rise and fall, but do not disappear, the path is straight but not always clear*" Now, Sophie. This land is threatened by a great evil, an ancient evil. Prevail North Star, save my people. And remember, I am always with you." she spoke, before disappearing quickly.

Sophie's eyes then returned to normal, and she recuperated herself, albeit still dressed in the armour.

"Soph, I don't know what to say," said Micky, emotional and almost traumatised.

"It is through sacrifice that we become anew," Sophie then uttered, repeating the words she had been spoken, before turning to Millie.

"You kept your promise," she said emotionally.

"Yes, I did..." Sophie responded. "Always..." the two then hugged.

"But there is no time to celebrate, I feel something is wrong." Sophie then said ominously, as the three of them proceeded to leave the scene.

Chapter: XVIII: The Southwick Job

The chaos of the past few days had effectively led the trio to forget that an election was taking place, and as it happened, that same evening following the events in Durham was the day of the voting itself, and from ten p.m., the count had begun.

Elsewhere, back in Sunderland, Eddie Scott sat mindlessly absorbing television, as he always did. Despite having been visited by the police several times over the past few days, who continually interrogated him about the whereabouts of his daughter, he seemingly expressed indifference towards her welfare, only revealing anger and revulsion to those he knew.

The situation however, only made him more depressed. Deep down, he missed her and wondered what was going on, pondering if he himself had anything worth living for if she was gone. The empty takeaway containers piled up at the corner of the room, crippled by his lethargy and lack of motivation to do anything.

At the least, of course, he had been out to vote for Fulton that day, because who else was there you could vent your anger through? But besides that, he preferred not to speak to anyone, his sense of shame and grief engulfing him, the same feelings, of course, that had plagued him for most of the past decade, and were directly responsible for the fragmentation of the relationship between him and his only daughter, the living legacy of that which he had lost.

That night, Eddie laid on the settee and tuned in to watch the election footage. The City of Sunderland had always made it a tradition to be the first place in Britain which declared their results in local and national elections, a claim to fame which, as mentioned, crystallised an iconic image amidst Brexit.

Thus, as the counting began throughout the North East of England for the mayoral election, Sunderland was first again, and unsurprisingly William Parker-Fulton had romped home with a tally much higher than anyone anticipated, scoring a whopping sixty four per cent of the vote against the rival candidates, and setting the tone for the night. Eventually, the neighbouring areas, including Newcastle, Gateshead, North & South Tyneside, Northumberland and the County of Durham, followed suit as the night rolled on.

In Newcastle, Fulton was defeated by the Labour Party candidate, and likewise by 0.1 per cent in North Tyneside. However, he then went on to secure another crushing victory in County Durham, before sweeping South Tyneside and Northumberland, of which at this point the outcome was already written on the wall. Fulton had been elected the Mayor of North East England, his Sunderland based strategy having made him triumphant.

At this moment, in the sports hall in Sunderland's suburb of Silksworth, an election official walked up to the stage and made an announcement.

"I now formally declare William Parker-Fulton as the new mayor of the North East Combined authority!" Which was met with a thunderous round of applause. Fulton himself, very cheerful, a big fat blue and white rosette pinned to his jacket, then stepped forwards waving his hands to the crowd with delight, before taking the microphone.

"Thank you, thank you very much! Today is a new day, the

start of a new era in this region, in this city! The voice of the people has spoken and it is one small step towards taking back our country. This city has been betrayed, betrayed by the treacherous metropolitan elites in London who have nothing but contempt for working class people. They despise you, they despise your values and your way of life. Now, the fight begins. We are in a struggle for our own survival. The forces of history and change threaten to sweep away everything that is precious and dear to you, and that is why we must work together to protect ourselves. And together, we shall fight back the tide of crime, we will end amnesty for illegal immigrants sponging off your taxes, and will ensure all local villains are firmly placed behind bars. It is my testimony that Sunderland and our region shall be heard again, and I cannot thank the people of this city enough for placing their trust and faith in me on such an overwhelming scale! Thank you, and good night!" He then said powerfully, as the crowd once again roared in ecstasy at him.

With the election finally over, Eddie managed to creak a smile onto his face, something he wasn't capable of doing often. He then looked at the clock, the time was midnight, it was almost certainly time to go to bed. He switched off the television, stood up and stretched. Suddenly, he then heard a bump coming from the direction of the kitchen. Confused, he made his way to the source of the noise.

"Hello... who's there?" he asked, entering the kitchen. "Sophie, is that you?" He then reiterated, with a particle of hope in his voice. "If it is you, stop messing about you're in enough trouble as it is." He then snapped in a harsher tone as he looked around, but there was nobody there, either in the kitchen or outside. Shrugging his shoulders, he then turned around and made his way to the hallway.

"Evening Eddie." A sinister voice suddenly called out from the hallway. Startled, he then looked to see Tony standing in front of them, wearing his long black leather coat.

"If yer after me money, I haven't got it!" Eddie then reacted immediately on seeing him in a helpless voice.

"I'm not here for your money, I'm here for you." Tony then laughed, before proceeding to pull out a gun and point it towards Eddie. "Are ya gonna be a good boy and give up nicely?"

Elsewhere, Micky drove his car at breakneck speed back towards Sunderland.

"It's Tony's payday tomorrow…" Sophie said in a panic. "We've got to get back to my home before he can try anything, and then we'll deal with him for once and for all. Once he's out of the way, we get the staff." She contemplated, as they passed the sign officially re-entering Sunderland. The roads were clear, allowing Micky to be liberal with his pace as they swerved back into Thorney Close.

On arriving at Sophie's street, Micky hammered the brakes with a resounding screech, with Sophie jumping out so quickly she could have hurt herself. She then ran up the steps to her house to discover the door was already swung wide open.

"Dad?" she then asked softly on entering, "Hello? Dad?" But nobody was home. At that moment, she then noticed a note on the kitchen table.

"*Come and get him, dear.*" it read. Furious, she then ripped it up in anger, before running back outside to where Millie and Micky were waiting.

"He's took him!" she shouted. Micky then looked at her for a moment.

"Hey, tell you what, I just read on me phone that Fulton won. He was meant to be supporting you through all this, aye? Why don't you give him a call?" he then suggested.

"Okay then..." Sophie said in frustration, feeling agitated and stressed, yet trigger happy as she was still dressed in her armour. Managing to retrieve her wallet and phone from inside, she then pulled out the small contact card he had given her a week or so earlier, and nervously dialled the number on it. She waited and waited as it rang, perhaps he'd gone straight to bed after the count, and of course, who calls at this time of night? But there was no time to wait.

"Hello?" A tired voice then emerged from the phone. "Mayor Fulton speaking," he said.

"Hi... Mayor Fulton, congratulations on your election... it's Sophie," she then said nervously, hoping that he would recognise her and stay appreciative, or so had he claimed.

"Sophie? Oh Sophie! Hello. Well what a surprise, I certainly wasn't expecting this given recent events... what do I owe the pleasure?" He said, sounding surprised.

Sophie quickly broke the ice by pressing him hard. "Look, you know I'm innocent and the charges are a stitch up. You said you'd help clear my name and work with me together to stop Tony. I've come home and he's kidnapped my Dad," she said harshly. "You told me to stop him, so what should I do here?" she then asked, putting him on the spot.

"Oh dear, I'm sorry to hear that. Yes but I only just got elected what? An hour ago? And there's not much I can do until you expose Tony and find the staff before he or Simm gets it. You've been looking, right?" he then asked.

"Of course! We have the riddle" Sophie groaned. "But look, we need to resolve this here and now," she said in a stressed out voice.

"Okay Sophie..." Fulton then hesitated. "It's quite clear he's taken your father to his base in Southwick. Do not quote me on this, and again, we never had this conversation, but you might want to go there and 'handle' him to put it lightly. Then once we're done, we can talk about David Simm." He then suggested in a serious voice. "You can't miss his base, it's located in an old warehouse in Southwick, just on the north bank of the River Wear."

"Okay then, I'm on it," Sophie said coldly.

"Do keep me posted!" Fulton then added cheerfully.

"Talk later then, night," Sophie said abruptly, putting the phone down. She then turned to Millie and Micky.

"We're going to Southwick, step on it," she ordered, as they got back in the car, just as the sound of police sirens began to emerge in the distance.

Micky's car then once again charged through Sunderland at the dead of night, swerving relentlessly around the empty roads and streets as they headed towards the River Wear. But as the sirens earlier had suggested, they certainly weren't alone or arriving unexpectedly. As they gained sight of the Queen Alexandra Bridge in the distance, they then noticed the road had been forcibly blockaded by police cars.

"Why aye man… they've blocked the road," Micky groaned, grinding the car to a halt at a safe distance where they wouldn't be spotted.

"Stuff that," Sophie then said as she suddenly opened the car door and dived out, proceeding to pace down the street at extraordinary speed towards the blockade.

"Oh Sophie man…" Micky shook his head as he watched from afar.

"Oi you!" The officers yelled, not armed, as they powerlessly attempted to stop her. Charging towards them, she then proceeded to leap over the blockade into the air as if it were a school gymnastics hurdle, landing on the other side and then darting across the bridge, which was made out of stone and steel columns.

"Come on, let's find another way across!" Micky then said to Millie, as they got in the car and disappeared out of sight before the police officers could respond. Meanwhile, having crossed the bridge, she then carefully moved towards a series of large warehouses which made up the industrial estate on the periphery of Southwick.

Southwick was a funny sort of place. Once an independent medieval village distinct from the town of Sunderland itself, a community had lived around its small village green for over a millennium. This gave it its own tight knit sense of community and identity. However, statistically speaking, Southwick was also the poorest and most deprived ward in all of Sunderland, which gave it, similar to places like Hendon, a notorious reputation amongst locals. Gangsters, such as Tony Radcliff, having based their entire operations from there, did not help.

Entering the industrial estate, Sophie looked around carefully. She didn't know which unit to enter, but it wouldn't take much for her to work out as suddenly, a Redcap and two gangsters emerged from along the road, screaming and running towards her. The gangsters fired rifles in her direction, as the Redcap this time boasted a giant black machete.

Sophie managed to block the shots, before proceeding to engage the Redcap in a fierce duel whilst under the threat of looming gunfire. With a better and far more proficient weapon, the Redcap slashed wildly at Sophie, which forced her to jump back to find more space, before deflecting two more bullets.

Frustrated, she attempted to outrun the Redcap and deal with the gangsters first. However, as she attempted to run, it pulled her over by the leg sending her crashing to the crowd with a clang. It then thrust its machete to the direction of her throat, leaving her with few good options to block it, desperately trying to push it away with her own sword as it leaned over her.

In a last gasp escape attempt, Sophie booted the Redcap's leg, making it fall back, before driving her sword through its calf and rendering it unable to walk, leading it to unleash an inhuman scream in agony. She then pulled herself up and charged in her usual fashion at the two gangsters who fired at her relentlessly, the shots bouncing off her armour.

Sophie then jumped forwards, flipping round in the air before landing her foot right in the face of the first gangster, knocking him out cold, and then proceeding to snatch the rifle out of the hands of the second as if he were like a child, before proceeding to punch him in the face and knock him out cold.

Having finished that, she then turned back to the Redcap, still on the ground and unable to walk, and quickly finished it off with her sword. She then casually walked away as it crumbled to dust, heading in the direction they came from before, identifying a big grey warehouse as Tony's likely headquarters.

Inside his base, Tony watched a CCTV footage feed carefully from a small upstairs cutaway room elevated on the top of a metal staircase. Smiling sinisterly, he then turned round towards a tied up and muffled Eddie Scott, who had been completely bound to a chair.

"Looks like Daddy's little girl is here to try and save you." He laughed. "She just doesn't know when to stop does she?"

At that moment, Eddie attempted to speak, making incomprehensible noises behind the tape sealed over his mouth. "Don't worry Eddie boy, she'll be filled with lead soon enough."

He then cackled, as he waited patiently, seemingly expecting Sophie to continue to cut through the defences as a knife to butter and soon be in their midst.

And soon enough, Sophie then burst into the warehouse, which was filled with boxes and barrels of kinds, a useful facade of course, to disguise a criminal hideout and a narcotics factory.

"Oi!" a big gangster yelled as she burst in, but before he could make another move he too was knocked unconscious with a swift punch.

She then looked up towards the monitoring room on the upper level next to the ceiling, calculating that Eddie was in there. She scanned the area for any further resistance, before darting up the thin metal staircase to reach the office. Upon seeing the door had been locked, she then kicked it open violently with her metal boot, and there was her father, sitting helplessly in the middle of the room tied up. But there was no sign of Tony Radcliff anywhere...

"Dad!" She then proclaimed with shock, before running over to begin cutting through his ropes. Eddie groaned as she untied him, before carefully pulling the tape off from around his mouth. He gasped, taking a deep breath as he tasted the fresh air.

"Sophie, you came for me," he then said emotionally, as if he couldn't believe it.

"Of course, I did, why wouldn't I?" She then smiled, before embracing him with a hug for the very first time. "Let's get out of here!" She then urged, guiding him out of the room and onto the metal balcony.

But the moment they left the room, a voice emerged from nowhere, ambushing them.

"Not so fast!" It cackled, as Tony Radcliff emerged from the side, holding a gun directly to Sophie's head, rendering her unable to move. "Did you honestly think it would be as easy as that pet?" He scoffed. "DROP THE SWORD!" He then roared, prodding the gun into her crown.

Seemingly checkmated, Sophie dropped her weapon and raised her hands above her head hesitantly, but Tony did not change his posture.

"It will be here, tonight, where the saga of the Scott family finally comes to an end, you meddling little bitch." He then growled at her. "The Redcaps think you're a king, but I just think you and your Dad are bad for business."

"Tony, let her go!" Eddie then shouted, defending his daughter fiercely for the first time. But Tony simply laughed.

"When have you ever given a toss about her mate? You had her slaving for you because of debts you couldn't pay, you probably would have sold her for a price if you could, you lazy fat, useless fool," he scorned. "Sure, I don't pretend to be a nice bloke, but even for me, it's plain obvious you were a bad dar to her!" He laughed. "Her death is on you, mate!" He shouted as he taunted Eddie further, who at this point looked on in horror as all the mistakes of his life came crashing down on him like a ton of bricks. Tony was a reprehensible human being, but he wasn't technically wrong, to some extent the entire situation was indeed a product of the bad decisions Eddie had made in life. Now, he faced the prospect of losing the one thing he had in the world, his precious daughter.

And for all Eddie had been lazy, negligent, selfish, inwards and irresponsible, deep down he loved Sophie. Thus, as Tony Radcliff proceeded to shoot her, he immediately jumped forwards.

"NOOO!" With all his strength, he then pushed the gun out of the way before wrestling Tony to the ground.

Sophie looked on in horror, grabbing her sword as fast as she could to intervene, but at that moment a loud bang forcefully rang through the air. She looked down to see Eddie lying on the metal with a gunshot wound to his stomach. Speechless, she then began to cry at the sight of it. But Tony was not done yet, picking himself up, he then cornered Sophie again with the gun.

"Now, it's your turn!" He barked. Sophie, still shell-shocked with horror, couldn't bring herself to move, and closed her eyes in panic believing she had finally met her fate. Then suddenly, she heard three more loud gunshots next to her. Was that it? Had she died this time for real? She opened her eyes to discover she was fine, and instead Tony stood in front of her, motionless, with three gunshot wounds through his body, blood sponging onto his shirt.

He then fell down to the floor lethargically in slow motion, revealing Micky and Millie standing behind him, the former holding the same gun Sophie had first snatched from Tony back at the museum. But before they said a word to each other, Sophie then dashed over to Eddie and embraced her father in her arms, who was groaning in agony.

"Dad, it's going to be ok, I promise. Hold on, please!" She pleased as she cried, holding him tightly. Eddie then looked Sophie in the eyes, and smiled.

"Sophie, this world is not for me. Listen, I want yer to know this. Am sorry for everything. I love you, and you were the only thing I had in this world. You made me proud, thank you." He groaned to her in a happy voice, exerting the last of his strength, before giving up the ghost, his face finally content and smiling.

"Dad? No, no, no, no, no…." Sophie cried as she then hugged him closely. As she did so, Millie and Micky then kneeled down and also embraced her. Eddie, was however, free now, and as painful as it was, Sophie was no longer cursed with the burdens of his life, with the evil of Tony Radcliff also having been vanquished from the earth.

But it wasn't over yet...

Chapter XIX: The Pilgrim's Path

Sophie was heartbroken. Unable to salvage her father's body from the scene, the trio decided to respectfully call 999 to the warehouse before fleeing in Micky's car to the area southwards of Sunderland. Eventually, they stopped in a secluded area of coastline, which was similar in appearance to Ryhope Beach with large limestone cliffs and a cobble filled surface. Unique to this area though was that parts of it were also lined with a mysterious orange and red hue, reflecting the presence of a former ironworks. Having parked, the trio spent the few remaining hours of the night sleeping rough on the seats.

Inevitably having been unable to sleep well, Sophie woke up early the following morning to watch the sunrise over the sea, looking into it as if she felt lost. The others soon followed.

"You know..." Sophie said to them in an empty voice. "...You just don't know what you have until it's gone. He was a prick to me for most of my life, and then the moment he realises what I did for him, he dies because of a situation I caused," she said slowly, still stricken with grief.

Millie then placed her arm on Sophie's back to comfort her.

"It wasn't your fault Sophie, but I can't imagine what it's like to lose both of your parents so young. You were unable to save him, but the love that you showed redeemed him. He sacrificed his life for you. He was miserable, but died a happy and satisfied man because of who you are. However heartbreaking it is, in a strange way it's beautiful, Sophie," she said thoughtfully and softly.

"Aye Soph, you did well. I'm proud of you. I've never met anyone in my life with the guts and bravery you have like," Micky added, seemingly tearing up. Sophie however, seemed unmoved emotionally, and continued to stare blankly at the horizon.

"It's not over yet though…" she replied ominously. "There's still David Simm. We need to get the staff before he does, or whatever he wants to do with it."

"We have the riddle though, he doesn't." Micky added positively. "When we work out the answer, of course." He then laughed with a hint of doubt.

"Yes, so thankfully I was able to record that voice on my phone when it happened and make a note of it," Millie then said enthusiastically. "Obviously, I've had zero time to actually study it given you know… everything going on, so I'm still stumped. I mean, what comes and goes but is always here?" She asked rhetorically.

At that very moment, the waves of the tide lapped off Sophie's bare feet, sparking inspiration in Micky as he looked on.

"Well, the tide comes and goes but it's always here, aye?" He then suggested randomly.

"That actually might be a really good guess!" Millie then responded with enthusiasm. "Because the tide also rises and falls! So it sounds almost like a path, connected to the tide somehow!" She raced around unable to contain her excitement.

"That's it! Holy Island! Lindisfarne!" She then proclaimed. "A holy place where the causeway comes and goes with the tide, but it's always there! Yes!" On hearing this, Sophie then smiled for the first time since her father's passing.

"Micky, you're a genius, ha!" She laughed lightly.

"Haha not compared to you man, thick as two short planks when you get down to the nitty gritty," he replied humbly. "Right, so when are we driving up to Lindisfarne?" he then asked, bracing himself and seemingly expecting Sophie to marshal them there and then.

"Nah, I still need some time to cool down." Sophie then butted in, as she sat down on the cobbles.

"You know what, I've just realised, where did your armour go?" Micky then asked curiously, as he sat down next to her.

"Wish I knew, just like the sword, it kind of just does its own thing when trouble is over I think," she said doubtfully.

"So, you don't control it?" Micky then asked again.

"Nope, or least I haven't figured how to yet," Sophie then replied, shrugging her shoulders.

"Right, so what happens if you lose that stone which turns into it, don't tell us we're done for, right?" he then asked further.

"Micky man, don't tempt fate!" She pushed back at him in a joking voice. "It's our only hope. Funny thing is, I found it on a beach just like this one. Well just up the road in Ryhope to be exact," she then added in a calmer voice, looking on to the waves.

"Okay, so are we going to be on our way or not?" Millie then added from afar.

"Yeah, but do you mind if I take some time to get washed first?" she then asked. "I haven't even changed in days," Sophie then looked down at her clothes, which were sweaty and greasy. "Overnight at Liam Heskett's house, then all that running around, and now sleeping here. I honestly feel filthy."

Millie and Micky looked at her blankly for a second, unsure what to say.

"I'm going to go wash myself in those isolated rock pools

around the corner, just hold on." Sophie then added abruptly, before quickly dashing off into the distance.

Alone, Sophie discovered some pools of shallow water amidst the rocks. It was crystal clear and sparkled in the light of the sunrise. Sensing peace, Sophie removed her outer clothes, placing them carefully on a taller rock with her stone in her jeans pocket, before dipping herself into the freezing water slowly, gasping with shock as the cold stung her body. It was cold, yet refreshing. Then, finally acclimatising to it, she gave a deep breath as she slowly relaxed, washing herself with it.

Suddenly, Sophie found herself shoved head down into the water violently by an unseen force. She screamed under the water as she squirmed desperately, with air bubbles pouring out of her mouth, desperate to pull herself out and see who it was attacking her she raised her arm and grabbed onto what was pushing her down in a bid to wrestle it off. It felt fleshy, yet thick and cold, as if it lacked the warmness of a human being. She then managed to look upwards to see a blurred image of something tall and black standing over her.

Desperate, she punched upwards at it as she struggled for breath, but at that moment the figure pushing her down was suddenly gone and she was able to get out of the water. Horrified, coughing and gasping for air, she looked around in a panic, but there was nothing.

"SOPHIE!" "SOPHIE!" She then heard voices screaming in the distance, leading her to turn around to see Micky and Millie charging towards her in a state of panic.

"What happened? We heard screaming!" Millie then said in a panicking voice. Sophie, in shock and embarrassment, covered herself up in front of Micky, before replying.

"Oh… nothing, the water's just very, very cold. Don't

worry!" She then laughed nervously, attempting not to startle them. "Anyway… we need to go… now…" She then added in a much more serious tone.

"Areet then. Hold on. I've got a towel in the car boot. I'm not looking, promise!" Micky then replied, seemingly accepting her excuse.

After Sophie dried herself and got ready again, the group then got back into Micky's car and prepared for the long journey northwards to the island of Lindisfarne, which was based far north in the rural county of Northumberland, near the Scottish Border. For a while, there was silence between them, for even though Sophie had said little about this incident, there was an underlying feeling of tension and unease, not least for where they were heading now.

But eventually, Micky spoke up.

"So anyway, why do you think they want this staff thing?" he asked.

"Well, it's been repeatedly speculated that it is magic, but remember, we know there's something bigger at play than him. What did she say to us? This land is threatened by a great evil, an ancient evil. That's more than Tony Radcliff and Simm surely…" Sophie replied thoughtfully. "When we fought those Redcaps, they said they worshipped a lord, and that he would soon return. Tony might have used them for his own gain, but he always seemed to be quite open to me that he didn't have full control of them. He was just a passenger, on for the ride. There's definitely something more." She then continued.

"Do you not think it could be the one Mr Marchant kept telling us about in class, Glanfeoil?" Millie then inputted. "Because here's what I put together. You, Sophie are the North Star, the anointed heir of King Oswald who by legend, as we heard in class, would return again. But think about it this way, that legend was also premised on the apparent return of Glanfeoil!" She proclaimed once again in another eureka moment. "These monsters, the Redcaps, were the servants of Glanfeoil after all!"

"So, does that mean, the staff rightfully belongs to that Glanfeoil? And that's why it's hidden?" Micky then asked.

"Possibly, but the question is now, has Glanfeoil come back? How has he come back? Who is he? And where is he?" Millie then asked rhetorically.

"Beats me," Sophie asked. "But let me tell you this, I think Glanfeoil is the one from my dreams." She then added coldly, returning to the serious tone she embraced earlier. "For so long now I've had nightmares of a man, a man in a black cape and hood, demanding I submit to him. For many years, I thought these dreams were some sort of trauma, as if I was living a moment again and again, but now I realise, it's because I'm the North Star and he threatens me."

"It all makes sense now, so that's why the staff has been hidden somewhere they deem to be sacred and sanctified…" Millie then pondered.

"It's no surprise like that hasn't worked out, because people don't believe in God any more." Micky then commented abruptly.

"Well, I don't see you running into a church." Sophie then teased sarcastically.

"Ah man, Sophie, I was never raised religious, I mean who is these days? Apart from you two going to a Catholic school aye?" he then asked.

"Don't think any of the students actually believe it. I only went for a good education because the kids at state schools are unruly little pricks," Sophie then replied in a negative tone.

"But what does that tell you? It tells us here in the North East today, people have nothing to believe in. Sure, it doesn't have to be in a God, of course, so to speak." Millie then presented her opinion. "But sometimes I feel in this country, there are no values, no expectations and no direction. It's so alien to what my parents taught me. So is it a surprise that if Glanfeoil was suppressed by faith of the people, he somehow is returning?" she then asked.

The car then fell silent. They drove far, far north, leaving the urbanised span of Tyne & Wear behind for the rolling hills and forests of Northumberland, the last true remnant in name of the great kingdom King Oswald had once presided over. Micky continued to instinctively travel north, until they spotted a jagged green island sticking out on its own in the midst of the deep blue waters.

"There it is, the Holy Island of Lindisfarne." Millie proclaimed as they looked out of the window.

"So just checking, the causeway is open right?" Sophie then asked with concern. "Because you can never tell with the tides," she added.

"Yes, I just checked my phone, I think we have timed it well. We have two hours before the tide shifts to look around, that should be enough right?" she asked.

"Why does it matter man? I mean it's not like we've got anywhere to be afterwards is it? We need to find it, and if we have to stay there all night to do it that's fine with me," Micky said in a tough voice.

As the car approached the beach, it stood before a long stretch of tarmac extending out into the sand, which was tinted green with moss and seaweed along the edges. At the end of the road stood a sprawling island with an almost romanticised castle structure perched on the top of a hill like mound.

"Look at it, it's so beautiful," Millie said thoughtfully. "This island was one of the first bastions of Christianity in England, a place which truly shaped Northumbria," she added, as they then proceeded to make the journey east across the tense causeway.

Reaching the island, Micky parked the car, before they got out and immediately walked towards the ruins of an ancient monastery, all of which remained were a series of crumbling stone arches and pillars, a mere fraction of its former glory.

"Okay, I think we should have a look around the ancient Lindisfarne site." Sophie then commanded, taking the lead. "Don't be afraid to get your hands dirty, but also don't arouse suspicion, remember, I'm still wanted…" She noted.

The trio then wandered slowly, glancing at every detail within the ruins as they walked through the jagged rock surface and crumbling stairs.

"Now if you were an Anglo Saxon monk, where would you want to hide an item like that in your sanctuary?" Sophie asked as she pondered.

"Beats me," Micky replied, shrugging his shoulders. "If it's evil, you'd want to block its power, so maybe somewhere really holy?" He then suggested.

"Yeah but the problem is everything here is holy!" she then replied jokingly.

"But what would be the most holy place then?" he asked.

"The thing is though…" Millie then commented. "This monastery was also destroyed by the Vikings in the 8th century, hence its ruined state. Now, making the clear guess they never found the staff, it also had to be placed somewhere beyond this building, where plunderers like that wouldn't think of looking for it," Sophie then replied puzzled.

"Then are you saying we need to look somewhere else?"

At that moment, Millie's eyes fell upon a small old church building opposite to the ruins. A sign read *"The Church of St Mary."* Running close to it, she then inspected an information board outside of it giving a historical overview. *"St Mary's parish church is reputed to stand on the site of the original monastery founded by Aidan. The earliest parts of the building date back to the 7th century, several hundred years before the close by Lindisfarne Priory was built. The church was largely rebuilt in the 12th and 13th century, with the bellcote added in the 18th century."*

"Sophie, Micky!" She then yelled with excitement, calling him over. "This church building is where the original monastery stood, and is older than the ruins, which were built later! This would mean logically, that not only is the location underneath it lost and hidden, but I'm sure it would be the most sacred place too, surely?" she then asked.

"Aye, I guess it would, let's go take a look!" Micky then agreed.

"Impressive once again Millie!" Sophie then smiled, before they pushed open a creaking wooden door to enter the chapel.

The interior of the church was small and humble, with a simple design of stone pillars which were far older and less sophisticated than the monastery ruins outside, or for that matter the glory of those seen in Durham Cathedral. At the top of the building three chasms of light shined in through narrow stained glass windows, which beamed onto the trio as they walked through. As they approached the altar, Sophie then felt a dark feeling run through her, which hit her as if it were a punch to the stomach. She fell to the floor, causing Micky and Millie to frantically go pull her up

"Sophie? Are you all right, what's happening?" Micky then said concerned.

"It's here, I can feel it." She groaned, pulling herself up amidst the agonising energy. She then pulled her stone from her pocket, which was glowing brightly.

"Then I think it's somewhere near here, underground." Millie then commented.

"Ha'way let's shift this carpet." Micky then urged, and they then rolled away a long and hefty red carpet from the floor which had been placed in front of the altar.

Looking at where the carpet had been, there was then a large square slab on the surface which appeared looser than the rest, as if it was designed to open and close as a trapdoor.

"Look at this!" He pointed out.

"Okay, you two lift that, I'm going to stand outside on guard in case anyone comes. I mean it is a public building after all." Millie then commented, before dashing back and outside. Sophie then looked concerned as she left, but had been too distracted to comment as the two then began to heave the slab out of place.

"Well, would you look at that..." Micky then said with surprise, looking down at a narrow man sized hole leading to a staircase beneath the floor.

"It's a hidden passage." Sophie commented. "Let's go..." and the two together slowly climbed down it, before carefully walking down the staircase, unable to see anything in front of them.

"It looks like a cellar or summit." Micky then commented as they entered a tightly enclosed room with a low hanging ceiling.

He then lit up the light on his phone. The two gasped with

horror as the light peeled away the blackness, revealing a series of ancient cobbled walls which had been plastered with wooden crucifixes from head to toe. Rats scuttled across a rough dirt floor, while a recurrent dripping noise could be heard echoing through the chamber. At the top of the room sat an elaborately carved stone block which was holding a long finely carved wooden object inside of it. The top of it seemed to contain a glowing purple jewel of sorts, with the wood around the top having been crafted to give the appearance of natural branches holding it in.

"Holy mother man, there it is!" Micky whispered loudly, but it was at that moment Sophie moved towards it that she randomly crashed to the ground in delirious agony again. As she convulsed on the floor, the whole room seemed to change. She looked up as she wrestled in pain, and Micky and the entrance into the room had vanished, before it then started to spin around her violently, the crucifixes turning upside down.

"Sophie... Sophie..." a familiar voice which only she could hear then hissed. "Submit, or die." It said sharply. A high pitched screaming noise then pierced her ears, as if it sounded like that of a little girl.

"Sophie! Sophie!" Another voice yelled. She woke up, breaking out of the trance, to find Micky by her side desperately trying to bring her round. "It's okay, Sophie, I'm here!" he then said softly, before helping her up. "It was like you had a seizure or something," he then added in a sensitive voice.

"I'm okay..." Sophie then said in a toughened voice, brushing the dirt off her jeans before walking closer to the staff. "I can get it for you, it might be better that way" Micky then suggested confidently, before he proceeded to walk forwards and grab the staff.

But at the moment he touched it, he then yelled in agony, falling back across the room violently as if some unseen force had repelled him. Sophie, as he did to her, then ran over in shock and concern.

"Micky! Are you okay?" she then panicked, helping him up.

"Uhh… I'm alreet." He smiled, putting on a brave face. "I've nee idea what just happened like, felt as if I was off me heed while on a rollercoaster." He laughed.

"I think only I should carry it," Sophie then said in a very serious voice. "It's powerful, a normal human can't control it…" she then said honestly.

Sophie then took out her stone, which continued to grow, placing it close to her chest. She closed her eyes, thinking deeply for a moment, before making a sharp rush to grab the staff. Again, on touching it, a dark force seemed to descend upon her, leading her to experience a myriad of negative emotions all at once, anger, sorrow, grief, anxiety. Yet she pressed against it with her mind forcefully and countered it as hard as she could with positive feelings. It exhausted her quickly, she then pressed on, holding it tight successfully.

"Bloody hell man, Sophie, you did it!" Micky then cheered. "Reet, let's get out of here, back to Millie," he said as he and Sophie raced for the exit, back up the stairs and out of the hole, before darting up through the church hallway and outside. Leaving the door, they then looked around confused; Millie was gone.

"Millie?" Sophie then said loudly.

"Millie?" Micky then yelled loudly through his hands. "Come on!" he then said anxiously as he and Sophie, while still carrying the staff, began frantically looking around the site for her.

"Please, please…" Sophie said to herself out loud. "Not this again, turn up Millie please." They continued to look, high and low, endlessly going around in circles even as they continued to call her name, until suddenly, as Sophie proceeded underneath what was known as the Rainbow Arch, she stumbled backwards with a shock.

"Sophie Scott, what a surprise!" A familiar voice said cheerfully, but menacingly.

"William Parker-Fulton?" She then reacted with horror, her jaw dropping.

Chapter XX: Evil Reborn

Under the arch stood William Parker-Fulton, his face smiling with an intimidating glare. Sophie stood anxious, realising something was wrong.

"What are you doing here?" she then asked, at least attempting to make normal conversation.

"Looking for someone, are we?" he then replied, again in a menacing voice, with a follow up question. "Perhaps, I can be of assistance!" He then snapped his fingers loudly, and at that moment a number of Redcaps then descended upon them from all directions, blocking their every route, but they merely stood and did not attack. At that moment, Police Chief David Simm then appeared behind Fulton, but he was not alone. He had his arm wrapped around Millie's neck forcefully, while holding a gun directly to the side of her head.

"Well then, it looks like our dear officer here has found your missing friend! Now it's just a question as to whether you want her alive… or dead!" Fulton then laughed in a psychotic manner, Sophie still having not uttered a word yet as she grappled to process everything in a state of shock.

"What's going on?" she then asked with panic. "I thought you were supporting me Fulton, I thought you were against all this!" she said, her voice slowly turning to anger.

"Sophie, my dear, I'll let you in on a little secret. I'm the one who has been truly seeking out the staff all along. It's no ordinary staff Sophie, this staff, or the Caenterstaff as it is so called, is one of the most powerful magical items ever created. Some things cannot be done by the hand of man necessitating new forms of power. But this was once mine, and for so long had I lost it!" He then announced in a triumphant voice.

"What? So you are Glanfeoil?" Sophie then asked in horror.

"You could say that, but the point is, I'm not just a politician my dear girl, but a magician, and through that staff you hold there, I shall rekindle what is mine and reverse the ill conceited ways of this land! Already, and even without the fullness of my power, I have created the magic lava, made the Redcaps out of the spleen of angry young men, won an election on top of all that, and of course, managed to fool you into doing my bidding!"

"I trusted you!" Sophie then yelled indignation to him. "I promise you will go the same way as Tony! You sleazy, lying good for nothing spiv!" She shouted, but Fulton simply laughed, feeling perfectly comfortable.

"It finally clicks! Poor Tony, useful, but an idiot. He certainly made for a convincing ruse, as all he cared about was money. However, it is you who has fallen hook line and sinker into our traps every single time, and now you've led me to the very thing I wanted to find!" He laughed. "Not so bright for a North Star now are you?"

"This isn't over yet," Sophie said angrily towards him as she glared into his eyes.

"Perhaps, not. You're impressive, Sophie, to have achieved everything you have so far, but you're also reckless. Whether it be battling Redcaps or even Tony himself, the running theme of all this is that you have placed those you profess to love in danger again and again, and it's eventually come to a terrible cost to you, hasn't it? And of course, here we are, in the same situation again. Perhaps you can kill me, right here and now, but I ask you solemnly Sophie, will the same cost of victory to your previous one be as acceptable for you as the last one was?" He then smiled at her viciously.

Fulton's mode of manipulation seemed almost perfect. Sophie suffered, lost for words, and simply muttered to him.

"You treacherous swine." She knew she was trapped. Fulton then smiled again, before saying in a superficial voice.

"Give me the Caenterstaff, and I will give you back your friend. Unharmed. However... try and fight me, your friend dies. Try and escape, your friend dies. I like to be a man of my word, I haven't lied to you in asking you to bring me this staff, only concealed part of the truth. I don't differentiate myself from other politicians for nothing you know. So how do you want to play this?" he asked.

Sophie just stared at him, paralysed with fear and resentment.

"How many more people will die in your name Sophie? Is your best friend's life worth more than this piece of wood?" He then followed up again. Overcome with guilt and anxiety, she looked at the staff in her hand, and then back over to Millie.

"There's no way I can ever let anything happen to her." She then sincerely told Fulton, who then grinned wickedly as he heard this. "You win, you can have the staff... just please let her go." She pleaded.

"Marvellous!" Fulton then said loudly in his usual jovial voice, as Sophie then begrudgingly walked up to the rainbow arch, handing Fulton the staff, who then proceeded to shake her hand in a patronising manner.

"Very good, David, please let her go," he then asked in a sincere voice, as David Simm unleashed Millie onto the ground, who then ran into Sophie's arms distraught. "Well..." Fulton then continued, turning back to Sophie. "It was delightful doing business with you, "North Star". If you wish to yield later, we can discuss that soon enough, but for now, cheerio!"

As Fulton grasped the staff, his eyes suddenly flashed red, appearing to turn completely blank with no pupils or eris visible. The head of the staff then glowed with him, as the trio watched in horror, as a blinding flash of purple light filled the area. Suddenly, Fulton, Simm and all the Redcaps which surrounded them had disappeared completely, as if they had never been there in the first place. Sophie, without saying another word, fell down to her knees in tears and disbelief.

Elsewhere, Fulton and Simm materialised with the staff into a large dark hall. It had a classical and intimidating look to it. The walls were painted a dark brown shaded red, while the floor was chequered in the pattern of a chess board. Around the room were scores of chairs and benches, all with bright red velvet padding, which were nearly arranged in a square pattern as if they were designed to accommodate some kind of audience or congregation. In the top of the room, stood an elevated throne. Up above, the ceiling was of a deep blue variety, of which in the centre of was placed a gigantic circular golden light which was divided into ripples as if it reflected the rays of the sun.

William Parker-Fulton, with the staff in hand, then took a seat on the throne. He then turned to David Simm, who looked upon him as if he were an obedient soldier of sorts.

"From this day forth, I shall no longer be known as William Parker-Fulton, but as my true name Glanfeoil!" He then beckoned to him, but Simm merely gave him a confused look.

"Okay, so what's the significance of that?" he then asked in his typical cynical and nihilist manner. "I thought this whole magic act was to remain discreetly hidden from the public while you used it to control them, not that you would actually adopt this wizard's name. Wasn't that the plan, no?" he asked unkindly.

"You have no idea." Glanfeoil then responded to him coldly. "In fact, you may have misunderstood a lot of things. Glanfeoil isn't a legend or a child's fairytale, and I'm not adopting his name as a title, I am Glanfeoil!" He then continued sharply. "There was never such a man as William Parker-Fulton, he was an identity I fabricated and hid behind after I finally returned to this mortal plain, having been banished for over one thousand four hundred years! I have spent the last thirty years quietly preparing for this moment, to be reunited with the full source of my power, to build up my influence base in Northumbria and then to reclaim this land which was stolen from my ancestors!" David Simm looked visibly uncomfortable as Glanfeoil ranted on. "Tell me, David, why do you serve me? Why did you choose to follow this cause and partake of these magical secrets?" he said in an antagonistic voice. Simm seemed stumped to answer.

"Well, I erm... really believed in your vision, and thought what you planned would help this region become a better place," he replied unconvincingly. On hearing this, Glanfeoil simply laughed.

"Do you honestly think I believe that drivel?" he then asked bluntly. "Let me tell you this, you are a corrupt self-serving law bureaucrat, who whilst being very helpful in helping rebuild my kingdom and keeping Sophie at bay, you did so for purely selfish purposes. You jumped on the bandwagon seeing money, power and opportunity for yourself! My goal however, is to establish a new political order, and I have been merely feeding on the rotting carcass of the existing one." Simm was stung with shock, as a man with no principles who had, of course, confided the fullness of his true self in Fulton's scheme, he could scarcely defend himself. "But now Simm, you are able to see what true power looks like…" he then hissed.

"You mate, are mental!" Simm then shouted, finding the courage to talk back. "I don't give a monkey's about your political goals! But don't pretend you're cleaner than me sunshine because you're no less self-serving! I'm going to end this now, and the world will hear how you were a mad cultist who conspired with Tony Radcliff, and we had no choice but to shoot you!" On saying that, Simm then withdrew his gun and pointed it at Glanfeoil.

"Go ahead and shoot me then, make sure you don't miss!" He taunted. Simm, seemingly overconfident, took the bait and fired his pistol several times, but Glanfeoil, as if by magic, blocked the shots with his hand effortlessly.

"Finished?" He then jeered sarcastically, as Simm's face turned white with fear. "Now, allow me to show you my true power." Glanfeoil then spoke in an insidious voice. Then suddenly, as if by magic, the door to the room closed and locked. The lights in the windowless facility then also began to flicker as he stood up from the throne slowly and menacingly.

"The time of awakening has begun. The dawn of a new era, and the House of Baldur shall rise in all its glory!" He then proclaimed, as the Caenterstaff then began to glow and pulse repeatedly. Simm, terrified, desperately attempted to open the door in vain, before then trying to kick it open violently. As he did so, Glanfeoil simply laughed at him, as a dark energy then began to radiate from the staff and surround the warlock. Again, his eyes transformed permanently white and blank, absent of any inner contents or sentiment, as a dark green robe then materialised around him.

"I no longer need you… David." Glanfeoil then hissed, his

voice now darker and deeper than before, as if it had become monstrous. "But I do need… your essence." He continued. Simm then turned round with a look of pure helplessness on his face as the lights continued to flicker amidst the dark energy.

"My what?" He then gasped horrified.

"Many, many Redcaps will be your legacy." Glanfeoil laughed wickedly, before suddenly appearing in front of him. A blood curdling scream of absolute horror was then heard from outside of the building, so great that a flock of birds loitering nearby flew away, cawing loudly as they felt unsettled.

Having dealt with Simm, Glanfeoil then transported himself in front of Sunderland City Hall. Standing in his dark green robes, with the Caenterstaff, he then took down his hold to reveal his empty white eyes to the world, and began to make a public address.

"People of Northumbria, hear my call! You shall no longer know me as William Parker-Fulton, but as Glanfeoil. After having slept many centuries, I have returned, and the house of Baldur has awoken in all its glory. We shall now rebuild our kingdom and purify this land! My people, I sense that your lives are filled with anger, disillusionment, and cynicism. Your society has failed you, and your politicians have failed you. You have lived on generations of lies, disseminated by those you trust, of which have never made you better off. While men enriched themselves at your expense, you have only suffered and been cast out on the wayside! Now, I make the promise unto you, that through my power, that we shall together destroy the old world and find salvation in a new order that shall deliver unto us truth and justice! Voting, my friends, was only the beginning!" He spoke again triumphantly in a style similar to his predecessor.

Of course, the people nearby looked on with concern,

amusement and disdain.

"What was this?" They thought to themselves. "Has Fulton gone mad? Why is he dressed like that?" All of these thoughts raced through people's minds as he now stood preaching a radically new doctrine to them seemingly premised on the overthrow of Christian-Judeo society in the name of Nordic Paganism. As crowds watched, people began livestreaming the event, which quickly went viral not just around Britain, but the world too.

But soon, the mockery would quickly dry up.

"I will now give unto you an ultimatum!" He proclaimed. "Submit to me as your new lord, or perish by the hand of my eternal power! Behold my servants, the Redcaps!" He then roared, as his staff glowed purple yet again. At that moment, a chasm of black energy volleyed out of its tip and into the sky, as it touched the clouds it then seemed to start spreading as if it were food colouring hitting water. Within seconds, the entire sky had been engulfed in blackness, causing the people on the ground to freak out in panic and confusion.

As that happened, Glanfeoil then held out his hand and a red ball of energy emerged within his palm, which then burst outwards as a storm of red lightning bolts which spread in every direction. From the lightning, the red outline of figures then began to emerge all throughout the city, as if something was materialising on a large scale. The outlines then crackled as slowly, thousands of Redcaps emerged within the templates, each one of them armed with various weapons. People screamed and panicked as the monsters appeared within broad daylight throughout all of Sunderland, who without any hesitation then began pursuing destruction and disorder on a massive scale.

They smashed people's windows, destroyed and burnt out

cars, senselessly ransacked shops and interiors amongst many more things, in what was collectively a massive show of force to coerce the people of Sunderland to submit. All as Glanfeoil stood rooted in Keel Square laughing and smiling viciously, the crowd that had frequented him having long fled.

Evil had been reborn.

Chapter XXI: Honest Questions

Sophie could hardly speak following the events at Lindisfarne. Crushed under the weight of her own perceived sense of failure and guilt, she truly believed she had betrayed everyone she loved. With her having shed tears, Micky and Millie escorted her back to the car supportively, albeit their faces also gloomy and shellshocked.

"I can't believe it…" Micky said quietly as he drove. "Fulton lied to us all, the spiv ," he then said with resentment. Millie bit her lips to try and stop herself speaking, being barely unable to contain an "I told you so," but chose not to for the sake of Sophie and digging up past arguments.

"I don't even know where we can possibly go now like." Micky then commented with frustration as he drove the car back over the causeway. "But listen Sophie." He then began, turning to her. "This is not your fault, and I need yer to know you shouldn't feel bad. You did the right thing," he then said solemnly. Sophie, still lost in self-doubt, nodded without speaking. "As I said before, I'm proud of you," he continued, attempting to brighten the mood. "And he hasn't won yet, the slimy prick," he then said sharply. "We need to make a plan on what to do next mind. I'm driving southbound but it feels aimless as I've no idea if we should even go back to Sunderland."

Suddenly, Millie's phone began to vibrate violently.

"Someone's calling, I think it's my mum," she said hastily as she picked up the phone. "Hello?" she then answered. "Mum, is that you?" she then asked, as something unusual seemed to be going on in the background. "Yes, I'm okay, what's going on?" Millie's face then dropped in disbelief, before she then put the call loudspeaker to share with the others.

"Millie whatever you do, do not come back home!" Her mother then said in a state of panic. "It's impossible to explain what's going on but there are monsters everywhere! Hundreds of them!"

"What in the dog's...?" Micky then commented on listening.

"Mayor Fulton has launched some kind of attack on the whole town. It's a full scale riot. Homes are being smashed, shops looted, vehicles destroyed, so wherever you are Millie please stay out!" she pleaded.

"Mum, are you okay?" Millie then asked, panicking back.

"Your dad and I are just hiding at home in the cellar. We've boarded up the windows. Please stay safe, I will call you later, okay?" The call then cut off suddenly.

"Mum? Oh she's cut out," Millie then said.

"I need to call me parents later as well," Micky said extremely unsettled. "Let me pop on the car radio so we can see what's going on." Micky then took one hand off the wheel and pressed a button, springing the radio to life, and a song started playing.

"*I'm the dandy highwayman who you're too scared to mention, I spend my cash on looking flash and grabbing your attention, the devil take your stereo and your record collection...*" Micky, pulling a look of disapproval, then changed the station instantly to find a news report.

"BBC Radio Newcastle, This is a breaking news report. Violent riots are sweeping the city of Sunderland this afternoon as the area has come under attack by unusual men, seemingly at the command of newly elected populist Mayor William Parker-Fulton, now referring to himself Glanfeoil. The sky over the city and surrounding area has been covered in darkness but the cause is not yet understood. All emergency services have been rendered unavailable. Residents are being urged to stay indoors and listen to pending advice from the government." A reporter then spoke in an extremely ominous voice. "If you are in Sunderland, and have any information on these disturbing events, please get in touch immediately," he asked.

"What do we do? I can't just leave mum no matter what she says" Millie then asked in an anxious voice.

"I know it's a crappy situation but we can't possibly just gan back there while Sophie's like this, they'll kill us. By the sounds of it like, there's hundreds and hundreds of Redcaps this time, as well as a bloody dark wizard," he said in a pessimistic tone.

"I agree. We need to get back as soon as we can and stop them though." Millie then asked.

"Aye, we need to wait until Sophie is better. My suggestion is we drive to some guesthouse near here, get some food, we sleep it out and make a plan," he then said, assuming the reins of leadership amidst Sophie's struggles.

"Yes, we do need some rest. I'm worried sick, but I get it." Millie then concurred.

"Areet then, how about we head for Bamburgh? It's just down the road, the nearest place coming up." Micky suggested.

"Sounds good," Millie replied. As he drove, an enormous stone castle appeared on the horizon mounted upon a hill, towering over a small country town with a rosy and romanticised feeling to it, as if it were something from a fairytale, dotted with colourful stonework houses with traditional chimneys. The streets were also lined with old style black Victorian street lights, while a red London style phone box asserted itself by the side of the road. It was as if time had stood still in Bamburgh, in a nostalgic way.

Scouting around the town, Micky then pulled into the carpark of a small and cosy looking guesthouse, titled *"Jean's Bed and Breakfast."* Leaving Sophie and Millie in the car, he then got out quickly and rushed into the reception, where a little old lady with glasses was sitting reading.

"Hello, dear, how may I help you?" she then asked kindly.

"Areet, I'm wondering if there's any room at the inn…" Micky then asked in a joking time. "Three people, just one night," he asked, trying to conceal his panic.

The old lady put her book down, and looked at a planner on the table.

"Yes dear, we aren't too busy today. I can give you one room, with a bunk bed and a single bed, for £70, one night. Is that okay for you?" she then asked.

"Aye that will do cheers," Micky then replied smiling.

"Okay, just a minute." The lady then got up and slowly walked over to get a key, as Micky dashed back to the car to bring back Sophie and Millie, before then paying with his own debit card.

"Okay, dears," the lady then replied as she brought the room key. "Breakfast is at eight thirty, enjoy your stay!" She smiled as they dashed up a small staircase to the rooms.

On opening the door and entering, Sophie then finally expressed some signs of life and enthusiasm.

"Dibs on top bunk!" She then said very quietly, but more happily, before racing up the ladder and lying down on the top mattress.

"Hey!" Millie then jokingly replied before settling on the

bottom, as Micky then sat himself on the single bed. The trio then rested in relative silence. As it had been an extremely long day, as well as an emotional one, with an extremely early start, backed by the fact they got very little sleep prior to that, Micky and Millie soon dozed off to sleep almost instantly.

Sophie, however, with the events of the day still racing through her head and emotionally draining her, had no possible way of putting her mind to rest. Worse still, Micky was now snoring, much to her disdain. She picked up her phone, which she had long placed on flight mode to stop the police tracking her, and looked at the time. Realising it was only three forty-five p.m. She then pulled herself up restlessly, put on her disguise and walked out of the room and the guesthouse as the other two slept. Walking out onto the street, she felt a bit liberated as the town was quiet and nobody, of course, was likely to recognise her.

She walked around the area as she tried to calm her emotions and manage her thoughts, as she had always done back in Sunderland, before heading down onto a wide spanning beach, which sat under the beautiful watch of the castle. She stood and looked at the fortress in front of her, pondering the nation of Northumbria, that this small town once represented as its capital, before heading towards the water, where she looked out at the horizon as the waves lapping gently onto the sand.

Still frustrated, she then began picking up pebbles and throwing them into the water. At that moment, she then took the North Star stone from out of her pocket, before looking at it and then back towards the sea. She then sobbed as the memories and experiences of the past few weeks hit her.

"How could I have gone through all this?" She cried to herself out loud." Will my life ever be normal again?"

"Sophie…" she then heard a voice call out very softly. It was one she recognised but couldn't quite put her finger on. Startled, she turned around to see a woman standing behind her, dressed in a white dress. Her hair was long and wavy, her face kind and benevolent.

"Mam?" she then asked with surprise, on recognising the woman as the figure that had repeatedly appeared to her throughout her journey.

"Do not be down," she then spoke to her lovingly.

"No, I failed you. I'm sorry," Sophie said in a depressed voice. "Fulton got the staff and now everyone's lives are being ruined, because of me," she said, looking down to the ground.

"No Sophie... You did not fail. While setbacks may be disheartening, I have seen within this moment, and throughout your journey you have always chosen to serve and protect the ones you love. Your sacrifice has been the hallmark of a true hero. You have grown up so much and you have come of age... my Daughter." The woman then comforted her.

"Mam, it really is you, it's all real!" Sophie then proclaimed in an emotional voice, hugging the woman.

"Yes, Sophie, it is me. I am your Mother. I have been watching over you, with hope and trust that you might become worthy and ready for what is to come, and you have long passed the test." She then explained.

"But, Mam, I need to know, you died, how is this all possible?" Sophie then asked honestly, still of course, confused at her appearance.

"My body has died, but my spirit is bound to the Earth. I am called as Viviane, the lady of the lake and the anointer of worthy heroes. This is my burden, to prepare you, the chosen North Star, for your destiny. When you have fulfilled your mission, I shall be free."

"But what do I need to do?" Sophie then asked.

"Banish Glanfeoil and protect these people, deliver them unto righteousness and hope. Vanquish their disillusionment," she replied.

"I will," Sophie then responded in a quiet voice. Viviane then placed her hand on Sophie's, touching the North Star stone she held.

"This stone, Sophie, is meant to be a prompt for you. A guide. The true power lies within you, and will always be yours providing you believe in yourself. I shall leave you now, but know that I love you, always. The fate of these people depends on you."

After she finished speaking, Viviane then disappeared by gently fading away, leaving Sophie standing alone on the beach, with a mix of sorrow, awe but also renewed hope. As she stood, a random man walked past with his dog and commented.

"You all right, pet? Seemed like you were talking to yersel there." Sophie smiled awkwardly and unconvincingly, before responding.

"No, no… just talking out loud, rough day that's all."

"Areet then, as long as you're all right, take care now," the man said cheerfully and he walked off.

Back at the guesthouse room, after a brief snooze, Micky woke up, sitting up in the bed, stretching his arms and yawning.

"God I was shattered like," he said out loud, looking around. "Looks like Sophie's gone out." He then commented, noting her empty space on the bunk.

"Ugh, what?" Millie then said in a tired voice as she also came round. "Is she okay?" she asked, concerned.

"I'm sure she'll be all right, just doing her thing," he replied.

"Yeah but you really don't know what to expect these days,"

Millie responded, getting up. "Have you spoken to your parents yet? They must be worried sick too, you need to check if they're okay."

"Not yet, been meaning to do so. They're used to me doing my own thing, mind," Micky replied.

"So different from what I'm used to. You see it for yourself, my Mum would freak out at the smallest possible things, so protective. Their expectations of me have always been huge," she said, opening up to him. "They're typical Asian parents, and that's why it's been so hard growing up in somewhere like Sunderland, so many people just don't care. And you feel so alone sometimes, as if you don't fit in."

"Aye, so many people have nothing to believe in, nothing to hope for," Micky then nodded.

"So, what's your dream then Micky?" she then asked curiously.

"When I was little, my dad wanted me to be a footy player, I mean seriously. He forced me into all the youth teams, would cheer and scream at me during games, bollock me for every failure, and you know what? I didn't even make it. I didn't do well at school or go to uni, so my goal has just been to take the most of it all, to remain cheerful and hope that one day, hard work might get me somewhere," he replied, thinking deeply about his life.

"I'm sorry to hear that, but yeah I'm sure it will, as long as you have some dream. You're a good lad Micky. I'll admit I didn't like you at first, but hey, I was a bit of a snob myself, but you get like that when you feel nobody else understands you or your values." She then added.

"Nee bother ha, the funny thing is you were right about Fulton all along. But a fellow misfit yeah? That's why you were mates with Sophie," he asked, smiling.

"Yeah, you could say that. She was different, I was different. We stood out together, and there was nobody else who would listen to me like she did. So I had to learn not only to not stick up for myself, but for her too," she then said in a more sad voice.

"But now, she's the one sticking up for you." Micky then commented in reply "And bloody hell man, what a friend you have in her... she's come a long way," he said in a sentimental manner.

"I know, I still can't believe any of this is real. But who knows what's coming next..." Millie then replied. "As we said, whatever happens, we'll be here for each other..." he then smiled. "Friends?" she then asked.

"Always," he replied. He then stuck out his hand for Millie to shake, before she grabbed it and then hugged him.

At that moment the two looked each other in the eyes deeply, but before anything else could happen, the door of the room suddenly swung open, causing Micky and Millie to jump back away from each other awkwardly as Sophie stood in the doorway, her countenance completely transformed.

"I've got so much to tell you both!" she said in an urgent voice.

"Oh, all right Sophie!" Micky replied, slightly embarrassed. "Good to see you're feeling better..." But Sophie was too self-engrossed to have noticed the situation.

"Okay, who's for some fish and chips? Lots to get through!" she then suggested cheerfully.

Chapter XXII: The Forest of Tribulation

Night fell, and the vast cosmos twinkled brightly over the Northumberland coastline. After Micky and Millie fell asleep, Sophie once again slipped outside and continued to traverse the town of Bamburgh on her own, her mind invested in her past, present and future. Too deeply saturated within her thinking to contemplate any tiredness, she walked up the steep hill towards the castle, gazing upon its mighty walls and towers with awe.

She then looked up into the sky, and smiled as she saw the North Star, Polaris, shining brightly above all the rest. Inspired, she took out her stone and held it up to the sky.

"For my parents, and for Northumbria!" She then shouted triumphantly, assuming nobody else was around.

"Hi, you all right there?" A voice then sounded suddenly from nearby, causing Sophie to freeze in embarrassment. The voice sounded familiar, but she could not put a name on it. She looked around frantically at where it came from, before spotting a man standing nearby.

"Wait a minute, haven't I seen you before?" she then asked in surprise, on seeing it was the same man with long brown hair and a beard that she had encountered back on Ryhope Beach previously.

"Yep, that would be me," he smiled. "How's it going?" he then asked in a carefree voice.

"Well... where do I even start?" Sophie then replied nervously. "You don't know me so I honestly don't know how I can explain my situation... right now." She smiled awkwardly.

"Don't worry Sophie, I know everything, of course," he then replied and smiled.

"Okay..." Sophie replied in a more comforting voice. "So, who are you then?" she then asked.

"I'm nobody," he then replied. "Don't worry about me. I just wanted to make sure you're okay, that's all. Mind you, nice night tonight isn't it?" he then asked, looking up at the stars.

"Well yeah... somehow, I mean I'm alive." Sophie then laughed.

"Trust me, you'll be fine. Confront your fears, own them, and relax," he said, as he smiled.

"Thank you, but do you really not mind telling me your name?" Sophie then asked, still puzzled at the man's identity as she also gazed on the stars. However, her words were met with silence. Confused, she looked back to where he was standing and he was gone. She stood alone.

Puzzled, she walked back to the guest house. The night passed without incident, before she woke up the following morning with the light piercing its way in through the curtains. She sat up and peered over the top of the bunk to see Millie awake and getting ready, with Micky still dozing off on the bed at the other side of the room.

"Morning Sophie!" she then said cheerfully as Sophie rubbed her eyes and climbed down from the bunk.

"Today is the day..." Sophie then told her in a very serious voice. "We're going to go back to Sunderland." Millie stood and looked at her, concerned but willing to listen. "We can't hide up here as nomads forever. It's time to stand up and be counted for…" She continued. "So our plan is this: get ready, pack your bags, grab breakfast, call your parents to make sure they're okay and whatever you need, then we're going." She ordered. Millie, curious about the situation, then scrambled to her phone and began searching for news.

"Oh no…" she said in a concerned voice as she read. "It's not good… Let me turn on the TV," she said, grabbing the phone and turning on the small television in the room, where a special news report again was underway.

"This is a special emergency broadcast from the BBC…" the reporter said in an ominous voice. "Violence and disorder has continued to sweep the city of Sunderland overnight, and shows no sign of ending. The government now understands the situation to be an insurgency started by populist Mayor William Parker-Fulton, with his followers wearing distinctive red hats or clothes. At least seven people have been killed in the chaos, as residents are again advised to take shelter where possible. All emergency services have been rendered unavailable"

Micky, on hearing the TV, woke up in fright.

"What's going on?" He asked, before pulling himself around and squinting at the screen.

"The prime minister will meet with the national security council to host a COBRA meeting together, where a decision is expected to be made concerning potential military action. Already, local garrisons have been deployed to blockade entrances to the city. Please stay tuned for more updates."

"Crap!" Sophie then snarled on seeing it. "We have to prepare quickly, and go!" she said urgently.

"But wait, your plan is to go back, but then what will we do when you're there?" Millie then asked concerned.

"As I told you last night, defeat Glanfeoil. How? Who

knows… But at least being there is a start." Sophie said as she rushed around getting ready. "We have to stop this before the army is deployed and any more people die. It will be carnage!" She then commented as she aggressively combed her hair.

"Aye, knowing the government, and seeing the redcaps can't easily be killed, they'll probably end up bombing the place or summit," Micky then commented cynically. "Ha'way, let's go," he said, pulling on his jacket and stroking his stubble, having not shaved and waiting at the door. "Always takes longer when you're with women," he then joked as he waited for them.

"Ha'way Micky, you know I have to look me best for the date with Glanfeoil," Sophie then joked back.

"Sophie, you couldn't possibly look any better." He then smiled, making her blush.

"Bloody hell man…" She groaned.

Finally ready, the trio raced downstairs and acted so quickly that they almost threw the room keys back at the old lady at the desk.

"You're in a rush aren't you, are you sure you don't want a spot of breakfast dears?" She then asked. Sophie then stopped for a moment and despite being in a rush, turned to consider her friends.

"Let's grab something and take it with us!" She snapped, and within a few moments they then ran out carrying coffee in paper takeaway cups, as well as a few slices of toast, bacon and plastic jams stuffed into a paper bag.

"Thank you!" Sophie said, as they raced outside. "Take care now!" The lady waved.

They then dived into Micky's car and he drove off, hammering the accelerator heading southwards.

"Am going to hazard a guess that the police are completely

buggered because of all this, reet?" He asked as he drove, looking at his speed dial.

"Yeah that's right," Millie then replied. "It's led to a surge in crime all over the region, even without the Redcaps. It's anarchy," she said in a worried voice, as they finally began to tuck into their belated and rushed breakfast.

"What we really need is to spark some kind of popular resistance," Sophie then said slowly as she chewed on some toast. "It's easy to say I'm the hero, but I can't do this alone. Sunderland itself has to do its part," she then asked.

"Aye, how so?" Micky said as he casually navigated eating and driving aggressively.

"Still trying to work it out, but from everything we've discussed so far, these Redcaps thrive on negative and angry energy, and that's why Sunderland has been a target. We need to get people to believe in themselves," she said. "You don't think?" She then asked.

"Aye, of course, but god knows how to do that like," Micky then replied as he chewed food in his mouth. The trio then said little more as their nerves began to sit in as they proceeded southwards, growing closer and closer to Sunderland. Noticeably, the areas they passed were eerily silent, as the growing unrest and terror emerging from Wearside sent ripples throughout the rest of the North East. Already, even passing through the City of Newcastle Upon Tyne, they spotted shop fronts and supermarkets that had been completely ransacked and looted, as the police force, their leadership having been compromised and then decapitated, had effectively disintegrated.

All of a sudden, as they drew nearer to the city of Sunderland, the sky above turned completely black as if it were completely separate from the cycles of night and day. There was simply no making sense of it.

"Gosh…" Micky gasped upon seeing it. "What time is it like?" He asked.

"Ten thirty…" Millie then said in surprise as they looked upwards.

He then slowed his car down carefully as he effectively entered the city boundaries proper. Looking for an exit from the motorway, the routes had been blocked by metal barricades and armoured vehicles, as soldiers in combat gear stood guarding them with assault rifles.

"Oh man, the army really has blocked off all ways into the city." He commented as they drove past slowly. "There's nee way we're getting in while it's like this," he then said in frustration.

"This is blocking off the central area of the city right?" Sophie then asked, remembering that Sunderland was wider in scope.

"Yes, that's right," Millie then replied. "The military perimeter has been erected around the A19 road to the west. They've set up separate blockades against Houghton and Hetton." She then responded as she checked her phone. "But not the area we're passing now to the west, Penshaw…" she said ominously. Just after Millie spoke, Sophie noticed a spear descend on the car from their right hand side.

"DUCK!" She screamed, as it then smashed through the car window with unbelievable force, just missing Micky, who swerved in a panic and hammered the brakes, just managing to maintain control of the car, with the front window broken completely.

Micky shouted expletives, before pulling the car to a stop.

"Can't drive like that… Ha'way let's go," he then said in a

serious tone, as he jumped out of the vehicle and gently brushed the broken safety glass off his clothes. At that moment, Sophie's stone then began glowing, and in a flash of light she was dressed in her full set of armour with sword in hand.

"Watch out!" She then yelled as another spear rocketed at them from a series of trees to the right side of the road. This time, Sophie slashed it clean in two with her sword, diverting the shards away from Micky and Millie.

"We're under attack, keep moving!" she ordered, as they paced up the empty motorway.

As they made their way cautiously up the road, they then spotted a small country lane further up.

"Sophie, there's no army barricade on that road there!" Micky then shouted as they ran. "It seems they missed this, you can get back into the city from there, heading through the forest and down through Herrington Park, bypassing this road!" He shouted, short of breath.

"What? You're joking right? Sophie then said with a look of horror on her face. "I'd rather not go to that area right now…" She expressed with great hesitation.

"What? Why not?" Micky then asked. "It's the only way from here," he said, confused.

"There's no other way?" she then asked.

"Not anywhere near here, no," he replied.

"Okay then…" Sophie stopped, hesitating. "I'll do it, but it's not going to be easy for me." She gulped, as the trio quickly darted up the lane.

As they reached the top of the road, it split into two directions. One route, bending left, spanned over a road bridge hanging above the motorway, which had also been barricaded by the army. The other loped down a bank into a cul-de-sac dead end, bordering a vast forest of trees spanning down the right hand side. A narrow entry in the trees was visible.

"See, we can go through here." Micky then pointed out, as they moved quickly down the bank, avoiding the attention of the soldiers. Sophie, however, looked mortified. On entering, they walked down a narrow dirt path, as the trees blockaded whatever light was left available amidst the darkness. All was silent, not even the singing or chirping of birds could be heard.

"Okay, if we keep walking we can get to the park," Micky said positively.

"I'm well aware Micky, because I've been here before, in fact many times." Sophie then added coldly.

"Aye?" Micky then responded confused.

"But this isn't easy for me, because if you really need to know... this is the forest from my dreams." She added uncomfortably.

"Oh, nee wonder then, I wonder why though, if you don't mind?" he then asked innocently.

"I'll tell you..." she then replied very coldly. "My Mam, she died in these woods," she then announced abruptly. Millie and Micky looked at Sophie sorrowfully.

"Come here and sit for a moment..." she said abruptly as they spotted several fallen logs on the ground, which were situated around a burnt circle of ashes that had been used as a makeshift camp fire. Behind them, through a gap in the trees, a Pantheon-like Greek style temple sat on a hill in the distance.

"I'm sorry I never told either of you this for all the time I've known you, but it hasn't been easy, of course... When I was seven we came here on an ordinary day out. Me, Mam, Dad... We were playing with a ball, it got stuck in the tree. Dad told me to just leave it and forget it, but I was so upset. My Mam went back and climbed up to get it, she fell and, and… well you get the idea," she then said emotionally, a tear emerging in her eye.

"Oh, Sophie man…" Micky then replied, almost tearing up, as he put her arm around her sympathetically.

"That explains so much…" Millie then added. "Thank you for sharing that," she then said softly.

"Yeah, Dad never forgave me, or himself for it… This is why he was the way he was. But ever since then, the nightmares of the figure… They've all taken place here. Every time, I am chased through this forest and then he… Glanfeoil, calls my name," She then said softly.

"It's like he's been playing on your trauma, mocking your insecurities all this time," Millie then commented.

The group then sat for a moment in a mournful silence, until all of a sudden, an unusual rustling noise sounded from amidst the trees, as if something was moving.

"What was that?" Sophie then asked, standing up in a state of alert and raising her sword vigilantly. "We should have remembered, we were followed…" She then added coldly, as she noticed a figure dashing through the woods in the darkness. "They're here…" she then said in a cold voice. "It's not a dream any more… it's reality, RUN!" She yelled, as a number of javelins suddenly emerged in their direction, narrowly missing them. They started running at full pace down the forest path, spotting an exit on their left hand side spanning out into some fields. Sophie then stopped and looked back into the blackness to see scores of Redcaps running after them.

"There's no way we can outrun them!" Sophie shouted. "Millie, Micky! Get out now into the field and hide, I'm going to distract them!" She barked, as the two of them fled for an entrance at the side. Sophie, knowing she was their primary target, then continued to race directly through the forest with the Redcaps giving chase to her, losing interest in the others. But at that moment, as she continued to run, she suddenly heard a piercing voice call out to her.

"Sophie... Sophie..." It hissed.

Eying another entrance to the forest, situated by a pond, Sophie kept running as the Redcaps kept pace, but the voice continued.

"Sophie... Sophie..." it beckoned. Then, just as she reached the main exit, a figure appeared in front of her, blocking the way. In shock, she tripped and tumbled to the ground, before looking up to see a man standing in dark green robes, his face not easily visible, and holding the very staff she had once retrieved, with his left hand.

As he emerged, the Redcaps, like they did at Lindisfarne, stopped in their tracks.

"Sophie, my old friend, the appointed champion of King Oswald, we meet again at last." The voice hissed. He then looked up, revealing his face and his cold, completely empty eyes. As Sophie looked at him, she recognised the face of William Parker-Fulton, but his countenance and cheerful glean was gone, replaced with a sinister, dark and emotionally empty look.

"I have made it clear to you, you are to submit, or die." He then proclaimed.

"Why do you do this, Glanfeoil?" She then asked coldly. "Why did you not only lie to the people of this town, but now inflict horror upon them?" She interrogated him in a tough tone. Glanfeoil smiled viciously.

"This kingdom, the land of Bernicia, or otherwise Northumbria, was founded by the House of Baldur, his clan and kinfolk. This is our land, and we were betrayed by the Christian folk who sold onto its people a lie, which has led them to suffer misery, rather than experience true power and justice. Their descendents now live in this dystopian world, believing in nothing and fighting for nothing. We will destroy this treacherous mistake, the lie created by those who have ruled you, and we will purify this land of these wretched people who believe in nothing and start anew!" He then answered coldly to her. "Tell me, Sophie, why is it you choose to fight against me and to keep the world as it is, when nothing in your life has ever gone in your favour? Why do you defend the world which has made you miserable?" He then asked.

"Well, not counting the fact you helped make it miserable, I might add it's because life is only enjoyed through the love that you share with others..." She replied humbly. "Yes, I have suffered great pain, but I did not lose my humanity through it all, unlike you."

Glanfeoil smirked dismissively.

"No, I was just like you. I had nothing, but I found that I was a fool if I did not fight for myself and rely on the necessity of brute force." He began to lecture. "I thought you were a good student Sophie, throughout your time, did you not read Machiavelli yet? Let me make it clear. This world will never reward good intentions, because someone is always willing to exploit them for their own gain. So you're better off doing it for yourself first than being someone else's fool! Just look at this country, across all of these centuries, from the Anglo-Saxon Kings, to the Normans, the Tudors, to those who sit in Westminster today. None of them care about you, or this wretched town. They are rich, you are poor. Yet, as a so-called hero, you give these fools your pittance while framing me as the real enemy of the people, just as King Oswald did so long ago!"

He then shouted.

"You are absolutely wrong if you think yourself and these monsters are the answers to the problems of today! You're a dinosaur from the Anglo Saxon times!" She yelled at him.

"I am but reclaiming my heritage and restoring my fatherland!" He then hissed back. "Enough talking, let's end this now!" Sophie then yelled, before proceeding to charge at Glanfeoil with her sword. Without breaking a sweat, however, he then raised his hand and froze her in complete mid-air, before swiping his hand to the left and sending her crashing into a tree.

"You have a lot to learn, child." He then chided her, showing no signs of alarm over her attack. "I'll ask you again, join me and embrace the glory of the revolution And embrace our power TOGETHER!" He then proclaimed. Sophie, hurt but enraged, did not give up. She then swung at him again with her sword, but Glanfeoil then suddenly disappeared. Sophie looked around confused, as the Redcaps looked on at her in silence with their poisonous yellow eyes.

Then, suddenly, Glanfeoil reappeared behind where she stood, before proceeding to blast her with a voltage of red electricity, causing her to scream in agony. Sophie quickly recuperated, before wielding her sword defensively to guard against any further attacks, her face angry and hardened.

She then swung several more blows in his direction, but Glanfeoil artfully blocked them with the Caenterstaff, demonstrating adept agility. But before she could strike at him again, he then stuck out his hand again and sent her flying through the forest path.

"What a fool you are." He then proclaimed in indignation. "How could you possibly kill me? What a grand and intoxicating innocence, how could you be so naive? I see you have made up your mind now, and what a foolish mind it is. Come, lay down your weapon… And it shall not be too late for my mercy. But if not, Redcaps, kill her!" He then ranted, before abruptly disappearing from the scene.

The Redcaps, who had been waiting unusually passively behind her, then roared ferociously and began once again hurling projectiles in Sophie's direction, before proceeding to rampage towards her. Sophie scrambled to her feet and belted out of the forest in the open park, performing a full leap over the duck pond to make distance with them, before then running up and over the hill and towards a series of fields lined with tall corn crops, allowing her to disappear into the blackness. Suddenly, as she ran, continually looking backwards, she crashed into someone, knocking them over.

"Ow!" An easily recognizable voice then cried.

"Millie!" Sophie then proclaimed. "Oh my goodness I'm sorry are you okay? I was legging it from the Redcaps!" She said in a guilty voice, pulling her to the ground.

"Oh, it's you! What happened Sophie?" she asked. Micky, who was hiding nearby, then appeared.

"Sophie, glad you're all right!" He then said with relief.

"You managed to lose them then?" He asked.

"Yes, for now, so come on!" Sophie said in panic, pulling them both by the arm as they continued dashing through the field.

Eventually they reached the bottom of the farm, climbing over a small wooden fence onto a dirt footpath, which directed them over a footbridge passing the motorway they were previously on, which was situated in a carved out depression below. As they walked, they saw housing estates appear in the distance ahead of them.

"We did it, we made it back into Sunderland!" Millie

cheered.

"Nice one Micky, although I did have to deal with Glanfeoil on the way…" Sophie then added in a less optimistic tone.

"Wait, what?" he then asked in shock.

"That moment in the forest, it wasn't a dream, it was a premonition, he appeared to me in that forest as I fled the Redcaps and asked me to submit to him. I tried to fight him, but it's impossible to even land a hit on him, he's too powerful…" Sophie explained, as they entered the city outskirts, having left the outlying fields. At that moment, their faces then drained with horror as they began to witness the reign of terror the Redcaps had unleashed on the city. Windows were broken, cars burnt out completely, children's playgrounds wrecked, and shops stripped bare.

"Christ… Herrington's had it rough." Micky commented as they walked.

Having walked for a while, Sophie then looked upon the stone sign of her home estate, reading *"Thorney Close"* which, in line with the surroundings, had been peppered with strange occultic vandalism in bright red paint, with entire buildings, walls and just about anything had been sprayed with the rune like inscriptions, as well as proclamations worshipping something.

"This is unbelievable…" Millie commented as she looked upon the damage. "I hope my home is okay.She then added in a worried voice. As they walked, there was not a soul to be seen.

"Where is everyone?" Sophie asked bewildered as she looked around.

"Hiding, I think." Micky then commented quietly.

"As I said on the drive down here, we need to inspire people to fight back. As I've just experienced, they are just too strong and too numerous to confront by myself," she then said, doubting her own abilities.

Then suddenly, with the trio having made their presence far too obvious, a number of Redcaps emerged from every direction, trapping them from both sides of the street.

"Well crap." Micky then proclaimed bluntly as he looked both ways.

Chapter XXIII: By the Glory of the People

Surrounded, the trio looked around tensely as the Redcap hoard closed in on them, as Sophie desperately attempted to shield her friends.

"We're trapped!" Millie said in despair.

"I've never handled this many of them before, but look if we don't try, and if we don't work together, we will never succeed!" Sophie then courageously charged at the group, cutting down one of them instantly and engaging several more. But at that moment, the Redcaps from the other direction then charged at Millie and Micky, who appeared defenceless.

Managing to dodge the attack, Micky then looked on the ground for anything he could find, before scrambling to pick up a glass bottle. Without any hesitation he then smashed it full force in the face of an attacking Redcap, who much to his astonishment, then fell back in shock and growled in pain. He smiled in surprise at his own achievement, before running over to help Millie, who panicked as several Redcaps attempted to attack her. He struck one of them with a piece of car debris, before another swung its axe full force at her. Millie bent backwards agilely, before then miraculously back flipping against another blow and then swiping a low kick against it, knocking it off its feet onto the ground.

"Bloody hell how did you do that?" Micky then looked on,

shocked. She simply looked at him and smiled as Sophie then intervened, shaking off more Redcaps and slicing down the ones the others had injured. However, the more they held off, the more that seemed to arrive. Every time one was defeated or knocked down, another seemed to emerge to take its place, with the alarm clearly having been sounded that Sophie was now active in the city.

"There's just too many of them!" She gasped, out of breath. "Run!" She then shouted on at least having broken the encirclement.

Just as the trio fled, Micky noticed that local residents, hidden within their houses, were discretely filming and livestreaming the battle from their homes, but as they focused on escaping he did not immediately speak up. As they belted around another corner in the Thorney Close estate, they were then stopped in their tracks by another mob of incoming Redcaps, repeating the same entrapment situation before.

"This is never going to end!" Millie then panicked.

"Don't give up!" Sophie then yelled defiantly. "We will fight you Glanfeoil until the last Redcap!" She shouted very, very loudly, which echoed throughout the street.

"Yeah, but what about until the last of us?" Millie said in a panic, as Micky then looked over to the houses again, where residents continued to secretly film them.

Sophie again took charge at the attackers, unleashing her anger onto them with a devastation she had never displayed previously. However, outnumbered again, a Redcap then got the better of her and struck her on the back so hard her sword went flying across the road. But unlike the attack at Foxy Island, there was no time or space for her to call it back, as she was forced to dodge a series of follow up attacks from multiple Redcaps.

Defiant, she punched one of them as she walked backwards, but as they gradually closed in on her the space she had begun to shrink and shrink. Micky and Millie desperately tried to intervene by throwing street debris at them, but they did not budge.

Sophie strained as a Redcap closed in on her, swinging its axe in her face. Forced against the side of a house, she attempted to push away its arms with her hands, but soon the others prepared to strike too. Then, a metal bollard crashed over its head, distracting it and allowing Sophie to escape. She looked round to see none other than Bertha standing and holding the bollard behind them. She smiled upon seeing Sophie.

"Bertha, are you joking?" she then said in disbelief.

"Nar pet, I'm here to help!" Bertha then replied carefree.

"So we're friends now, right?" Sophie then joked.

"We'll see." Bertha then smiled, before Sophie called her sword back and charged at the approaching Redcaps again, while Bertha swung the bollard at them in tandem.

Suddenly, a roar of motorcycles came surging from in the distance, growing louder as it seemed to emerge in that direction. Millie and Micky looked across the street to see an entourage of young men, wearing a rainbow variety of exotic nylon tracksuits, emerging on dirt bikes, all equipped with baseball bats, hockey sticks and similar equipment on their backs. Pulling in front of the Redcaps. Stopping, they then leaped off their bikes and drew their weapons.

"Ha'way man then!"' one of them wearing a woolly hat ferociously roared. "This is our town!"

The group then charged at the Redcaps, beating and striking them. Sophie then called back her sword to her hand and then began slicing through the distracted creatures effortlessly.

"Areet Micky!" A voice then proclaimed. Micky turned

round to find Liam Heskett, holding a wooden bat, while being cheerful and relaxed as usual.

"Liam man!" Micky then shouted out joyfully.

"We've all seen this owa Facebook, so me and me mates thought we'd come and give a hand. Nee one misses a fight in Sunderland man. Let's Send these Radgies packing!" He then said enthusiastically as the group battled the Redcaps in a series of duels, miraculously matching their strength and resolve.

At that moment, Sophie then rushed over to Micky and asked urgently.

"Micky! I need you to film me, livestream me on social media!" Micky then quickly got out his phone. "I'm going to send out a message to everyone in this city!" She said in a serious tone before clearing her voice, as Micky positioned the phone towards her.

"People of Sunderland!" She then proclaimed. "It is time to rise up and take back our city! Do not let the world trample on you any more, stand up and be accountable! Do not be scared of these monsters any more, they thrive on your negative emotions, fear, hopelessness and resentment. I want you to know that you can do this, before the British government sends in the military! Come on Sunderland, believe in yourself! Let's get them and expel this evil!" She yelled into the phone, before confronting more oncoming Redcaps with gusto.

Within the space of minutes, people then poured out of their homes all over the surrounding streets and throughout the city, armed with whatever they could find, including pots, pans, kitchen knives, shovels, rakes and rolling pins. They congregated in the streets together fearlessly before charging at the occupying Redcaps, overwhelming them with the sheer force of their numbers.

"Yessahh!" Micky cheered. "Sophie you've did it, people are fighting back!" As the crowds continued to lash at them from every angle, the Redcaps then began to retreat, disappearing into the darkness.

But even as people celebrated, Sophie's countenance did not brighten, as something else sprung to the front of her mind.

"Show me the news!" She snapped to Micky before practically snatching his phone out of his hand. She pondered on it for a moment, before streaming a live BBC broadcast, reporting from Downing Street in London. She then turned the volume up to maximum for everyone around her to hear.

"This is BBC news live, London, where we have just had word from the COBRA meeting that the Prime Minister is to give authorisation to the use of military force against the insurrection in the city of Sunderland, and that martial law will be declared for the entire North East of England region. The riots, which have swept the city for the past 24 hours, show no signs of abating as residents continue to battle each other in unexplained circumstances, and a concurrent crime wave sweeps the surrounding towns and cities." The reporter then spoke into the microphone as he stood outside the black door of ten Downing Street.

"The Prime Minister is expected to come out now and give a speech." He then noted. At that moment, the door opened behind the reporter, and a slender looking British Indian man walked out, his hair groomed smartly and his teeth glaringly white. He smiled charmingly as he took up a podium behind the correspondent, as the cameras shifted to him.

"Today, we are gravely concerned by the events in Sunderland." He then started to speak, in an extremely serious tone. "An entire city has descended into chaos and anarchy, impacting a whole region. Lives have been lost, and our own people are fighting each other in the streets like animals. Because of this terrible situation, I am obligated to take into account the best interests of everyone in Britain. After meeting with the COBRA council today, we have decided on a series of actions in order to guarantee national security and protect our country. Therefore, my government is declaring martial law within the North East of England with immediate effect, and I have given express authorisation for the use of military force to restore order in Sunderland and uphold the rule of law. We are issuing, starting from now, a two hour ultimatum that if those leading this insurrection do not surrender, we will be forced to intervene. Secondly, we are now imposing a mandatory lockdown in the city. You must stay indoors and take shelter. In the event of military action, all people present in the streets will be treated as an enemy combatant, you may be arrested and we cannot guarantee you will not be shot. We will do everything it takes to restore law and order. Thank you." The Prime Minister then smiled, before heading back inside of Downing Street quickly.

Sophie, as well as now everyone else around her, looked on as they listened in a state of disbelief. She then looked around, even though the Redcaps had retreated, everyone seemed confused and disoriented, with their eyes sat upon her as if they were all waiting for her to instruct them on what to do next.

"What do we do?" Millie then asked.

"We have to defeat Glanfeoil and tell them to call off the attack as soon as possible!" she then said urgently.

"They don't seem to distinguish between Redcaps and ordinary people." Millie then noted.

"Aye, so where is he then?" Micky then asked.

"That's the thing, I don't know…" she replied doubtfully.

"Come on, where's the one place he could dwell around here, away from all the chaos? Where does he run his administration?" Millie then asked, encouraging them to think.

"That's it, city hall!" Sophie then said enthusiastically. "It's where he made his first speech leading up to this!" she added.

Sophie then looked around at the crowd that had gathered to fight the Redcaps in the streets, who gazed upon her with awe.

"Okay, I will go to city hall to confront Glanfeoil! I do not want any of you to get hurt if things go wrong, so I encourage you to stay home. I will handle this alone." She then suggested softly. The crowd however, looked at her with dismay.

"Nee way, we want to support you!" Liam Heskett then shouted out, as many heads nodded in agreement.

"You told us to fight for Sunderland, now you want us to go home and let this government threaten innocent people like that?" Another person shouted. Sophie looked on with concern.

"No bloody government is going to force me back inside, we've had enough of it with their bloody lockdowns!" An older man in the crowd then shouted out cynically. On seeing the crowd's reaction, Micky then turned to Sophie and spoke to her quietly.

"Sophie, earlier you said you couldn't do this alone," he said close to her, putting his arm on her shoulder. "Sure, you're the one with the powers, sword and armour, but as we kept telling each other, we're in this together. Always. It might be terrifying what the government is planning to do, but as you said, it's time to take a stand. The world is watching..." He said kindly, practically whispering.

"Yes you're right I guess, my Mam told me to be a champion of the people." Sophie then pondered, reflecting on their encounter on the beach.

Sophie then took a step back, before then putting her fist into the air and shouting.

"Let's go and get him!" The crowd then roared in jubilation and applause.

"Sophie! Sophie! Sophie!" They chanted in unison.

"You are right!" She proclaimed. "The true power and glory of Sunderland lies within the hearts of its people, and together we will show the British government what a terrible mistake they have made, and stand for our town!" As she finished speaking the crowd again erupted, before she then began to march with them towards the city centre.

Chapter XXIV: From the Ashes, and from the Heart

As Sophie and her friends walked through the streets of Sunderland, many followed behind her, while others looked on from their doorsteps, cheering and clapping, seemingly unmoved by the scenes of destruction and carnage which had surrounded them. It was as if they possessed nothing, but also had everything.

"I've never seen the people of Sunderland united like this." Micky commented as he travelled next to her. "And believe me, I've been to plenty of our football matches..."

Sophie did not fixate on the crowds, but her eyes were locked on the route forward, her emotions high and her heart beating tensely. Making their way into the city centre, Sophie then stopped abruptly upon seeing the Dun Cow, the bar where her humble journey had begun. The building itself had not been destroyed or badly damaged, but its windows were broken and its contents had been looted.

"Memories." She then uttered to Micky and Millie. "Funny how I've come to miss a job I once hated though. It only goes to show how this whole journey started upon a hope that I might be able to have dreams like anyone else..." She continued sentimentally, before smiling and moving on. From there, the group moved into the focal point of the city centre, known as Keel Square, of which above it stood the mighty City Hall. It was, to some extent, one of a few buildings which had not suffered any damage or repercussions at the hands of the Redcap army, illustrating perfectly where the balance of power lay. The square itself, however, was completely empty. Its sculptures and decorations, built as a commemoration to Sunderland's shipbuilding past, had been vandalised and destroyed, the paving sprayed with runes paying allegiance to the North East's new proclaimed demi-god, Glanfeoil.

Sophie stood in the square patiently as the crowds gathered behind her. She then looked towards the City Hall with indignation, before shouting at full blast.

"GLANFEOIL!" SHOW YOURSELF! HEAR THE WILL OF THE PEOPLE, AND STAND DOWN!" But nobody responded. She stood still for several more minutes, the crowd becoming confused and agitated. Suddenly, a blinding flash of red lightning struck the square, causing everyone to cover their eyes. Sophie, moving her arm away, then looked forwards to see Glanfeoil standing a few metres in front of her, donning his green robes and the Caenterstaff.

"So we meet again…" Glanfeoil then said menacingly.

"This ends here!" Sophie then yelled at him defiantly.

"It certainly does, and it seems you have learnt little from our last encounter. You have chosen death, and so be it!" He hissed.

"No, for I have chosen the city of Sunderland, and together we will rise from the ashes!" She then proclaimed, and at that moment, before she could make any move herself, the crowd who had followed her and flocked there from other areas, already angry, then began rampaging towards Glanfeoil at full throttle, shouting and raging.

"GET HIM!" They yelled, as the lynch mob charged at him. But Glanfeoil simply grinned at the onslaught, waving his hands forwards abruptly and at that moment, sending scores of people ricocheting into the air in every direction, crashing onto the ground throughout the square.

Many of them tried again, only to be pushed back and thrown away a second time. Glanfeoil, unphased, then laughed to Sophie.

"Did you think these degenerates could truly stop me? When you say the people of Sunderland, do you bid them to die in your name Sophie?" He mocked, as he flicked off the crowd as if they were merely annoying insects. Soon, people lay in agony all around the pair, their attacks fading away. Without replying, Sophie then held up her sword and jumped at Glanfeoil in indignation, but again, as it were before, he simply froze her in midair with his hand, before sending her crashing to the ground, laughing sadistically as she groaned.

"This has been fun, but I've trifled with you long enough!" Glanfeoil then snarled, before raising his hand to levitate a mix of broken glass and debris on the ground and send it flying towards Sophie. She narrowly dived out the way, avoiding the attack. Jumping towards Glanfeoil again, she then attempted to swing several blows on him, but he again stopped the attacks in mid-air putting out his hand, and proceeded to then bash Sophie in the face with the Caenterstaff. She fell back onto her backside on the ground, disarmed. Her nose was bloody, groaning in agony.

"He's completely invulnerable with the staff..." Millie said to Micky, as they watched on in horror. "We can't just stand here and watch, we need to do something!" She then panicked.

"Sophie!" Micky then shouted "You need to get the staff off him!" He then suggested. Glanfeoil's head then turned towards him with a furious look on his face. Snarling, he then sent Micky flying several metres.

"MICKY!" Millie then cried out in horror, running towards him.

Sophie, having gained a moment to recuperate, then dived at the distracted Glanfeoil and grabbed onto the staff with both her hands. As she had experienced back in Lindisfarne, an immense pulsing of dark energy then rushed through her entire body, leading the world to spin around her in some kind of seizure. Every negative emotion conceivable invaded her brain, including anxiety, resentment, disillusionment, hatred, jealousy, despair, as negative memories also flashed before her eyes. But she did not let go, and nor was Glanfeoil able to dispatch her.

She cried out in anguish as the staff's power psychologically skewered her, and in a desperate bid to break the deadlock she then kicked Glanfeoil with all her might, sending him backwards with the staff shooting up into the air. Sophie looked at him, realising for the first time she had been able to land an attack on him. Without even pausing for thought, she then raced forwards, neglecting the staff, and proceeded to punch Glanfeoil in the face with the full force of her Gauntlet. The crowd, hurt but still watching, then roared and cheered.

"GO ON!" They cheered, as if it were a football match. "HA'WAY!" They then shouted as she jumped forwards, punching him again and again. But before she could summon her sword and land a decisive blow, Glanfeoil regained the staff and sent Sophie crashing into a brick wall with overwhelming force, disarming her again.

Before she could make another move, Glanfeoil then blasted a chasm of electric red energy at Sophie's sword, and to the horror of everyone watching, it then reverted back into its stone form. He then laughed as he walked over to it, before forcefully stomping on it with his foot, crushing it to pieces. At the same time as this happened, Sophie's armour then disappeared into dying flickers of light, leaving her lying in her ordinary clothes. On seeing this, Millie and Micky, as well as others gasped out loud.

Smiling again, Glanfeoil then walked over to Sophie and forcefully yanked her up with her hair, pointing the staff directly at her head.

"It's over North Star, you have lost," he then snarled into her ear. "Do you have any last words?" he then said amusingly.

"No..." Sophie groaned resentfully, defiant but unable to exert resistance.

"Very well, now because I am merciful, I will not kill you, but I will put you out of your misery by banishing you to a distant corner of the universe, where you can live out the rest of your days..." he then smirked, as the top of the Caenterstaff began to glow blue.

At that moment, Sophie's life began to flash before her in her mind. The images in her head recounted the journey she had been on, from fighting with Bertha in school, to arguing with her dad, to confronting Tony, to the many memories she had made with Micky and Millie throughout their adventure, both the good times and the bad. At that moment, she then recalled what Viviane had said to her on the beach.

"*This stone, Sophie, is meant to be a prompt for you. A guide. The true power lies within you, and will always be yours providing you believe in yourself.*"

Then, suddenly, as Glanfeoil prepared to cast the spell, his guard down and holding Sophie, Micky then dived at him in a full force rugby tackle, crashing him to the ground and sending the staff flying tinto he air again. Sophie, seeing the opportunity, then jumped up and grabbed it. Again on grasping it, she was then captivated by the onslaught of dark energy, which struck at her at such a force it seemed it might tear her apart completely. The world began spinning around her, as a high pitched screaming of an inhuman nature pierced her ears and made her head vibrate in agony. The dark forest then flashed behind her, the spectre of Glanfeoil standing before her, grinning wickedly.

But Sophie did not give in. She then wrestled back control of her mind, thinking of her Mother's words to her, the dying moments of her Father, the promises she made with Millie, and then her friendship with Micky, and the hope, faith, bravery and love she had manifested not simply for herself, but on behalf of others. At that moment, the spinning darkness and screaming around her were swept away by a blinding bright light. Sophie then woke up, finding herself again in Keel Square, clutching the Caenterstaff in her arms, as everyone around her watched on. Glanfeoil then stood in horror, helpless without the staff, and the smirk having been wiped off his face.

Sophie then looked down at herself, her armour and sword had suddenly returned, with a white aurora now surrounding her. As she held the staff, its core now also glowed white, as if the evil had been sanctimoniously purged from it through the sheer force of her will. Sophie then looked over to Glanfeoil, smiled and said in a cheeky voice.

"What was that you were saying mate?" Before pointing the staff at him, and with the same spell still readied, blasted a chasm of white energy in his direction.

As it exploded upon impact, another blast of light then filled the area, and Glanfeoil was gone. At that same moment, the darkness imposed over the sky above then disappeared miraculously, as the warm light of the sun penetrated the clouds and shined down on Sunderland again. Concurrently, the Redcaps, still out and at large throughout Sunderland and battling others, also all spontaneously disintegrated into dust, their debris blowing across the streets in the wind.

Upon seeing this, the crowd then erupted with euphoria, cheering, clapping and celebrating. A mob of people descended on Sophie instantly and began hugging her, including Micky and Millie. She stood there awkwardly, and did not celebrate herself, but simply smiled, looking up to the sky as a tear filled her eye, where she saw an image of her mother standing in the clouds. She then heard her voice, speaking down unto her.

"Sophie my child, you have accomplished your destiny, and fulfilled the prophecy. The North Star has risen, vanquished the ancient evil and redeemed these people. You Sophie, are the champion of Northumbria, and are now free to pursue your own dreams. However, the people of this land will still continue to look upon you for protection, you must continue to guide and protect them, be their hope and light. There are many secrets yet to be revealed, and if new evils arrive, you must always be ready. Now Sophie, I am free... the curse is lifted and we must say farewell... I love you."

At that moment, as Sophie looked up and cried, Viviane then disappeared. With everyone around her in such a state of jubilation and shock simultaneously that they did not seem to notice what she was looking at. However, a sense of urgency then returned to her, and she slowly wriggled some room away from the crowd before proclaiming.

"The government deadline! We need to stop them!" Everyone then paused in shock, remembering the course of action their leaders had set for them, who seemingly had no acknowledgement of the reality of the situation whatsoever.

Sophie then stood up on a bench, still clutching the Caenterstaff in her hand.

"Film me!" She then commanded again, as she prepared to make another speech. The crowd, gathering round her, pointed their phones in her direction and began to livestream.

"I am addressing this message to the British government, but also to the people of Sunderland and the world!" She then proclaimed.

"The evil and disorder that has beset our town is gone! We have prevailed! While you may know me as the North Star, I do not attribute this victory exclusively to myself, but through each other! All of us here today! Today marks a new beginning for our city, where we together have found our inner strength and understood who we truly are. We have shown the ability to persevere and to overcome, as well as experiencing the true value of friendship, love and solidarity. Sometimes living here we have felt we have nothing, but we can find the greatest riches in each other. I may be the North Star, but in the end I'm just like anyone else, I'm a seventeen year old girl, I have hopes and I have dreams, and I started on this path because I did not want them to be taken away from me. The evil today was not caused by the people of Sunderland! It was caused by William Parker-Fulton, or better known as Glanfeoil, who beset an army of monsters on it known as Redcaps. He also used local gangsters and an organised crime ring, which peddled a mysterious drug all over town in order to make more of these beasts! He is now defeated! Now, we have won, and the events today marked only our resistance. Therefore, I ask the government to call off their assault, before the blood of any more innocent people is spilt! Order has been restored, and we will go back to our ordinary lives! Thank you!" She then ended abruptly, stepping down, to another thunderous round of applause from the crowd. But before they could gauge any further reaction, the crowd then gasped in horror as intimidating and bulky military vehicles then rolled into the square in multiple directions from the surrounding roads.

"What's going on?" Micky then asked in a state of fear. "The two hour deadline isn't even up yet!"

Intimidated, the crowd watched silently, not daring to move, as the vehicles abruptly grinded to a halt in front of them, as their doors swung open and a number of soldiers in combat gear, equipped with assault rifles stepped out, followed by an officer wearing a peaked cap and a smart green jacket with golden buttons and red insignia on his collars. His face was stern and extremely serious, as if he did not know to smile. Upon exiting the vehicle, he walked immediately over to Sophie.

"Are you in charge of this rabble?" He then barked at her in a formal voice. "I am Colonel Henry Asquith Fox!" he then said sternly. Sophie looked at him nervously.

"Yes, sort of..." she replied.

"I am carrying direct orders from his majesty's government and have been placed in charge of the North East England military administration! Listen carefully! We have just received word that the attackers, as well as Fulton, have been dispatched, is that correct?" he then barked.

"Yes sir, that's right," Sophie then replied fearfully.

"Very good! The ultimatum has been fulfilled and the planned military operation has been called off!" he then said very loudly. As they heard this, the crowd then cheered and comfortably came back to life.

"However..." he then added. "We have still been asked to peacefully restore public order to the city and region. These will be temporary measures to ensure security. The government will likewise be dissolving the regional administration and conducting an official investigation into Mr Fulton and his insurrection," he then announced. "And in doing so, Miss Scott, we'd like to now take you in for questioning!" He said to her in an intimidating manner. "Please step this way!" Holding his hands towards the vehicle.

Sophie then made a very uncomfortable smile as she headed with the Colonel into the vehicle. As she walked, she looked back on Micky and Millie, as well as Bertha, Liam Heskett and others who had joined her.

"Sophie! I'll catch up to you soon!" Millie then shouted in a somewhat upset voice and waved nervously as the soldiers then slammed the door and drove off as abruptly as they appeared.

Chapter XXV: The National Security State

Sometime later, after a long and unsettling drive, Sophie sat nervously in a dark room. She had no idea where she was. The room had no windows, and nor did it have anything else in it but a table, two chairs and a single light hanging down from a bulb without a shade. Now in her ordinary clothes again and without her sword, she waited nervously for what felt like an eternity, unsure what lay ahead.

Suddenly, the door swung open abruptly, briefly pouring in the superficial light of a white corridor outside, as a young man wearing a shirt, tie and black trousers walked in. His hair was gelled and he had a youthful, relaxed look on his face. Entering the room, he then smiled lightly, before he sat on the other chair in front of her, and took out a small tablet with a digital keyboard.

"Hi Sophie, nice to meet you," he then said politely enough. "My name is Jason Greenard, I am an intelligence officer for MI5, and you are Sophie Scott, right?" he then asked.

"Yes, that's me," she replied. He soon began to type away on the keyboard as they talked.

"Very good, nice to meet you. Now first of all, I need you to understand before we begin, you're not under any form of arrest or detention, okay? But we do need to question you about your role in everything that just happened. It will be best if we cooperate, and you speak truthfully, right?" he then asked.

"Okay…" Sophie then replied nervously. "I thought I was in big trouble." She then laughed.

"Well, you might be, who knows? Although hopefully not," he then said jokingly with an underlying degree of seriousness.

"Right, okay then, but also one more thing before we get started, if something you know happens to be supernatural or unusual, please do not hold back. We are well aware of what's been going on, of course…" He then said in a more serious tone.

"So on this video you recorded this afternoon, which I have here on my tablet, you said you are the North Star. Can you tell me what this means?" He then asked, beginning his question. Sophie hesitated for a moment.

"Okay… I know it all sounds so crazy, but the North Star is the title of a hero, originally from Northumbria, which I have been given." She then began explaining.

"Okay, given by who?" He then asked in an interrogative voice.

"A lady who described herself as Viviane, but was actually the spirit of my dead mother, claiming to be a guardian of sorts," she then said bluntly.

"Okay, and what did this Viviane ask you to do?" He then asked.

"She first appeared after I started to get attacked by those monsters, known as the Redcaps, and told me I had been chosen. She later gave me the clues to finding that staff, the one I brought in, and then to save the North East by defeating Glanfeoil, or Fulton as you know him," she explained.

"Okay… interesting…" he commented as he typed rapidly, his keyboard making a loud noise as he wrote. "So did you have any interactions with William Parker-Fulton, what was your relationship to him?" He asked, this question making Sophie nervous.

"He exploited my family situation and the publicity about me to trick me into thinking he was supporting me, and used this as a set up to get this staff for himself, before turning on me and using it to unleash all the chaos." She then said uncomfortably.

"Right, so where did you meet him?" He then followed up with another question.

"He simply phoned me one day after seeing me in the news."

"I see..." He then continued. "So this staff, where did you find it?" He then followed up.

"It was hidden under the chapel, in Holy Island, Lindisfarne..." She replied.

"Fascinating, we had no idea where it came from, or that such a thing even existed..." He then commented. "Okay, so do you know anyone who conspired with William Parker-Fulton in this plot?" he then asked.

"I do yes..." she added, smiling. "He hired a local gangster, known as Tony Radcliff, as well as the Police Chief, David Simm. Both of them tried to stop me in my quest, and framed me for serious crimes." She answered earnestly.

"Okay, so where are they now?" Jason then asked sharply.

"They're both dead I think. Tony, as he died in a shootout at his base as I tried to save my Dad, while Simm disappeared after Fulton got the staff. I reckon he killed him," she replied.

"So Fulton co-opted the police force and a local crime syndicate simultaneously to pull this off?" Jason then asked, surprised.

"Yes, he did, and I ended it, all of it." She then proudly.

"Right, I see... But I'm curious, how did this happen? You, a seventeen year old girl, made the decision to stand up to them, why?" He then asked.

"Because they stood in the way of my dreams, attempting to take away everything I had to look forward to in my life," she then said in a serious tone. "Whether there was a North Star prophecy or not, these people extorted my Dad, tried to kill my friends and arrest me. Even before I understood truly what was going on, I was fighting for my future."

Jason then sat in silence for a moment, as he typed notes. He then looked up at her again, the look on his face brightened.

"Sophie Scott... I want to say you are the most inspiring young woman I have ever met in my life. Obviously, it's my job, and given the seriousness of what has happened, to fully get the bottom of this, and of course, you were irrevocably connected to it, but I am satisfied even with this brief exchange that you have done no wrong, and it is at least my opinion that your testimony is truthful," he smiled. "However..." he then added in a more ominous tone, which wiped the emerging comfort from Sophie's face. "We do have to make some stipulations. First, I am going to tell you bluntly you can't keep that staff I'm afraid. That's a dangerous magical artefact, and as you can see, its destructive potential is limitless. Secondly, and by orders of my superiors, you are forbidden to use the title of 'North Star' as you termed it, to claim any sort of political privilege or leadership over the people of your region or city, outside of the bounds of law and democracy. You also have no right, in turn, seeing as the role is linked to an Anglo-Saxon king, to make a pretender claim to any throne or kingdom pertaining to this country... As ridiculous as that might sound," he said very sternly.

"Oh, right... Well, of course, not," Sophie replied, baffled.

"It's a national security concern, here at MI5 our mission is to subdue any 'threats' so to speak, to Parliamentary Democracy and the rule of law in Britain. Fulton just got himself elected and attempted to create his own dark magical kingdom in the North East. Even though you are not like him, in terms of intentions or values, you always have the potential to be so. You are thus to be monitored as a potential 'mythological' tier national security threat."

"What?" Sophie responded, perplexed.

"I mean, to say it straightforwardly, don't use these powers you have irresponsibly," he then added. "That doesn't mean you can't do good with them or you know, be a hero. But it does mean that we're going to be acting as a check on you, tentatively and you must recognise the authority of the British state in everything you do…" He then said in a much more menacing voice. "Which leads to the final point, we may, from time to time, solicit your cooperation for other matters that may emerge that threaten this country."

"Okay then, I have a question myself…" Sophie then replied in a more confident voice. "If you're that tuned in, how did you not see any of this coming with Fulton? Even to the point the Prime Minister contemplated using the army against innocent people?" She asked, leading him to stumble awkwardly.

"Um… well, the less said about that the better. I think Fulton "slipped through the cracks", just not really someone on our radar. It's rare, but it happens." He then admitted uncomfortably.

"I think the truth is, if the government actually cared about this region then the likes of Fulton would have been stamped out years ago." She then commenced harshly. "The truth is, the government has failed the North East for decades, even to the point they unwittingly elected a dark wizard into office." She then added, putting her hand on the table towards him authoritatively.

"Surely not! But anyway Sophie, thank you for your

cooperation. We do hope you pop in and visit us in London, but either way you will be hearing from us again. Right, you're free to go anyway, I'm pleased to announce we will also step in to clear all charges against you influenced by the Fulton-Simm regime."

    He then clasped his hands together and closed the tablet, as Sophie then smiled with a sense of relief.

Chapter XXVI: The Light at the End of the tunnel

Sometime later, Sophie stood solemnly, dressed all in black, with a fine dress and a hat over her head. Before her, stood a gravestone. It was white in colour and neatly decorated, with gold text etched into it. At its base lay a cohort of red flowers. The inscription on it read. "*Eddie Scott, 1968-2022, much loved Father & Husband "Greater love hath no man than this, that a man lay down his life for his friends"*.

Next to Sophie, as she looked at the grave, stood Micky, finely dressed in a suit, Millie, as well as Liam Heskett, Bertha, Joe Goya the next door neighbour, her teacher Mr Marchant, Derek the pub manager, Gemma Burlison the sports teacher, Matthew James, the young boy they rescued, the parents of Micky and Millie as well as her younger sister Ayesha, alongside Katie Clough the journalist, who now had a remorseful look on her face. Micky then turned to Sophie and said softly.

"You know, he would have been so proud." Sophie then looked at him, saddened, and replied.

"I'm the one who's so proud. I know it sounds odd, but without my parents I could never have done it."

"Thank you Sophie for saving us, and I am very sorry you had to go through all of this, especially from me." Bertha then said to her, filling up.

"It's okay," Sophie then responded to her softly. "I forgive you." The group departed from Bishopwearmouth Cemetery. A week or so then passed, and Sophie soon found herself sitting in another office. It had windows, of course, plenty of light and many pretty posters too, yet in mood and substance, it had little difference to the dark, menacing and geographically unknown interrogation office she had been brought to, being likewise a place which in her mind could only be associated with trouble, fear and punishment. But that wasn't the case this time.

"Sophie, on behalf of myself and the school, I cannot apologise enough for what has happened. The past few weeks have been a shock to us all, and I hope you will understand these unprecedented events caught us all by surprise, and we were wrong about everything." Joan the headmistress said in a rare voice of humility, as Sophie sat opposite her with Millie, both smiling gleefully.

"Well that's an understatement…" Sophie then sarcastically sniggered to Millie quietly.

"Because of this, as we informed you by email, we're ending your suspension effective immediately. You're also incidentally in luck. Due to the large-scale destruction from the attacks and the disorder it has caused, the entire term has been postponed as we need to give everyone and everything a chance to recover. Meaning, you now have new time to catch up with the lost time!" She then said, straining a cheerful note out of herself.

"Yes!" Sophie cheered.

"Okay then, be on your way now… See you when term restarts." The headmistress then followed up, returning to her usual serious and soul sucking tone, as Sophie and Millie left the office feeling triumphant.

"So, what do you want to do now?" Millie then asked enthusiastically as they left the school grounds, gazing upon the building, with numerous workmen dotted around it, both cleaning and repairing it.

"I want to study, study, and study!" Sophie then smiled enthusiastically.

"My house then? I think my mum would be really pleased to see you again!" Millie then said excitedly.

"Ha, let's do it then!" said Sophie, and they walked off... The next few months then seemed to fly by, as the city of Sunderland rapidly recovered from Glanfeoil's reign of terror. Windows were replaced, graffiti was cleaned off, sculptures and parks rebuilt, and the debris of destroyed vehicles was cleared off the streets. It was the same town they always knew, but the people were different. Because of that, everything had a new, energetic and positive energy about it.

"I'm surprised you're still working here, you know now that your dad and Tony situation has been... resolved," Micky said awkwardly, as Sophie returned to the Dun Cow, which had been repaired and refitted.

"Well, who else is going to pay for my house? At least until I get to uni," Sophie replied cheerfully. "Reduced hours though, studying comes first obviously. But after the summer, yeah I'll be leaving Micky." He smiled, but had a sad look in his eyes.

"Ah well, better make the most of it while you're here, but I always knew you were too good for this place, to be truthful." He then added.

"Keep up the good work Sophie!" Derek then said positively as he walked past, his entire mood being transformed.

Months passed, and soon enough, July came. Sophie got ready peacefully and at her own pace, proceeding down the stairs to make breakfast. The house was now fresh, clean and anew. As she cooked for herself, she looked over the empty table and chair and almost cried. After eating, she then picked up her school planner and looked at the term schedule, with "EXAM RESULTS" etched into the square of the day's current date. Her heart then started beating rapidly, before she grabbed her bag and proceeded out of the house and down the streets of Thorney Close with not a moment to waste.

"Areet Sophie!" A voice then grunted cheerfully as she walked.

"Good morning Goya!" She then replied and smiled.

"Keep up the good work love, I'm proud of you," he then said happily, before raising his signature thumb up to her as she walked on and grabbed the bus. Having got on and sat down, she then once again grabbed a copy of the local newspaper, the Sunderland Shine, before her eyes fell on a headline titled. "LOCAL HERO" written, of course, by Katie Clough.

"*A Sunderland girl was wrongly framed for a series of high profile crimes as a result of police and political corruption, an official inquiry has ruled.*" She began to read. "*Last year, Sophie, now 18, from Thorney Close, was subject to politically motivated charges by both disgraced former Mayor, William Parker-Fulton, and Police Chief, David Simm, both who seemingly died in their failed attempt to launch an insurrection on the city with their followers, known as Redcaps. Sophie, who showed incredible bravery to ultimately foil their wicked plot, as well as their cooperation with notorious local criminal, Tony Radcliff, was wrongly accused, with charges being dropped soon after by the Justice Secretary following the intervention of MI5. Sophie, who also attributed her victory to her friends and the people of the city, told the Sunderland Shine the victory was 'bittersweet' following the loss of her father, but she was 'delighted' to get her life back on track to study at University.*"

Sophie smiled as she put the newspaper down, before getting off the bus and walking down into the school, where as always, she had greeted Millie at the gates and hugged her.

"Today is the day!" she then said excited, but nervous. "I still bet I haven't done well!" Sophie chuckled.

"Don't say that Sophie, as I said, you have a bright future ahead of you," Millie reassured her. As they walked, they then encountered Bertha, who this time smiled at her sincerely.

"Hi Sophie, how are you doing luv?" She asked, embracing her in a mini hug.

"I'm great thank you Bertha, good to see you, and good luck for today!" Sophie then responded hastily as they hurried into class.

"Good morning girls!" Mr Marchant said as he waltzed into the class in his corduroy trousers. "Today is the day! And guess what? I have jolly, jolly good news for ALL of you!" He said in an excited voice. "Yes, your final exam results are in! So let's get started handing them out!" He said, with a large paper envelope in his hand. Sophie's heart then began racing as he slowly began walking around the classroom, distributing the papers one, by one. What seemed like a minute or so felt like a millennium for Sophie as the tension bubbled inside of her, her stomach tingling with glee and anticipation. He first put Millie's down next to her, who scrambled to open it.

"Oh my god, I got an A star!" she screamed loudly.

Then, eventually, Mr Marchant stood in front of Sophie's desk.

"Sophie…" he then said ominously and paused, leading her to look up in horror. "WELL DONE!" He then said very loudly, before putting her paper down. She picked it up, barely being able to concentrate on it.

"I got an A star too!" She then screamed jumping up with both of her hands in the air, before embracing Millie in a hug.

With the results she hoped for, later came more good news. One afternoon, Sophie sat alone in her bedroom, sipping a cup of tea as she looked incessantly at a computer screen, aggressively clicking refresh again and again. The corner of the website read *"UCAS- University Applications"* with some text below reading *"Durham University- Submitted - Pending."* Sophie moaned as it refused to update.

"Come on man, where is it?" She said to herself in frustration, as she clicked away.

Then suddenly, as she made one more click, the page had changed. Her eyes enlarged at the screen in shock, which now read. "Durham University: OFFER- History BA HONS" Sophie jumped up again so fast and with so much power the cup of tea went flying onto the floor.

"YESS!" She screamed again, as she scrambled to get her phone, which she could barely keep hold of, to phone Millie.

"MILLIE! I did it! You did too? YESS!" She screamed, jumping around the room in hysterics. "Let's go for a walk! I'll invite Micky! Talk soon!" she then said excitedly, before quickly hanging up and racing downstairs, putting on her shoes.

That evening, Micky, Millie and Sophie gathered next to the fields they had previously ran from the Redcaps across, before walking up the narrow country lane to a large mounded hill which towered over the houses of Sunderland on the eastern side. Micky, who had already heard the news, smiled.

"Sophie, I'm gonna miss you at the Dun Cow like." She smiled, before replying with a sad look on her.

"Can't believe I'm saying this, but me too…" She laughed, as the group climbed up the hill, which at the summit gave a wide panoramic view of all of Sunderland and the surrounding region.

"My legs are knackered going up here like." Micky laughed as they walked up.

"It's only Hasting Hill man, not Mount Everest." Sophie laughed. "Maybe you do need to take up footy again!" She then jokingly suggested to him.

"Ha, I'm nee good, that's why I'll be a lowly pub servant forever." He laughed humbly.

"Nah, if there's anything we should learn from all this, it's never let someone take your dreams away from you, or give up!" She replied thoughtfully. "We just toppled a gangster, a dark wizard and his army of monsters. Why can't you do something footy related again?" she then asked him.

"You know what Sophie… You're right," Micky then replied, feeling inspiration.

The trio then reached the summit of the hill and then gazed upon the view around them. Sophie looked down, where immediately opposite to them across the road stood the dreaded forest that tormented her for so long. She then turned to look south, with the spires of Durham Cathedral sitting twinkling on the horizon. Finally, she gazed northwards upon the hills of Northumberland, of which beyond sat Bamburgh and Holy Island.

"Mint view like. You can see pretty much everywhere we went." Micky then commented. "Mad like to think of all we've been through. But I tell you what, I love this town, I love the North East and I wouldn't live anywhere else in the world…" he then said, tearing up.

"Best friends for life," Millie then replied.

"And here's to a new future, and a new chapter in our lives!" Sophie then said jubilantly, as the three of them embraced in a group hug.

As they stood on the hill, amidst the twilight sunset, the North Star was visible directly above them, shining brightly in the sky.

THE END